Ron Mueller

Books by Ron Mueller

Bram Nielson Series-Science Fiction
The Fold
The Message
Fold Wormhole
Negative Fold
Ripples in Time

The Alex Evercrest Series-Detective
The River Front
The Girl on the Grill
Missing
Maggot
Racist
Votive Candles
Windy City
Country Road
Pool of Blood
Sins of the Daughter

The Taelo Series-Prehistory America
Taelo: The Early Years
Taelo: The Golden Feather
Taelo: Journey of Discovery
Taelo: Dangerous Passage
Taelo: Condor Clan Slingers
Taelo: Circumvention
Taelo: The Journey of Sages

A Taelo Story
The Name of the Child
White Swan and Quiet Pheasant
Broken Spear
Floating Cloud
Quiet Rabbit
Busy Bee
Little Otter& Talking Wren
Burley Bear & Meadow Flower

A Feather-in-the-Wind Story
The Eastern Elk Clan

The Door Series-Science Fiction
The Door
Delivery
Journey Beyond

The Savitar Series-Science Fiction
Journey's End
Savitar
Confluence

The Problem Solver Series-Secret Agent
The Beginning
Drug Lords
Border Crosser

Current Past and Future-Science Fiction
Event Survivors-Science Fiction
The Door--Science Fiction
Imagination by Courtney Huynh and Chloe Parker

The Fold

Ron Mueller

Around the World Publishing LLC
4914 Cooper Road Suite 144
Cincinnati, Ohio 45242-9998

The Fold, by Ron Mueller © 2021
Republished December 2022, February 2023

ISBN 13: 978-1-68223-309-2
ISBN 10: 1-68223-309-X

Distributed by Ingram
Cover Picture by NASA IC 335 Gsfc 20171208
Cover Design by Ron Mueller

Dedicated to those whose dreams:

take them out beyond.

Table of Content

Chapter 1: Conscripted

At five in the morning the far and faint twinkling starlight and the hint of the Cheshire moon provided the only light. Bram moved cautiously as he took each step up the narrow foot path he had made through the ragged greyish green leafed sage brush of the desert.

A slight breeze put a chill in the air. He was glad that he had on his warm windbreak it held back the surprisingly frosty chill of the desert air.

At this time in the morning all vegetation looked black to his eye and seemed to challenge the existence of the path he had made in the days since he had arrived at the camp, that he thought of as his personal gulag.

The sharp brown glass like particles crunching beneath his hiking boots spoke of some ancient volcanic activity in the region.

He envisioned the large boulder, which was his destination, being pushed the glacier for thousands of years until one side was worn flat. This flat area had become his morning throne.

The large commanding boulder appeared ahead and loomed above him. Using several projecting knobs and several pock holes, he climbed up and claimed his East facing throne.

Soon after his discovery of the boulder and while sitting and waiting for the sun a friendly desert mouse befriended him and joined him each morning to watch the sunrise. His little friend always waited until the morning sun was ready to warm them both. He was a great listener and they got along admirably.

The sun broke over the far horizon and Bram turned his face to let the morning light fall on and warm it. He watched as Einstein, the name he had given his small, brown fluff of a desert mouse, scurried up and sat by his side.

In the flat valley below lay the airfield, the few houses with yards, the helicopter hangar and the expansive block building that housed his apartment, his lab and housed the rest of the people in what had become his home. The facilities were new, luxurious, and well appointed. He knew the whole complex had been built specifically to house him and everyone that was there to keep him in and to make his stay comfortable.

He had been surprised when told that a chef would cater to everyone's desire. He knew that his current life was more lavish than he had ever experienced.

His previous years had been much more utilitarian. He had been an assistant professor living in Boston. He had discovered that the combination put him on the edge of starvation.

Yet, being held in luxury against his will and not being told where he was made him feel like a well-kept prisoner.

They would not tell him where in the world the compound was located. This was a point that irritated him and made testing of his theory more difficult.

He was dead set on finding out where he was being kept and on changing how the program, he was the center of, was managed.

For the last one hundred and eighty days, with the exception of a few trips east or to other secret locations, this had been where he was "kept and protected."

He had established his morning routine that began by greeting the morning sun, then feeding and talking with Einstein and then hiking out into the desert.

He had logged many hours among the sage brush. He had surprised many unwary jack rabbits or had been surprised by the rattle of an angry rattlesnake upon whose territory he had encroached.

He learned that rattlesnakes were sluggish in the morning cold but chose to wear high leather boots with a metal lining slipped in.

The warmth of the sun and the aroma of a cup of hot mint tea held between his hands, slowly wore away the early morning chill.

The sun rose slowly and created a shadow that pulled away from the base of the boulder he was sitting on.

He had positioned a timing stone. When the shadow hit that stone, it was time to leave for his hike in the desert.

Einstein and he had shared many a morning in this manner. Bram thought he and the mouse would have been well known to each other had they been able to converse.

The routine was consistent.

Bram would arrive just before sunrise and climb to his perch. As the sun broke over the eastern horizon, the mouse would poke its nose out from a hole at the base of their mutual boulder and climb up the boulder and sit with him.

Bram had told Einstein all his woes at least once, maybe more. He had asked him for advice and to review his scientific theories. He now felt an attachment to his lone desert mouse and always brought it a morning treat of biscuit or cookie crumbs.

The mouse would turn his head and seemed to agree with many of the complaints and comments Bram threw his way.

The surrounding desert, with its sage brush and yellow desert flowers was his one escape from himself and the government that was now "helping" him fulfill his goal.

He was virtually their prisoner. Well treated but monitored and tightly confined.

Sitting out on this boulder or hiking through the desert was a victory that he had gained by consistently refusing to work if he was not given the time to get out.

He was sure he was being monitored even when he sat on his boulder. He wondered if those monitoring had seen him talking to Einstein. If they had Bram figured that by now, they would have taken him away in a straight jacket.

Each morning he would wish his mouse well and he would then head out on a brisk walk away from the complex in a specific compass heading. His first four excursions had been the main compass headings of North, East, South and West. For the last half, a year he had gone out hiking on one degree increments clockwise away from North.

Each time after approximately an hour a helicopter would arrive and tell him he must return to the lab. The first few times he hiked back. Then he began to ride the helicopter back. This saved him time and he enjoyed bantering with the pilot. She seemed to be about his age. He wondered how she had been chosen for this duty.

This morning, day 185, he was now traveling south plus five degrees. He was slowly plotting a circle with the center being the site of his lab.

Bram carried the instrumentation that transformed him into an altimeter. He was creating a detailed topographical map of the terrain around the lab. This information had already reduced the possible location of his lab to just three areas in the United States.

On a daily basis, in a morning project meeting, he requested the information about where he was, and he was always politely refused.

He continued to ask about the location every time there was a meeting. He had decided that until the program leaders changed their mind about how they handled the team he would not provide them with any more information about his space-time Fold breakthrough.

He thought of his breakthrough as having stumbled on the knowledge that when activated would change how travel through the universe would be achieved. He was close to opening the universe to humankind.

He was not going to let his breakthrough remain a secret but publishing the concepts of his ideas in a leading scientific journal had gotten Bram into his current situation. He had been sitting at his desk running his fingers through his hair in frustration when the doorbell rang. He looked through the peek hole and saw a very beautiful woman dressed in a black business outfit. He opened the door and she introduced herself as Ms. Erica Wilson with the US government.

Her shoulder length black hair that swept over a perfectly formed ear and exposed the right side of her smooth, flawless face placed her looks in the beautiful woman category. Her smooth introduction, smile and greeting put her in the good sales ability category.

Her smile though clearly was not genuine but lit up her face.

He took it all in as he listened to her polished introduction and her pitch about how his article had captured her imagination. He wondered about her imagination since he had not described anything that might be imagined but he invited her in and pointed to the couch.

She explained she was with NASA and invited him to come to Washington and share his knowledge with her team. The invitation was enticing and of interest to him. When she highlighted Elizabeth Miller renowned the theory of Ethical Behavior in Science as a member of the team and a person he had read, as a member of the team, he agreed to attend the meeting.

He asked a few questions about his theory, and it was clear that Erica had little understanding of his article, but he was excited that his work had been deemed significant enough to get him invited to a NASA team meeting. It was important enough to send their project leader to personally recruit him.

Erica informed him that the meeting was for the following Wednesday. He was to review his article with a team that was focused on the same problem. She asked if he could make the meeting, as she reached into her purse. She hinted that there was a hefty salary if he made the team.

He said that the timing was very tight, but he would attend. He was about to tell her not to ruin things by trying to buy his participation but thought better of it.

Erica pulled out an envelope and handed him a plane ticket and hotel reservations as she stood to leave. She informed him that he would be met at the airport and escorted to the meeting. It was clear to Bram that she had come prepared for him to say yes.

He stood looking at the tickets in his hand as he realized that over the weekend, he would need to arrange to have his classes covered by his graduate students. He had not expected anything to happen this fast.

He looked out the window and watched as Erica got into a black limo. He was surprised at her ride. It seemed to him that she was well connected.

The weekend was a scurry of calls to his graduate students as he assigned them to cover his lectures.

On Wednesday as Bram was getting ready to leave to the airport, he was met at the door leading down to the street by an individual in a dark blue suit. Bram was intent on getting out to the walk where he expected to be picked up.

He excused himself and proceeded down the steps. He was followed down the steps and out to the edge of the walk.

There the man continued to engage him and invited him to meet with the president of the firm that was interested in funding his research. After giving Bram a card with the time and place for the meeting at a posh restaurant in Boston, he walked to a black limo and departed.

Bram had the card in hand as he got into the car taking him to the airport. He noted that the article had stirred the interest of more than the US government. He wondered what funding a private firm would pay.

He now had doubts about Erica's team.

Clearly people thought his idea was important. He had two people that had come to his apartment and that alone gave him cause for concern.

He wondered why was there this sudden interest in his theories?

The flight to DC left Boston early. He took note that if things didn't go smoothly with the US government, he now had a private company that was interested in supporting his research.

As Erica had promised when he walked into the arrival area, he saw a person holding a sign with his name on it. The sign welcomed him and had Erica Wilson written below his name.

He had not checked luggage, so he walked out with his escort to a waiting grey Ford sedan.

He was taken to NASA Headquarters at East Street Southwest. He felt good that NASA was so interested in his work. Its reputation was another reason that he had agreed to the meeting.

He wondered what group he had interested and what they wanted with his breakthrough.

He went through security and then was guided down a long corridor around several bends and finally guided into a meeting room where he was seated at the end seat on a long table.

Bram noted that all the seats had been taken. He looked down the table at the rather handsome Asian heritage person sitting directly across from him. Erica was sitting to that person's right. Bram recognized only one person from the rest of the people at the table.

The meeting was called to order, and everyone gave a brief introduction of themselves. Jeffrey Mikelson sitting at the head of the table, introduced himself as the Space Technology Mission Director. He was currently leading a program named STCP (Space Time Continuum Program). He welcomed Bram and then asked everyone to introduce themselves.

As Bram listened to the introductions and watched the team's interactions, it seemed to him that this team had been formed quickly and had done little work together.

When Elizabeth Miller, a person who he had admired and followed for years and now sitting to his left introduced herself, Bram stood and extended his hand. He said that she was one of the persons who had inspired him.

They shook hands and Elizabeth pulled him in for a hug. She whispered that it had all been set up for him and that NASA wanted him badly, but it was real. Bram smiled at her and nodded his head. If she was on the team then Bram was certainly interested.

After the introductions, Bram was asked to go through the presentation that he had brought with him.

The five-slide presentation that he presented to the team confirmed his suspicions. The team was of top talent, but they didn't seem to know each other and seemed to only know what he had written. He noted that the few questions asked were general and lacked depth.

He thought that the team was fresher than just churned butter. He now understood Elizabeth's whisper.

He concluded his presentation and after a final question and answer session, everyone on the team but Jeffery and Erica left the room.

Elizabeth patted him on his shoulder as she past him on her way out.

It was clear to Bram that the meeting had been rehearsed and that the participants had each played their part. He knew that the two persons remaining in the room were the decision makers.

Bram put his left hand on the spot that Elizabeth had patted. Bram knew Elizabeth, was globally known for her focus on human ethics in space exploration and would not have participated if she had not thought it important.

Jeffery made him the offer to get on team.

Bram was surprised that there was no small talk, and the offer came with a title, the highest government ranking and pay possible and a signing bonus.

Bram was offered the technical leadership of the team.

The salary offer was more than twice as much as his current salary and the signing bonus of five thousand dollars made it even more attractive. It made him wonder if the offer from private industry would be significantly more. When he asked for time to think about it, the atmosphere in the room changed.

Jeffrey and Erica looked at each other.

The answer surprised Bram.

Jeffrey quietly said, "No!." We are aware of an offer that might have been made to you this morning and we know about several additional offers that will come with conditions that would seem to be more attractive than the one I just offered, but each would make you their captive.

We are concerned about you and about the US national security.

Bram listened as Jeffrey emphasized that he was giving him everything that could possibly offered, and it was an offer that could not be refused.

Bram realized that he was not being asked but told that he was on the team. Jeffrey went on to inform him that he was immediately being put under government protection because of the importance of his scientific work.

He had been given best possible deal but the choice about joining was not an option.

Bram asked how it was possible that he had been noticed by so many organizations at the same time.

Erica assured him that he was already on the most wanted list of people to either recruit, abduct or eliminate. She shared that his actions since his publication had been monitored and that he was put under guard since the moment she had met with him.

Two men in black waited outside of the meeting room. Jeffrey introduced them as FBI bodyguards that would guard him until he interviewed and selected four that would live with him. They escorted him, Jeffrey, and Erica to lunch.

There they briefly discussed the arrangements that were being made on his behalf.

He would retain his position on the MIT staff, but he would be posted as taking a sabbatical.

That was the end of lunch.

He and his two men in black were flown to an undisclosed location. He arrived in the dead of night and was escorted to a spacious and well-appointed corner apartment on the top floor of the building. He walked slowly through his new two-bedroom apartment that had a huge common room and large open veranda. It was an apartment that could have been featured in one of the luxury apartment magazines. It made his apartment in Boston seem like a squatters shack.

The spacious exterior deck provided a place to sit and enjoy the desert view at sunset and it was large enough for him to practice his Tae kwon do and Aikido.

Windows formed two walls of the apartment. He was using one room for his office and the other, that featured a shower stall, for his bedroom. The apartment came with someone to cook his meals and with another person to clean it periodically.

It was clear that if he were prisoner he was a pampered one.

He was, by his own estimation of the circumstances, a valuable asset that was getting the best treatment possible but, in all respects, he was now a prisoner of the government. He wondered if it was the same situation for the rest of the team.

He would soon find out who would be staying at the compound with him.

He decided to enjoy his deck and sit and relax.

When his belongings arrived, he arranged his meager belongings and developed a schedule that he would follow.

He recalled both of his martial arts master's asking him what he planned to do with the capability and knowledge they were giving him.

He replied that he planned to do good.

They both seemed pleased with his reply. He really had no clue why he felt the need to pursue these martial art skills, but he had become a third-degree black belt in each.

Now he put the exercises to work to reduce the stress he felt by his current situation.

Tae Kwon Do and Aikido became his early evening exercise routine.

He added the early morning hikes into the desert to his exercise routine.

That is where he met his confident and counselor Einstein.

He thought about the fact that he had been given a brain that had a capability that was taking him on a journey that if he succeeded would be change the world.

He wanted that to be used to do good.

This morning like all the mornings for the last six months, he said good day to his pet mouse as he left the boulder. Bram then focused on his footing as he walked carefully down the rocky slope. This was his one hundred eighty fifth radial hike away from the compound. At the bottom, as he rounded a ragged boulder about twice his height, he came to a dark gapping opening. A cool breeze washed past the beads of sweat that had already formed on his brow.

The breeze surprised him. He was not sure what he had discovered but he was intent on exploring it. He pulled out his flashlight and entered the ten-by-ten-foot cave entrance.

The breeze meant that there was another opening somewhere ahead. He let the breeze guide him through the dark cave. His light bounced off the smooth well-worn ancient path and he slowly made his way forward.

He realized that what he was doing would certainly confuse his routine helicopter pickup pilot.

Amy began suiting up, it was time to retrieve Bram from his radial hikes away from the compound. She was not sure why he went out on his morning walks, but she had come to believe he was mapping the surrounding areas. Anything else made little sense to her.

She rated her current assignment as an easy one but very visible. She had heard this assignment was high up on the recognition list of special assignments, so she had volunteered in hopes it would look good on her service record. She was one of a short list of volunteers and she was the only female.

The assignment was not highly sought since it was an assignment that put a person in the middle of nowhere. She however was happy to have gotten the assignment.

She knew her performance ratings had always been high. What she wanted was a gold star in her record to improve her chances at getting accepted into the space program. She wanted to be an astronaut and the barriers leading to that opportunity were many.

She finished suiting up and walked out to her helicopter. The red beauty sat on its skids on the landing pad. The tail rotor with a shark like fin above the bright red rotor shrouding and the long thin white tubular connection to bright red main body brought a dragon fly to her mind.

But her toy had a sleek body that could host at least seven people and if necessary, it also had a winch to lift a person from the ground. It was the best ride she had ever piloted. She looked forward to each of her morning flights.

Amy climbed into the cockpit, went through her flight checks, and brought the engine to life. She slowly lifted off the pad and headed out on the heading of one hundred eighty-five degrees toward the south. She dutifully added the one degree each morning. She had figured out Bram's pattern.

She soon knew something had changed. She had flown out slowly, so she could spot Bram. This had become a normal morning routine. She would spot him hiking through the desert. He would wave at her as she passed over him and then she would swing around, land and he would approach and jump into the seat beside her. He always had a desert flower or some other small trinket to give her.

Today he was nowhere to be seen.

Her immediate reaction was alarm. Had he fallen down some ravine?

After several circular search runs, Amy made a call back to the base. She asked if Bram had returned to the base. A few moments later she was informed that he was in his lab.

Amy cursed under her breath and headed back to the landing pad. She was pissed. She figured Bram should have let her know that he had not taken his normal hike.

Amy took off her helmet and carefully hung it on its hook. She was fuming mad at Bram. For more than six months she had made this same flight and she had always found him. After the first two weeks he had always flown back with her. It had become like clockwork. She wondered what had happened to change the arrangement.

Still mad, she decided to go ask him what had happened and if the change was permanent.

A second person was also going to find Bram.

Erica was free to come and go from the compound as she pleased. She did not have to be at the compound but none the less she was upset that Jeffrey had given Bram a salary that was at least twenty per cent higher than hers and he had put him in the best apartment. She privately had her eyes on it and had been planning to move into it. She figured she deserved it. Instead, she had been assigned a one bedroom on the second floor. Jeffrey told her that she would only be there part-time and did not need anything more.

Damn him. She was the one who was supposed to be in charge of the project logistics.

He was getting the best of everything.

She bit her tongue and moved into an apartment she felt was below her paygrade.

She was sitting in the meeting room where she held her daily meeting when she was on-site. She watched as Bram, Marcus, Elizabeth and Mallica walked in chatting. They seemed to have developed a good working relationship.

It had become clear to her that Bram did not need the support of any of his team in the realm that he was working in. He was quite independent and engaged the rest of the team in philosophical discussions but seldom in the science he was engaged in.

Elizabeth seemed to be the exception but when Erica asked, she was clear she had no clue about the math and science that Bram was developing.

Erica decided she needed to have more control of what Bram was doing. She needed a timeline to the completion of his work. She would insist on a work plan from him.

Bram saw the look on Erica's face and knew that she was going to push. She would be trying to get control of the science part of the effort. This was a part of the project that Bram knew she had no clue as to what was happening.

He did not want her involved.

He put her in the category of a person too self-engrossed and not really interested in the science but interested in control of the environment around her.

She was only interested in getting herself recognized and rewarded.

Bram categorize her as self-aggrandized. He saw little use for her in the scientific arena.

He decided to try to shock her. He had determined the location of the base. He was ninety-nine with six nines after the decimal point sure where the compound was located.

He stood and looked at Erica but instead of asking his normal question about where the compound was located, he gave a latitude and longitude and stated that it was the location of the compound and gave the specific altitude of the room in which the meeting was being held.

Bram looked at her and softly said I know where I am and unless you quit playing games with me the rest of the world will know as well.

There was total silence in the room.

For the first time in her life, Erica did not know how to proceed. She had never faced anyone like Bram. Why was it so important for him to know where he was?

She put up her hand as if to deflect what he had said. She wanted to shout obscenities at him, but this was beyond what she had anticipated. Her self-control won out.

She canceled the meeting and said that she was bringing Jeffrey into this discussion.

Bram nodded and said he was pleased to meet with them both.

The sky was still a somber grey the next morning when Bram climbed on his boulder and looked down at the compound. The lights gave the complex an eerie shimmering appearance as the early morning mist began to rise.

The scene really looked like area 51 in all the sci-fi movies. In this case, Bram felt like he was the alien. He knew that the upcoming meeting focus would be on him.

The sun slowly drove the grey mist from the air and filled it with its clear rays of warmth.

The morning came awake like sleeping beauty after her lover's kiss.

Einstein came out of his hole for his morning treat. Today he listened to Bram's analysis of what would transpire at the coming morning meeting.

Bram left the rock and headed out at one hundred ninety second degree clockwise from North.

The morning air was brushing past him and hitting him on his right cheek. Now that he knew where the compound was located, he could almost predict what his hike would encounter. The few surprises were made up of boulders and cactuses that rose up in his path. But the elevation and the up and downs were visible in his mind's terrain map.

The location had never been of any concern to him other than as a lever to pull that would cause the mouse trap to open.

It would make it easier to test the space-time Fold transmitter, but he could have done it without knowing his current location.

He had patiently baited the trap so that he could force a change.

He heard the chatter of the helicopter and gave a wave as it passed overhead. Amy had told him he had scared the hell out of her when he had disappeared on his 185-degree hike and had not let her know he had found another way back to the compound.

He had promised not to scare her again. He was becoming very fond of her and enjoyed their morning chatter on the way back to the compound.

Marcus watched as Amy and Bram walked toward him. He was there to warn Bram about Erica's continuing bad mood. She had almost bitten his head off when he had given a simple morning hello.

He greeted Amy and then turned to Bram. He quietly told him the situation and that Jeffrey was already in the meeting room with a fuming mad Erica.

Bram smiled as Elizabeth joined them. He always felt better when he had his morning hug from her. She was old enough to be his grandmother. Her mind was the most powerful one in any room she was in. Bram used his interactions with Elizabeth to clarify his mind.

He let out a mental sigh of relief as Mallica joined them and they walked into the meeting room together.

Bram greeted Jeffrey and said good morning to Erica who was seated to Jeffrey's left. He was not surprised but disappointed that she did not reply. He concluded that Marcus had been right about her current mood.

Bram purposely chose to sit to Jeffery's right, so he could look directly at Erica. He also took noted that Elizabeth chose to sit next to him. It was clear to him that everyone expected sparks and fire.

Jeffrey opened the meeting by describing Erica's frustration with the behavior of the team. He went on to describe the concern over Bram's determination in constantly requesting the location of the compound.

Jeffrey listened to Erica, as she vented her fury at the disrespect she felt was being shown by Bram. Jeffrey said he understood her frustration but was surprised at her intense emotion. He thought to himself that it was clear that she would not last in the long term if this was how she felt.

He turned his attention to Bram to find out about his interested and focus about the location of the compound.

He looked at Bram and asked what the issue could be.

Bram looked around to each person on the team and then focused alternately on Jeffrey and Erica.

He began by stating that he cherished his freedom. He made the point that the breakthrough he was working on would affect the entire world. He went on to state that changes needed to take place if he was to continue his work.

Bram stood up and described how he envisioned the breakthrough being managed. It would be managed similar to the joint space station or Antarctica. It should be a concerted effort by a team made up of representatives from all the major countries of the world.

Bram sat down and asked if such a team could be formed.

Jeffrey looked to Erica and saw her face was a livid red. It seemed clear to him that she did not think much of Bram's vision.

He in turn stood. He looked at each team member and asked each to state their opinion of the Bram's proposal.

Elizabeth was first to support the idea. Then the entire team supported Bram's approach.

Ok, I will pursue this program change with my superiors. However, I would like to reserve the right to time the sharing of any breakthrough so how and the timing of the information can be planned and controlled.

Now what is the fixation about knowing the location of the compound? You have driven Erica crazy with this constant request.

Jeffrey sat and looked at Bram.

Bram looked across at Erica.

He asked her how hard would it be to ask someone to meet her if she didn't know where she was.

It would be impossible she blurted out but what the hell does that have to do with your request.

Bram leaned back as she leaned across the table as if to grab him.

He looked at Jeffrey and asked him the same question.

Then he looked at the rest of the team and asked them as well.

Elizabeth smiled.

She stood and took a piece of paper and made two round spots on it. She then slowly folded the paper, so the two spots met. She pointed out that she was able to do it because she knew where each point was located. It required her to know the location, so she could properly Fold the paper. She went on to say everyone should think of the paper as the fabric of Space.

Erica slapped the table and shouted, "Why the hell didn't you just say so?

Bram knew he could have made a similar point, but he had wanted to bring the issue of how the project was managed to a head. He also knew that he didn't need to know the location at all.

He stood and stated that now it was time to talk about freedom. He was not going to continue to work on the concept and had not for as many days as they had been in the compound.

He stated that the team should be free to come and go as they desired. He made the point that top security was provided to many people who were doing much less important work.

"Who the hell do you think you are," Erica blurted out?

She looked to see if Jeffrey was as mad as she was and was surprised that he was completely relaxed.

Jeffrey remained seated, but he was nodding in agreement.

He let the team know he agreed on both points. He asked the team to leave the room. He asked Bram to stay.

Jeffrey looked from Bram to Erica.

He made the observation that the two of them seemed to interact like oil and water and that it was clear to him that the technical side of the project did not need overseeing.

Bram would lead that part of the project.

Erica would manage the project resources and logistics of the effort.

The three of them would have weekly meetings to ensure a successful outcome for the effort.

Erica stood and left the meeting room without saying a word. She went out to the plane that would take her back to the DC area.

Jeffrey stayed to verify that Bram would continue his work in earnest.

Bram agreed but highlighted that they had not set up a work plan that would lead beyond the invention of the hardware to implement the breakthrough. He needed assurance that he would be involved all the way through the first use of the space-time Fold capability.

<u>Chapter 2: Elizabeth</u>

Elizabeth had given Bram a squeeze on the shoulder and winked at him as she left the meeting room.

She had covered the bullshit about needing to know his location to do any of the work he needed to do.

She was also aware of the ton of work he had been doing in building a variety of electronic control systems.

She might not understand much of what he was doing but she was certain that he was making progress. His behavior and attitude indicated that he was moving steadily ahead. His private workshop was a series of tabletop experiments.

Bram had invented a magnetron like honeycombed chamber that created the space time Fold.

Interacting with Bram made her wish she was forty years younger. She would have loved to be one of the people that would make the first trip to some distant star.

If she were forty years younger, she would certainly have been vying with the young helicopter pilot for his heart.

The daily conversations they engaged in were all focused on the ethics and impact of the ability to instantly leap across hundreds and thousands of light years.

Bram was of the view that such an action should be done in unison with all the people of earth.

He was keenly aware that his technological leap would leave the current development of the space program in the same position as the discontinuity the advent of the car created for the buggy makers.

Tremendous financial business crashes would occur. People at all levels would suffer. He felt those at the bottom of the ladder would suffer the most.

He had shared with her that he would not disclose the mathematics and the method of folding the fabric of space until a global approach was agreed to.

Even then he would try to limit the scope that would be shared.

A balanced, secure global group like the United Nations Security Council would need to be formed. He doubted the countries of the world could come to an agreement in time to be part of the implementation of the Fold capability.

They would need to come together to guide the long-term implementation of Fold destinations and potentially the interactions with intelligent life that might be discovered.

He had also expressed his concern about the actions various companies and countries might take to either gain access to or to gain control of the effort.

He was not sure Jeffrey and Erica were ready for such an onslaught. He placed himself in the too naïve to know what to do category.

The question Bram had posed for her was if Jeffrey wielded enough power?

Elizabeth had come to one realization.

Bram was the most disciplined and fair individual she had ever met.

Thinking about Bram took Elizabeth back to her days on Coochiemudlo Island in Australia.

She and her husband had lived there for twenty very pleasant years.

The Island was in Moreton Bay and was shielded from the Pacific by several larger islands.

Her morning swims were invigorating. Her daily morning and evening walks were soothing, and they provided time to think and ponder.

She was the typical Australian pad-old lady. Her husband went to work each day and expected his breakfast, lunch, and dinner ready and waiting when he walked through the door.

Twenty years of living with her mate had taken a toll on her. She had fought back and developed herself by reading the classics. She then continued her mental journey into exploring the sciences.

Her husband had stayed mentally where they both had started their union. He came home one afternoon and demanded a steak instead of the soup and salad she had prepared.

She complied and prepared steak, fried onions, and asparagus. She ate her soup and salad. He got up from the table after only eating half of what he had served himself.

He told her the food tasted terrible as he sat down in his recliner.

After clearing the table and cleaning the kitchen she came into the study to see if he wanted coffee or tea.

She discovered that he had passed away while sitting in his recliner.

She called the police. She did not know what else to do.

She immediately felt liberated, and she always felt guilty that she celebrated his death as the day of her freedom.

The year after his death she entered the University of Southern Queensland. She sold her home of twenty years and rented one on Fleet Street in Toowoomba. She bought the home based on its location. She was within an easy bicycle ride through the Japanese garden to the university. She would not need to own a car. She wanted to grow her mind and to live a simple life.

Her move of a little over one hundred fifty kilometers might as well have been a move of a thousand miles.

She went from being a pad-old lady to a reborn old lady of forty-eight.

She was at last free to pursue her own way. This thought did not escape her. Even though she had been comfortable and able to pursue her mental growth, she had been living an empty life. She recognized that it lacked a clear purpose.

Her educational goals were like a cross-stitched scarf.

On the one hand, she enjoyed the penetration of the minds psyche and intellect. She marveled at how the mind functioned and ticked and the personality each person developed to protect the being that was sculptured by the choices they either made willingly or were pressed into making based on their fear.

She had concluded that fear was the prime lever that formed a person's personality and guided many of their actions.

Her interest in the expansion of mankind into space and the science involved with astronomy and space drew her into the cross-stitch of the fabric she was weaving for herself.

This fabric was a mix of studies in many fields. Her advisors did not know how to advise her. It was clear to her that she was a student anomaly to her advisors.

She earned a Bachelor of Science degree in Spatial Engineering.

She was not satisfied. She went on to get a master's degree in Phycology.

She then applied to the most prestigious schools around the globe.

She was surprised by her aggressive approach.

She did not really expect to break into the next upper tier of universities.

Several months went by and just when she was about to look for work, she was surprised to get accepted to Oxford. She must have read the acceptance letter at least twenty times.

Each time she would laugh and hold the letter up and shout.

It was a shout of victory.

It was a shout against her fears.

Elizabeth realized her move to England and attending Oxford would deplete her finances.

She feared becoming destitute.

She began to write and submit articles in hopes of selling them to various publications. She hoped to make a small living to finance her PhD.

Her submittal to the Quarterly Journal of the Royal Astronomical Society was accepted!!!

The submittal was for a series of articles focused on the ethics of travel by humans into the vast areas of space.

This was more than she had hoped for. It would not pay her way, but it would give her more credibility as a published author.

She submitted articles to at least twenty additional magazines. She was accepted by at least a half dozen. She was able to establish a credible story arc that was accepted by each of the magazines. Each had a slightly different slant. Each flowed easily from her fingers and to her typewriter.

Each magazine provided a small but steady income that together was a significant income that made her quest for her PhD a much surer and comfortable journey.

She sold the possessions she could and gave the rest away. She left Australia and made the move halfway around the world to England. She had only one large chest and a small suitcase with her.

She arrived at the city of Oxford. Oxford was a city of almost ninety thousand and had a vibrant environment that was a mix of about forty percent factory working people and forty percent university students and the remainder in various supporting office and store work functions.

She learned that the university was teaching as far back as 1096, making it the oldest university in the English-speaking world and the world's second-oldest university in continuous operation.

She also learned that the University of Oxford was spread throughout Oxford. It did not have a centralized campus.

Elizabeth rented an apartment that was close to and convenient to the parts of the University she would be attending. She purchased a new bicycle and then began her pursuit of her PhD.

A short time later, Elizabeth was completely surprised by being chosen by the Royal Astronomical Society to receive a grant that covered her expenses. The grant was like found gold. It made her life that much easier.

She continued to publish and to explore the concepts and implications on human space travel. She was able to consolidate all her writing into a single manuscript that was more than five hundred pages long.

It became a best seller among the scientific community. This meant it sold at least a thousand copies. It did not, however, pay her living expenses. She knew she had been very lucky to have received a grant. And it did get her invited to several scientific conferences. The conferences in turn made her name recognized in the world of science.

It took her several years to earn her PhD. With her PhD in hand, she became a guest lecturer. She traveled to Amsterdam where she lectured for a year.

Then it was on to MIT where in the second year there, NASA approached her to engage the NASA leadership in a series of discussions on the ethics of human space travel and the risk posed on the persons sent out into space. The offer was not employment but came with a significant stipend. The stipend was large enough and renewable on a yearly basis that she would be set for life.

Elizabeth accepted. It seemed she would be spending time with people interested in the same field as herself. She was not exactly clear about her role, but it seemed that her book was the reason for the offer. She thought more highly about her book after that. In the end it had paid for all of her effort in writing it.

It was Jeffrey who had made the offer. He engaged with her in the topics covered in her book and seemed to be deep into the concepts presented. She enjoyed his perspective and was impressed with his passion for the topic.

She spent a great deal of time over breakfast discussions with him. He sponsored several workshops with a variety of government leaders. A few weeks later Jeffery asked her to be on a team working on the topic of folding time and space. She had no clue how or what the topic entailed but she was willing to be part of the effort. She did wonder where in the world Jeffrey had come up with that concept.

Elizabeth came back to the present. She had just met Bram. It was clear he was being forcefully recruited and that everything about the team Jeffrey had pulled quickly together had been aimed at him. She was about to leave the meeting room. She knew Bram was in a trap. She wanted to help him.

She made a comment to Jeffrey about his personal quest and that of the ethics of the situation.

She continued to look at Jeffrey and made the simple statement.

"Let's have breakfast and discuss the ethics of this meeting."

The look on Jeffrey's face let her know he understood her message to him.

Chapter 3: Project Control

Jeffrey sat calmly as he watched the team members leave the meeting.

He understood Catherine's comment and its implication. The many breakfast discussions on the ethical concerns associated with individual countries trying to use space travel and technology to gain the upper hand on the politics of the earth grew in fertile ground. He had wondered and worried about this from the beginning of his assignment.

Bram had clearly stated that this project was beyond the boundary of any one country. It must be a global effort. He felt the same. He had come to that conclusion some time ago. He had not acted on in because it was unclear how he could clear the formidable barriers he clearly saw ahead.

It was clear Erica was not listening. For her it was a matter of control, of being in-charge. It was "her" project. She was not looking at the larger longer term as it applied to the world.

Jeffrey was about to make a radical change. He was not sure Erica would accept the change. She was a hard-charging individual. Hopefully, she was still flexible enough to accept a role that had less overall control but was essential to the success of the effort.

He gave Bram new respect for how patient and methodical he had been to bring the issue out in the open. He hoped Bram would be as effective in making the effort a global one.

Jeffrey thought about himself. He in fact had folded his time and space.

He had grown up in the German section of Shanghai.

He had played in a time that no longer existed. He had gone to school a few city blocks from his home. The family's living quarters where above his father's shoe shop. They never had many material goods, but they ate well, and he played with friends out in the street in front of his father's shoe shop.

His mother insisted on him eating breakfast and then he went to school.

His favorite eatery was the noodle shop less than a half block from home. He would come to the noodle shop for lunch and then return for dinner at home.

Looking back, he thought of it as a great way to have grown up.

His mother had insisted on and enforced a rigorous study regime. He got away with doing little work with his father by claiming the need to study. His mother always backed him up.

It worked. He was the number one student in his high school class.

He received a scholarship to attend the University of Shanghai. He was good at bookwork and excelled but he had no clue what he wanted to do. Once again, his mother's guidance, to get a degree that could make good money, paid off. He graduated top of his class with an Engineering degree.

His engineering degree opened the door to go to work for a Global Western company. Their salary offer had been four times what any Chinese company offered.

He had changed his name from 杰佛瑞 （Jié fó ruì) to its western equivalent, Jeffrey

The teamwork, fair treatment, culture, and the attitude of the people in the company invigorated him. He excelled and went smoothly and consistently upward.

He had assignments in the US, Europe and then back to China as a Vice President.

He ran out of corporate ladder to climb. The work became less enjoyable, the environment much more political and the people around him seemed desperate and not motivated by their work or environment. They were not having fun. He was beginning to wonder about his own motivation.

He again folded time and space and made the leap away from the corporate ladder to his current position at NASA.

He had been aided by the desire of the US government to diversify their leadership. He realized it was proving to be a very challenging leap. He was on a slippery slope and needed both spiked ice boots, ice hammers and someone to hold his safety line.

He hoped that Bram would be that someone.

He looked at Erica and saw the same desperate need to succeed he had seen in the corporation he had left. She wanted to feel the surge of power when she was in command. He felt a little sad for her. The need for power usually preceded a fall.

He looked at Bram and recognized a person who had total confidence in his actions and was centered on fundamental principles of honesty, integrity, and the belief that everyone was valuable.

Bram was fighting the system of secrecy and confinement.

Jeffrey was sure he would win.

Jeffrey looked back and forth between the two. He said, "let's make some changes."

Both Erica and Bram looked at him in silence.

He asked Bram how he wanted the project to be organized. He could see Erica's face go red in anger.

Bram looked at Erica and carefully thought through his next words.

He had nothing against her.

She was smart, capable, and very aggressive.

He wanted her to see that there was more to the work they did than who was in control.

He began by surfacing the need for global participation. He verbally speculated that getting participants from the various countries would be a monumental task. It would require someone who would recognize the attempt to place spies that would be recommended with the legitimate placement of top scientific talent.

He stated that it would take someone that would confront those who were not honest or not acting with the true intent to make the project a success. The intrigue and the political machinations would be a challenge for anyone, and it would take someone who had a tough backbone, commitment to success and who would make the tough calls.

Bram pointed out that Erica had such capabilities. He went on to say that she would be the perfect person to negotiate with each of the world's country representatives.

He continued by saying she would also be the perfect person to stand the onslaught of the news media. She would be the best public face the project could possibly field.

Bram then looked at Jeffrey and made the point that he too would be in the spotlight on the world stage and would need to back Erica. The two of them would need to collaborate and negotiate and maneuver the politics of the entire program.

Jeffrey would need to face the internal US government challenges while Erica would need to face the global challenges.

He then recommended Elizabeth as the person to manage the technical and scientific team. She would be a tremendous asset as the three of them took on the world.

He saw the look of surprise in both Jeffrey's and Erica's faces. He knew they had been expecting that he would name himself as the leader of the technical team.

He smiled, nodded, and said, "I want to be left alone to accelerate the program through my discoveries." I don't need help. I need support.

I will need a top project manager to ensure the hardware and equipment for the project come together in record time.

I will need technical help in the field of electronic hardware and in the field of sensors and data gathering and analysis but only when I ask for it.

I don't want to participate in meetings to discuss the details that need to get done. My mind dies in such meetings.

I need the space to maneuver and experiment. I don't want to wait for approval of my actions. I want to make and prove the breakthroughs and then get on with improving them.

Jeffrey looked at Erica and asked, "What do you think?"

He then went silent and waited for a response.

Erica looked across the table at Bram. She came to the realization that her feelings and understanding had just changed.

She had a new respect for Bram.

She thought he had wanted her job. Instead, he had promoted her into the most visible role. It was a role she was already looking forward to and she was already trying to figure out how to make it a success.

She realized that she had just experienced a life change and undergone some life-changing personal growth in this new understanding of the environment and the people around her.

Tears came to her eyes. She stopped to wipe her eyes.

She nodded and thanked Bram for recognizing her as the person who could make the team into a global one.

She quietly said she would be honored to do just that.

Jeffrey looked back and forth at the two.

The world had also changed for him. He felt they now had a team.

He felt a sense of relief.

Perhaps the oil and water aspects of the two could be leveraged to enhance the chances of project success. He knew the hurdles ahead were high, but he now had confidence that together they would clear them.

He stood and extended his hand to Erica and thanked her for expanding her vision.

He thanked Bram for his persistence and his global vision for the project. He called for a lunch break and called for a meeting of all site personnel after lunch.

Jeffrey walked out of the meeting and located Elizabeth. He wanted to have a brief conversation with her to make sure she agreed to lead the technical team. It would mean a little more work on her part, but the technical direction would be mostly in Bram's hands.

He invited Elizabeth to lunch where he shared the outcome of the meeting with Bram and Erica.

Elizabeth was not surprised and was pleased with Bram's view of the future direction of the break-through Fold effort. She agreed to her role in the short-term.

The long-term role was questionable. As the team grew it seemed that she would need additional help.

Jeffrey assured her she would have a proper support staff to handle all the requirements for the team.

To Jeffrey, lunch tasted wonderful. He would later remember that feeling and realize he could not recall what he ate.

Later after lunch, Jeffrey approached the podium and looked out at all the site personnel. There were somewhere around thirty military personnel with duties of providing services, guarding the base, and up keeping the one helicopter assigned to the base.

He knew Amy as the pilot of the helicopter.

Bram had shared her desire to be an astronaut. Bram had also asked that she be recommended to be in the next class.

Jeffrey had agreed to make it happen.

He marveled that it took so many people to support a technical team of only four people. He shrugged his shoulders when he thought about the additional set of people back in Washington.

He looked at Bram and realized there was only one person that they all looked to for success.

This realization put one more action he would need to take.

As tight as the attempt to isolate Bram had been, he was not protected properly. He would need night and day bodyguards. Jeffrey decided he would immediately approach the FBI for such help.

He looked around and shared that some changes were going to occur. In the short term the site would continue to function as it had.

Jeffrey made the point that Marine Major Edward Sharp would retain all his current responsibilities.

No changes were expected in that arena.

He announced Elizabeth's change in role but did not mention the broader changes. He needed to evaluate and come up with how the team was going to function. These changes were going to come out later. He had lots of organization redesign work to do before making any observable changes.

He thanked everyone for the great job they were doing.

He then asked Elizabeth to say a few words.

Amy was sitting in the first row. She sensed that much more than putting Elizabeth in charge of the technical team was happening. She looked over at Bram only to see that he was wearing his poker face. This was all she needed to know that there was more.

She made up her mind to somehow corner him and find out the real scoop.

She would get it out of him when he went out on his next desert walk. He was due for his last walk the following day.

She intended to sit with Einstein and Bram. She would enjoy the morning sunrise, scratching Einstein behind the ears and while listening to Bram explain what was happening

Chapter 4: Breakthrough

Time slowed to a crawl, slower that a snail inching its way along a wet garden steppingstone.

The meetings had come out better than he had expected. Change was in the air.

Bram went to watch the sunrise from the perch on top of his boulder. Einstein, his pet mouse, came out to sit with him and listen to his explanation of how the meeting had progressed.

Periodically Bram would credit Einstein for helping him clarify what had been accomplished and how the project should proceed.

Einstein seemed to understand and would turn his head when asked a question.

The heading for today's hike was three sixty degrees clockwise. Each compass degree represented a calendar day. This was his one full year at the facility.

Getting agreement to have the program become a global effort made the morning seem to be more peaceful. He was ready to attack his work with more vigor and knew that he would make the breakthroughs he still needed to make.

Jeffrey had let him know that agreement on making the effort a global one had been accepted but it would be carefully controlled so it would not affect the effort.

Erica had enthusiastically engaged in getting the bios of potential team members from countries around the world.

He thought all seemed to be going well.

Bram's discussions with Amy had gone to a deeper level. She shared that she had been accepted into training as an astronaut. She had expressed mixed feelings about leaving her current assignment, but she was still eager to become an astronaut and get a chance to go into space.

Bram took his hike heading on the three hundred sixty degree on the compass. An hour later Amy landed the helicopter to take him back.

On their return, Bram invited Amy to watch the sunrise with him the next morning.

Bram walked slowly to his office. He was eager to continue his work but once again the rest of the day went by at a snail's pace. He had the breakthrough and had a working model.

He had figured out the physical design of the transmitter. It looked like a honey combed magnetron. He powered it up and the combination of the oscillating chambers and the enveloping magnetic field created a Fold that linked two special three dimensional coordinates. The chambers dimensions and their oscillating frequencies translated his mathematical equations into the magnetic space time Fold.

Amy walked away wondering about the timing of the sunrise invitation. She had shared the fact that she was going to accept the invitation to be trained as an astronaut.

She spent the day cleaning and re-cleaning her helicopter. She had no idea what Bram had in mind, and it made her nervous. She knew she was attracted to Bram but was not ready for any type of personal commitment.

Bram spent the day preparing for the next morning. He encapsulated two apples and two bunches of grapes in two clear plastic bubbles. He set them aside and completed the work on the two boxes that to the eye of an observer would appear to be square aluminum suitcases.

The content of these suitcases held the electronics and magnetron he had personally designed and had the lab machinist and computer specialist build.

The following morning would be his maiden test of being able to Fold time and space.

He wondered what the team would later think about his minimalist approach to testing a world changing breakthrough.

In the late afternoon, he set the two bubbles, one on each suitcase and left his lab.

He met the rest of the team for dinner. The conversation escaped him. He was wrapped in the fabric of time and space.

He was living tomorrow.

He knew it would be hard to sleep.

Early the next morning he walked by the lab and briefly looked in. What he saw excited him. His system seemed to be acting as he expected. He was hoping to see success at the destination of his morning walk.

He walked on past the lab to meet Amy.

Then together, they walked to the boulder where he hoped the verification of his efforts would be waiting.

He was having trouble controlling his breathing and his pace. This was the moment he had worked so hard to get to.

This was the proof of his many months and years of driving himself both mentally and physically.

Amy walked into the empty lobby and gave small groan. It was five in the morning. She was not a morning person. She hoped Bram would not keep her waiting in her morning misery.

She smiled as he walked in on the tail of her feeling sorry for herself. He seemed wide awake and chirpy. How that was possible was beyond her.

She could see excitement on his face. She hoped that she was not going to be ice water on his good feelings.

Bram walked in and gave Amy a hug. This was the first time he had greeted her in this manner. It was how the team greeted each other every morning.

It was not until he had done it that he worried about whether it was a proper greeting.

He decided to get up to the boulder before saying or doing anything else. He headed for the door with a follow me over his shoulder.

The star's twinkling and the Cheshire moon provided meager light for the ten-minute walk through the dark. Once on the trail, Bram could make the walk with his eyes closed.

This morning he was having trouble making his way.

He was on his three hundredth and sixty first trip along the trail.

This time it was different.

What was ahead would change how mankind controlled the world, controlled travel in space and across the Universe. It would most certainly change his life.

This time he was straining to see what was on the boulder. Finally, he could make out the top of the boulder.

He came to an abrupt stop. He asked Amy what she saw.

Two balls floating in the air was her reply.

Her response was what he hoped to hear.

He took her hand and walked up to the boulder and helped her up. She took a seat to one side of the two bubbles. He got up on the other side.

Amy commenced to pass one hand under the bubble on her side. She asked how it was possible that they were floating in the air.

Bram moved his hands under and around the bubbles.

This was a first for him and he too wondered how the bubbles remained in their position. It was the position and elevation he had specified in the space time location of the algorithms running on the computers located in each of his suitcases in his lab.

How the two bubbles floated in the air would require more analysis on his part. He pushed on his bubble and got it to move but when he let go it returned to its original position.

Bram told Amy that one bubble was for her and one for him.

He opened his bubble and took a big bite of the apple that was inside.

Amy continued to look at her bubble.

All she could think about was how it possible?

What was the trick.to make the bubbles float in thin air.

How had the bubbles been placed here?

She wanted to ask these questions, but she knew that Bram was enjoying his success at getting the bubbles to this location.

Bram told Amy to enjoy her breakfast fruit.

He told her that she was the first to witness the breakthrough he had been working on.

He would tell her more right after the sunrise and after greeting Einstein.

Amy was surprised at the globe holding an apple and a bunch of grapes. She twisted open her globe and popped a large purple grape into her mouth and let the sweet juice infuse her mind. She smiled and went to think, "her disoriented and twisted mind." She felt relief when it struck her that it was not about romance, but it was about science.

She looked at Bram and knew she was looking at a genius. One that seemed to care and look out for all the people around him. One that took the greatest breakthrough that could possibly be made as a moment to share with a lowly helicopter pilot.

She watched the sun slowly break above the horizon and felt the warmth of the first rays on her face.

She scooted away from Einstein as he came out of the hole at the base of the boulder and quickly climbed to sit between them but really next to Bram.

Bram took a napkin from his pocket and opened it. The remains of a cookie drew Einstein to the napkin. He thanked Einstein for helping him with the breakthrough.

Bram turned to look at Amy.

He repeated her desire to go into space. He then made the point that he would need a pilot when bubbles like the ones holding their apples and grapes took people across the universe.

He told Amy she could be that pilot and told her to go get the astronaut training but to come back to help design and then to pilot the bubbles that would cross the vast distances of space.

Amy was overwhelmed. She also wondered how she would be selected to be the pilot of such a craft. There would be many candidates that would outrank her for the job.

She asked Bram why he was so certain that she would be able to be the pilot of such a craft.

Bram understood her concern about being able to come back as that pilot of the first across the Universe spacecraft.

He stated that he would determine the passengers and crew of the first few trips across the universe. If she wanted, she would be the pilot on one of the two initial spaceships to cross folded space.

Amy sat trying to take everything in. She had been worried about some romantic advance but was now being rewarded for their current friendship with a future offer to be among the first to cross space.

She was also aware that Bram had let her be the first to witness his success.

This was more than she had ever expected.

She scooted over to sit next to Bram and gave him a hug as she thanked him.

She then said she was going to leave him with Einstein, and she would go to get her bird ready to pick him up.

She was going to go to her helo and scream her head off.

Her world had taken on a new meaning.

She was having trouble breathing as she stumbled back to her domain.

54

Chapter 5: Participants and Master Plan

The tension in the room was as strong as black phantom pepper sauce on a bleeding steak. It burned just to breathe the air.

Bram looked from one strained face to another. Meetings like this had been going on for months and little progress was being made. He had now sat through two of these.

He had no clue how Erica had survived so long.

He had received a request for him to join her in handling the situation. This had been a great surprise to him. He learned that more than two thousand names had been proposed. Every country had at least one entry. The larger countries had multiple candidates.

Erica had no clue on how to select the right candidates. She had been told select between fifteen to twenty candidates. She had finally concluded that she needed someone to help her reduce the number of candidates.

Her meeting with Bram had at least reduced the stress to where she was not contemplating shooting herself.

Bram seemed to think the situation was normal. Maybe for him but she was at the end of her rope. The representatives from the various countries were at best pushing hard and at worst they were just plain assholes.

Bram laughed when Erica vented her frustration. He made the point that he had been certain that he did not want the job of selecting the candidates but that he would be glad to help figure out how to evaluate and select the best candidates.

Bram had not only spent two days in unpleasant and contentious meetings, but he had also reviewed the list of candidates and was no more able to make selections than Erica.

Since the candidates were from the fields of astronomy, physics, math, and a variety of other related sciences he decided to get the whole team involve. He went one step farther and put Amy on the list of people who would review the candidates.

He did not anticipate her knowing anyone on the list, but it provided a way for her to be noticed.

He knew that would be important later.

Bram anticipated the rest of the team would have some say about certain candidates.

He sent his request for total team participation to Elizabeth.

When Elizabeth received the request, she immediately called the team together. The team agreed to take a shot at the more than two thousand names.

They discussed the request.

Both Mallica and Marcus confessed to not knowing any of the names on the list.

Elizabeth admitted she knew only four names on the list and had heard some information about another dozen.

The three of them agreed to split up the list and review the resumes, look at publications and the exposure on the web.

They agreed on Bram's suggested priority process.

First, they had to get candidates from all the countries on the UN security council.

Then any candidate that had been published in their field.

Then one from each of the five major religions.

Then one from each country by population size.

Bram also wanted; a planetary scientist, an earth scientist, a helio-physicist, an astrophysicist, a chemist, a biologist, an astronomer, an engineer, and a historian.

Elizabeth asked if there were any other consideration that Bram might have that could make the selection process a little more complicated.

He laughed and replied that if he thought of any others, he would let her know.

Amy received Bram's request and wondered how she had been selected to review the list of candidates. He must certainly know that she would not know anything about the candidates. She also noted that he had copied most of the NASA and Army command.

She realized that he had put the spotlight on her. She had grown up as a Lutheran and submitted her long-time pastor's name for the religious representative position.

She thanked Bram and gave him her one candidate as part of her reply. She made a point of mentioning her commitment to space and to her continued desire to complete her astronaut training. She copied the distribution that Bram had used.

Thank you, Bram, went through her mind as she pressed the send key.

Jeffrey reviewed all the messages with a focus on the expanded team. He believed Bram was orchestrating the situation so that the choices made would have a solid selection process that could be explained.

He was surprised at how well Erica and Bram were getting along. He was aware of the strain Erica had been under.

Bram's approach had provided an explainable means of managing the process.

He faced a similar storm within the US political and military hierarchy. Every agency and military branch wanted control of the Fold program.

He was keeping them all at bay by leveraging his connection with President Natorly.

He would keep Bram in mind when it came time to break down the next barrier.

He asked his administrative support to set up a meeting with Bram and Erica. He needed help and would explore his next steps with them.

Elizabeth cursed quietly under her breath. Bram had set them up with a lot of work. She smiled and asked Mallica and Marcus about their progress in prioritizing the list of candidates.

Mallica complained that she had spent more time than she had expected in researching each candidate.

Marcus just said ditto.

Elizabeth echoed Marcus.

After a quick discussion, she agreed to send their composite list to Bram. It added some depth to the information, but it said that Bram was to make the final selection.

Jeffrey's requested meeting was a Saturday morning breakfast meeting. There were no weekdays that worked. His support had found a secure location on the base. The normal kitchen crew would cater the breakfast.

He was sure it had been a long week for all of them and felt some guilt about a Saturday morning meeting.

Guilt yes, but the need was great.

He met Bram and Erica in the empty parking lot. He apologized about taking part of their weekend and then led the way to the breakfast meeting.

Jeffrey suggested they eat breakfast first and get into the meeting afterwards.

He noted that conversation was non-existent, and he wondered how the meeting would flow.

Bram had reviewed the recommendations and finalized the list as best he could. He was ready to layout the way forward as he saw it. He hoped that Erica had worked through an initial master plan for the massive work that remained to be done.

When the after-breakfast coffee and tea was set up, he stood and after filling his teacup said he was ready to share his participant selection, to share a rough work logic and a list of things that needed to get done for the project to move forward.

Erica was relieved. She wanted the participant selection to end. She wanted a normal project with logical actions and steps that she could manage.

Anything to bring the chaos to an end.

Bram left the planning wide open for her to step into.

Her response to Bram's statement that he had a participant selection list was that she was all ears.

Jeffrey echoed Erica.

Bram expressed the fact that he was glad to be able to close the participant list. He handed out the list of seventeen names from twelve countries to Jeffery and Erica.

He also stated that he did not need any of them for the Folding of time and space effort. The global team was a way to engage the other countries but until the Fold effort became a reality and was ready for sharing the global team should not be brought together.

He noted the surprised look on both Erica's face and on Jefferies face.

He apologized and said that he still held the view that the Fold program should be a global effort, his participation of selecting a global team had convinced him that it would just add chaos to the program.

His current team was all he needed.

Bram then suggested they develop a plan to build the space bubbles, the data collection, and analysis systems that would be required.

He highlighted the bubble construction as perhaps the critical path but that was something that Erica needed to handle.

Once again Bram surprised Erica. He was very clear on his capabilities and what he preferred his focus to be.

He said that delaying setting up the Global group freed her up to do what she liked best.

Erica was surprised with the sudden change in direction but immediately agreed and felt a sense of relief. She stood and walked to the white board and began asking the questions that would lead to a project master plan that would ensure a winning logic to guide the remainder of the effort.

Jeffrey shook his head and thanked Bram for simplifying his world and wished that he would have done it earlier.

Bram agreed that he too should have reached that decision earlier, but he had shared his conclusion as soon as he had come to it.

He then responded to Erica's questions and identified the need for two plastic bubbles each to house twelve people. They would need to have the supplies to sustain the twelve crew members for a year.

Four members would be data collectors. They would manage and maintain sensors and telescopes in the visual, the infrared and x ray spectrum.

Four would be data analysist.

One would be an instrument maintenance specialist.

One would be in command.

The remaining two would be the pilot and co-pilot of the bubble.

A third system of data collection would be housed on Earth.

The additional selected participants would utilize the data for analysis. Some of them might or might not go out in the bubbles.

He looked at Jeffrey and let him know all was ready as soon as the bubbles were done. He would need to get his time-space Fold equipment enlarged to make a sufficiently large Fold and to move the bubbles to the Fold location.

Bram identified two support items. He needed a company that would work with him to test his extrapolation of the power required for his space-time folding equipment.

The other need was to design the transport bubble he envisioned.

Jeffrey asked Erica if she had enough to get started and would she work with Bram to get more detailed on his needs. She replied yes but she would need more people to get all the work done. She was especially worried about the time it would take to construct the bubbles.

Jeffrey looked at the draft work plan that Erica had put on the white board.

He pointed to several of the task items and had Erica put NASA, Boeing, and the Air Force next to them. If speed was required, he would see if he could leverage existing resources that were already contracted and active.

Jeffrey felt great about how the three of them were working together.

He highlighted that he would need to get an increase in his budget.

He thanked both Bram and Erica and suggested they meet again on the following Wednesday.

<u>Chapter 6: Power</u>

Bram could not determine the amount of power he would need to Fold space around the structures of the space vessels. The amount of power to simply move an apple and some grapes had blown the power supply. He went through his equations several times trying to figure it out how he could determine the power required.

He could not determine it mathematically.

He had decided to try moving different blocks of steel of specific sizes through a Fold and monitor the power draw for the series of folds. He would then have the data to determine the power supply the project would need. He was certain the power requirement would be extremely high. He needed to quickly learn just how high.

Bram looked out at the collection of steel blocks he had shipped in for his testing.

The first one was a one by one-foot cube.

The next was a three by three-foot cube.

The next was a ten-foot cube.

The largest was a thirty by thirty-foot cube.

Viewed from the side they looked like the base of an asymptotic curve. This he thought was an appropriate view.

Once he was able to move all these cubes from one point to another, he would have the data to determine the mathematics to design the actual space time bending power unit and magnetron units on the scale he would need to move his plastic bubble spaceships.

His concern was how steep the asymptotic power curve would be.

His new lab was located outside of the Seattle area in an abandoned National Reserve helicopter hanger. To Bram it seemed like a huge facility. His steel blocks seem like tinker toys relative to the size of the hangar. He later learned it was not the size of the hangar that was of any concern, but the size of the power supplied to the hangar.

He was alone in this endeavor. He did not know how to engage someone to help him.

Well, he was not alone, he had a crew of twenty technicians working on building, the transport power supplies and a local machine shop making the space Fold magnetrons. He was having successively larger power supplies and space Fold magnetrons made for each size of steel cubes

Two bodyguards now accompanied and shadowed him day and night. There were four bodyguards. Two for the daylight hours and two for the nighttime.

Jeffrey had informed him that there was credible intelligence that numerous groups, countries, and companies were looking for him and that several subversive groups had interest in kidnapping him. This information was troubling to Bram, but he was focused on getting his space bubbles powered.

The attempt to move the one by one-foot cube had blown the power supply and the site transformer for the hanger. His control unit was also toast.

That clearly demonstrated his lack of knowledge of the power draw.

The power company upgraded the substation by tripling it in size. Bram asked that his power supplies were also tripled in size.

The rest of his technical team had remained in the original desert location. He talked to them daily and was trying to get them to help in defining the power requirement.

Once a week the entire team lead by Elizabeth met to discuss their activities.

Bram, Erica, Elizabeth, and Jeffrey had a separate meeting each week to review the program master plan. Erica was keeping everything moving. She laughed and commented that Bram was creating the critical path by regularly blowing up his work.

It was not his work plan that he was blowing up. He was now being guided by the power company crew supervisor and being shown a whole substation that he had recently blown up. The power surge when he tried to create a Fold to move his three-foot block of steel through had not only blown out the substation but had blacked out the three surrounding counties.

The power company refused to set up the substation again. They suggested he find a site that was located near or at the power generation site that had the capacity to support his power needs.

Bram returned to his office and called Mallica and gave her the data from the first two experiments and asked her to calculate the power required for the ten by ten and the thirty by thirty-foot blocks of steel.

Mallica spent the entire night working on what the power requirement would be. She extrapolated that it would take at least one thousand megawatts.

Mallica qualified her estimate by stating the parameters for the asymptotic curve she had developed. She was not sure of the accuracy of her estimate. She feared it could be more and she did not know if the distance of the Fold would need more power.

Bram thought about this huge power requirement. He needed to be as close to the source of power generation as possible. He also needed to be isolated from the general public population centers.

He called Erica and requested a location that would allow him to use the output of an entire power plant with at least one thousand megawatts. He made the point that the power requirements might be even more for the crafts being built. He doubled the power request.

Bram was surprised at how fast Erica and her staff located a plant that had that much power. They settled on a site south of the Dalles hydroelectric plant on the Oregon side of the Columbia river. They would need to erect a new building, but it would be surrounded by at least two thousand megawatts.

The dam provided power to a wide area but there were one thousand megawatts that was sold and flowed out on the grid. When the time came for the use for the power, the grid could adjust to cover it.

Erica called Jeffrey and assigned him the task of making the site available for the Fold project. She specified the building size, erection location and time to completion. She was confident Jeffrey could make it happen. She knew that he had a direct line to the NASA director and had visited the White House several times.

Jeffrey listened to Erica. He then put in a call to Bram, so he could hear for himself about the power need. Bram shared the experiences he had so far with blowing up substations and the fact that the power company had told him that the current location prohibited them from quickly giving the site any more power than they had made available.

Jeffrey then put in a call to the US Army Core of Engineers District Commander at the Dalles site. He asked who the final decision maker would be if he were asked to accept a project that might take all the output of the Dalles hydroelectric plant.

President Natorly was identified as the one needing to make the decision.

Jeffrey put in a call the John Morgan the NASA director. It would take both of them to convince the President. John would have to share the vision for NASA if this technology panned out. Jeffrey would share the Fold program objectives and share some of the specifics of what a Fold meant.

John listened as Jeffrey explained the need for the large amount of power required to Fold time and space. He went on to explain how much total power that would be needed was not yet clear. Jeffrey gave the current estimate to be two thousand megawatts to be continuously used during the time needed to see the mission through the Fold. He had doubled what Bram had told him.

John responded that the suggested location provided a good base and agreed that another two thousand megawatts should be installed as backup. The request would be for almost a billion dollars for the current location. A second location should also be included and be planned.

Jeffrey was surprised at how quickly John accepted the need and how quickly he planned to act. It was only a week later that they were set to meet with President Natorly. Jeffrey knew who the best person would be to convince the President.

The following week Jeffrey entered the White House meeting room and looked around the table. The entire cabinet was there. He had been asked to present the project to the group, but he had no clue how to communicate the details that would be needed to convince President and his team to support the project.

Bram walked in with him and took a seat beside him. Jeffrey stood and introduced himself. He proceeded to give a general introduction of the Fold project and then introduced Bram.

Those sitting around the table were silent and did not seem to understand and were not looking very supportive.

Bram knew that none of the people in the room understood the concept of Folding time and space. They certainly would fall asleep if he went into the math and science of the project. He had thought about how to communicate the need for the tremendous power to Fold time and space and had arranged that with the White House maintenance supervisor.

A demonstration would be the best way to get the support the program needed. He slowly and dramatically put his briefcase on the table. He looked in the case at the bubbles placed in their holders. He took out a thick massive power cord and connected it to one that had been made available by the White House maintenance supervisor. He told everyone around the table to pay attention and reached into the briefcase and pressed a button.

The lights in the room dimmed and flickered. A small bubble appeared and floated in front of President Natorly. He pointed at the bubble. Then he repeated the process two more times. Each time the lights flickered and dimmed. A bubble appeared in front of the Vice President, and the Chief of Staff.

He asked each of them to verify the bubbles were indeed floating in the air. The three did as requested. President Natorly pushed his with his finger and then let go. The bubble returned to its original position.

Bram asked each to grab the bubble and open it. He made the point that each bubble contained a candy kiss that was intended to persuade them to support the Fold program.

Bram took out a candy kiss for himself put it in his mouth. He stated that everyone in the room had just witnessed the process of folding time and space. He pointed out the dimming of the lights before each bubble had appeared. He explained that the bubbles had traveled from his briefcase through space to float in front of each person.

He then asked the White House maintenance supervisor to share the amount of power that had been consumed. The response was that a whole month of power had been consumed.

Bram smiled when President Natorly said his support could be had for one more candy kiss. He reached into the briefcase, placed a bubble in the appropriate location and pressed the button. The lights dimmed, and a bubble appeared in front of the President. Bram watched as the President passed his hand under and around the bubble.

Why doesn't gravity cause it to fall the President asked?

Bram answered that it was a great question and one for which he had no answer.

He volunteered that as soon as he solved that problem he would get back to him.

President Natorly looked around the table and said the project had all the support it would need. All resources of the US government would immediately be made available.

Jeffrey complimented Bram on his presentation. He then turned to the President and thanked him for his time and that funding was needed immediately to prevent the delay of the "Fold in Time" FIT project.

The reply that the funds would be released immediately to NASA pleased Jeffrey.

Bram was surprised at how quickly funding had been agreed to. A billion dollars seemed to be something that would take months to get.

On the way to the airport, Jeffrey complimented Bram on the way he had used the Fold breakthrough to get President Natorly to open the purse strings.

On his return to the west, Bram decided to go out to the new site and get the lay of the land. He would also go and check on the progress being made by Boeing on getting the bubbles built.

Amy learned from Elizabeth about Bram's funding success. She was close to the completion of her astronaut training. She would be one of two females in her class. Patricia Fleming, the other female candidate, had become a friend during the training. They had supported each other as each felt the bias against them by the male astronaut students in their class.

There were no scheduled space flights for them anywhere in the near future, so Amy asked Pat if she was interested in a side adventure. Pat asked what that might be. Once she learned of the specific details of the Fold project, she was not only interested she was eager to be included.

Bram recognized the ringtone on his phone and greeted Amy with their familiar greeting of *Babe.*

He stopped what he was doing and sat down. His bodyguards sat down on each side. They were in an empty field surrounded by power stations and overhead power lines. He listened to Amy and agreed to interview Pat.

He replied that he was planning to attend the astronaut graduation ceremony. He would interview Pat during his time at the graduation ceremony.

Bram stood up and thought about his relationship with Amy.

He really liked her but was she the one?

It was unclear to him.

He decided that time would tell. He looked around at the new location that would house the space bubbles and be the project's command center. He decided it was certainly secluded enough that any new construction would go unnoticed outside of the immediate community.

He returned to his Portland hotel and decided to drive up to the Boeing factory just south of Seattle.

He not only had bodyguards, but he was assigned a limo. He rode in back where he could relax.

Though he had planned to take in the view, he was soon asleep in the comfortable back seat.

His two bodyguards sat up front. The four assigned to guard Bram took turns in their day and night coverage. Bram knew that the current set of bodyguards were temporary until he interviewed the potential long-term applicants. He got along with the current set, but they all had families in the DC area.

Bram was met by Jose Estrada the project manager for the construction and assembly of the two bubbles. Jose was accompanied by Ester Mannerly, Jose's NASA counterpart. She reported directly to John Morgan the NASA director.

Bram was informed that the four half shells for the space bubbles had just arrived and were being put into their assembly position at the very moment. He was led out to the assembly area. This was one of the locations where the Boeing 787's were assembled.

It was clear to Bram that two assembly locations were set up. The four-story plastic bubble halves were being placed into position. They were mounted above a very large forty by forty-foot square, low-slung platforms. The bubbles were held in place by two cables that suspended them at what would be the center of a wheel like living and work area.

Bram followed behind Jose and Ester as they led the way to the first assembly area.

Bram took in the crew of about twenty personnel. He learned they were immediately starting to install the telescopes and sensors that he had specified.

He walked over and examined the sensor and computer equipment. He asked how they had been obtained so quickly and learned that NASA had redirected them from the next four space shuttles.

Bram asked how they planned to move the spheres to the launch location.

Ester smiled and replied that she had been told that he would take care of that problem.

Bram laughed. He realized that would be a great way to test the Fold power requirements.

He asked that the co-ordinates for the very center of each bubble be determined and sent to him. Yes, he replied that he would take care of getting the spheres to the launch location.

Bram spent the rest of the day with Ester inspecting the bubbles and the equipment to be installed.

The three of them agreed to meet for dinner. Bram made sure that the dinner was for seven people. He was making sure his protection team was well fed. Bram enjoyed the dinner and the genial conversation shared by all of them. He was pleased with the two of them having been selected to manage the assembly process.

He was headed for the airport and a night flight to Houston.

As he climbed into bed, Bram knew he was getting spoiled. He was on a private plane on the way to Amy's astronaut graduation. On any other airline it was called the red eye special. On this plane Bram figured it was just special.

His guilty feeling did not last long. Bram was almost immediately asleep

Chapter 7: Fold Pilots

Bram slept throughout the four-hour flight. He was awakened just prior to landing and took a seat. He looked out the window to see that the sun was threatening to come over the far horizon.

Bram did not feel even a bump as the plane landed. He complemented the pilots for the smooth as glass landing as he passed them on his way down the steps.

Bram looked up at the still visible stars. His watch showed it was five in the morning.

He was bracketed by bodyguards as he went to the waiting limo.

Bram learned that they had landed at NASA's private airport. It was not even shown on the normal Houston area map.

The driver commented that he and his partner would be with him during his stay. They drove to the Villa where he would stay. It was a three-bedroom furnished condo that had been recommended by John Morgan's support. The driver stayed behind the wheel, but his partner quickly stepped out to open the door of the limo and proceeded to get the bags out of the trunk.

Bram's guards talked briefly with the limo driver. Two of them got back into the limo. They were staying at a nearby hotel and would return in the evening.

Bram stopped long enough to thank the driver and his assistant. He asked their names and was told it was Jim and Joe. He again thanked them by name and then went into the condo.

Bram was impressed by the open feel of the condo entrance area. Two bedrooms opened to each side of the entrance hallway. The kitchen area was to one side of the hallway and the living room was on the other side. A third bedroom was to the right and a fourth bedroom was to the left.

Bram took the back-left bedroom. The two guards staying with him for the night each took one of the other bedrooms.

The sun was threatening to light up the far horizon and it was making the few clouds turn into pinkish yellow fluffs in the morning sky. Bram thought that it was the making of a wonderful day.

His two bodyguards entered and quickly checked out the apartment. Then they cleared Bram to go on his own.

He wandered through the suite to take in its layout. Once he had wandered around the suite, he stood looking out as the sun slowly rose on the far horizon.

The smell of fresh coffee reminded him that he had a busy day ahead. He was ready for a long hot shower and then he would go on to breakfast to meet Amy.

He was expecting a very hectic day.

The restaurant where he was to meet Amy and Pat for breakfast had a great view of the Gulf and when he entered it was empty. He and his guards had entered just as the restaurant opened and had selected the two tables that seemed to have the best view.

He ordered a pot of tea and some honey to sweeten it. He took in the view and when the tea arrived, he put in the honey and slowly stirred it. He sipped on the tea as he waited.

Bram came awake as he took in the two very good-looking women entering. One was Amy, her dark hair framed a calm and serene face. She looked very different in her current outfit versus the military garb he had always seen her in. Her friend, Pat, had long curly red hair, freckles and green eyes that immediately caught his attention. She too had the looks that would turn heads.

His two bodyguards and the four other persons now in the restaurant all stopped to look at the two women. Bram stood and waved to get the attention of the two.

After introductions they all sat down. After a brief discussion they ordered breakfast. Bram felt an immediate attraction for Pat. He took note that she was as direct and as confident in herself as Amy. The two were a contrast in looks and in mannerisms but both were stunning in their appearance

Bram put his evaluation of the two into a back mental compartment. They both impressed him.

Bram wanted to make sure of the schedule for the day and asked to go over it.

The graduating astronaut class had only six persons. The ceremony would be held at the NASA main training area at one in the afternoon and then there would be a dinner at the training center's director's home.

Bram had received his formal invitation more than a month ago and had sent in his acceptance.

He mentioned that he would attend with four bodyguards, and he hoped that it would not cause any problems.

He invited Amy and Pat for lunch at the Galveston waterfront. Amy accepted but Pat declined saying she had a couple of things to do before the graduation ceremony.

After breakfast Amy and Bram went to the NASA space center. There Bram followed the flow of the space program development. It was clear to him that his breakthrough was the next S curve of improvement in space technology. The current rocket technology would suffer the same fate as the horse and buggy when the automobile came on the scene or that the propeller plane faced when the jet engine was developed.

Bram listened to Amy describe her training routine. She shared that Pat had finished first in the class and she had finished third. He congratulated her on her performance and said that it qualified her to command one of the two, Fold, modules.

They returned from their walk and took seats facing the Gulf. They sat making small talk until it was time for lunch. After lunch they departed to the graduation.

Bram estimated that there were about fifty people attending the graduation and that the graduation class of six was greatly outnumbered. Half of the people attending were family and friends and the other half various officers, a state representative, and several sponsors for the astronauts.

Bram sat quietly and observed the reactions of each of the astronauts. He seemed to be Amy's only sponsor and that one of the state representatives was Pat's sponsor.

The ceremony lasted for about forty-five minutes. Afterwards there was some small talk among all the guests as they shared some hors d'oeuvres and drinks. The gathering did not last long. Except for the graduates, the rest of those attending did not know each other and were soon leaving from the gathering.

Bram walked with Amy and Pat out to the parking lot. They agreed to celebrate with a few drinks at a local night spot not far from the apartment that they shared.

The ten-minute drive to their apartment gave Bram time to contemplate on the accomplishment of the two women.

On the way to their nightspot, he heard them talking about the end of their training. They both commented on the fact that no space missions were planned, and they would probably be old ladies when the next one would occur.

Bram liked the fact that the background music at the nightspot remained low and allowed for small talk and periodic serious discussion. Part of Bram's discussion was Pat's interview. He was interested in her background and experiences.

Amy reminded them it was time to go to the Astronaut graduation dinner. Pat let out a small groan. She voiced the hope that it would not be too boring.

Bram stood up and led the way out to their waiting limo. He thought about Pat's comment about the dinner being boring. He knew that he would not be bored escorting the two of them.

Bram's limo took the three to the base commander's home. The limo easily held all of them in the spacious back seating area.

The dinner turned out to be a backyard barbeque. A cooling breeze kept the outdoor venue comfortable. The NASA training commander had selected only those close to the graduates to be invited.

John Morgan, NASA director gave a small speech about the future of space travel and the expectation he had of the new astronauts. He made the point that several of them would get a chance of a lifetime.

The dinner of steak, grilled shrimp, grilled asparagus and grilled corn with a mixed side salad and the backyard venue made for a more relaxed meal then Bram had anticipated. He made a point of sitting next to John, so he could request both Amy and Pat join the Fold team.

John expressed his concern in taking in rookies for the piloting.

Bram replied that independent of age or gender everyone was going to be a rookie. There were no Fold veterans. He pointed out that he was not sure what a Fold pilot would do.

John nodded and said he understood Bram's view, but the other two pilots he was recommending would be based on seniority and their performance in the NASA space program. He made the point that he was accepting a hot potato by naming the two women to be the pilots.

Bram said he understood and that having two long term NASA astronauts made sense. He was satisfied with the acceptance of the two astronauts he had requested.

Bram, Amy, and Pat were the last of the guests to depart the dinner. They thanked Major Wellington for choosing such a relaxing way to host the new astronauts.

Bram shook John's hand and reminded him of the request he had made.

His two guards and the limo drivers had discreetly enjoyed the backyard barbeque. The limo drivers commented that they had never attended an astronaut graduation, but they would try to be the drivers when Major Wellington again hosted such an event.

Bram made the comment that if he returned to Houston in the future, he would ask for them by name.

Bram wished he were staying another day, but he had arranged to go on to the East coast and meet with Jeffrey and Erica. He had also agreed to interview the FBI candidates that had volunteered for the role of being his permanent bodyguards.

He would then return to Seattle and meet with Ester and Jose to monitor the arrival and positioning of the main control and living quarters sections of the space bubbles. Together the three of them would make the acceptance inspection of those sections. The internal components of these sections were also arriving and would also need acceptance inspection.

Once on the plane, Bram ordered a ginger ale. He sat for a while thinking about Amy and Pat. He knew that in the future he would need to sort out his feelings about each.

After takeoff Bram walked to the back and got into bed. He knew he would need all the sleep he could get.

<u>Chapter 8 The First Fold</u>

For Bram, the months after the trip to Houston both flew and dragged by. He saw the work on the bubble as an Indy car going at breakneck speed around the track. He experienced the work on the Fold apparatus and equipment as moving at a snail's pace. The snail's pace was riddled with various and dramatic explosions as power supplies overheated when trying to move an object to a Fold coordinate. Bram was finally confronted by the Boeing power utility manager and informed that the power company would no longer deal with the surges that he was causing.

He resigned himself to wait to the time he would have access to enough power to complete his Fold transmission development.

Bram turned his attention to working with the crews of the two bubbles and began conducting simulated launch trials.

John kept his word to Bram. Amy and Pat had received their assignment by NASA to the Fold program. Two senior astronauts, Daryl Nazda and Harold Redat were teamed up with them as their backups. Bram instinctively assigned Pat and Daryl to Bubble 1 and Amy and Harold to Bubble 2.

Bram surprised Elizabeth by asking her to be in command of Bubble 2. Elizabeth gave an uncharacteristic shout and with tears in her eyes she rushed Bram and gave him a hug that made it hard for him to breath. Bram listened as she whispered into his ear that he had just fulfilled her personal dream of going out into space.

The bubbles became known as Bubble1 and Bubble 2. On his next visit from the NASA headquarters, John commented to Bram that the names were very clear but lacked creativity.

The building of the launch facilities at the Dalles hydroelectric plant had become the project bottle neck. The bottle neck was not the Launch building but the power generators, the power line infrastructure and the gas turbines that would back up the hydroelectric dam power.

Bram had pressured Erica to make it happen. Erica in turn forced the redirect of all the orders the turbine manufacture had to the Fold project. The manufacturer had objected but Erica invoked national security and made it happen.

Bram was pleased with the tour of the computer hardware and inspected the facilities that each of the two-bubble analysis teams occupied. Each bubble analysis group had a separate office area.

He really liked the large theater sized screen that was the center piece of the common gathering area. This was where everyone would gather during the observation periods. Bram felt the pull of the screens like the urge to jump when standing on the edge of a cliff.

Bram encouraged every participant on the team to select and decide on the observations to be made at the selected Fold locations.

It was Pat that asked if a powerful enough telescope to view the other side of the hole was part of the package. Bram listened to the discussion that followed and agreed with the team's recommendation that one Bubble should focus on the long-range mapping with a powerful telescope and the other Bubble should focus on the closer area of space.

Elizabeth took on the role of organizing the analysis teams. She spent her days working with each team on the aspect of the data gathering and the subsequent analysis to be done on the data. An initial analysis would be done at each Bubble and the data would be sent out in a continuous feed back to Earth. This transmission would not always reach Earth before the Bubble returned but it would be the safety valve in case of a major disaster.

Bram commented that any message sent out from across the universe might never be received. He made the point that Earth may have perished in all that time even if the message was traveling at the speed of light.

It was clear to him that the team needed to think differently about how data should be backed up.

Bram focused on the work with the Bubble one and Bubble two crews. His initial focus was on how to use and repair the sensors and the computer data gathering programs. He also worked through how navigation would take place.

The Fold was totally computer controlled but both systems had manual overrides that were the responsibility of the navigators. He made sure that Amy, Pat, Daryl, and Harold received training on how to program in new coordinates and what the home base coordinates were.

He was eager to get to the Dallas site. Erica had told him that the Fold program was also building homes to house the entire Fold personnel. He learned the housing area was at the entrance to the Dallas power plant area. His house would be first and would be at the top of the hill of the complex. She let him know that they were building on a hillside that had a great view but that looked more like the desert that they had left behind that what land should look like in Oregon.

Elizabeth joined Bram, Jose, and Ester on the inspection of the completed Bubbles. Bram's specification that the bubble was to maintain as close to one G rotation as possible had resulted in an expanded section and a composite shape that looked more like a spoked motorcycle wheel and tire with a globe at its center. The work and living area were on the inside of the outer tire like area. The bubble sensor area was connected in the center of the wheel by eight tubes that created the spokes. Bram noted that the center bubble area would have no gravitational pull orientation.

The week-long inspection tour of each wheel section was Jose's responsibility.

Bram briefly reviewed the plan with the four of them and clarified the process. He knew each day would be at least twelve hours long. He wanted a brief walk-through tour and then planned to step back and concentrate on his Fold power problems.

Bram commented that the name originally used for the two space vehicles no longer applied and the team should be thinking about better names.

Each day Bram noted that the wheel was rotated so each quarter of the wheel could be thoroughly inspected. Jose had an inspection checklist for every room and installation.

The control room and systems were checked first. Elizabeth, Jose, and Ester were the primary inspectors.

The plumbing and living area checks were done by activating each item. The lighting, showers, faucets, and stool were all tested. Each wheel occupant had their own small room. A common eating area able to hold the wheel team would function as both an eating and meeting area. Several minor defects were found in each area but overall, the work had been well done.

Bram had Amy and Pat and the other NASA pilots simulate their control actions. Bram evaluated the system response by attaching his computer to the control system.

Bram was impressed with the thoroughness of the checks and the immediate response to the defects list the team generated.

He invited the inspection and support team out for a steak celebration dinner.

At the dinner Bram suggested a name change from Bubble One and Two to Space Wheel One and Two. He watched the expressions on the faces around the table and knew that he had missed the mark.

After some discussion Amy and Pat suggested USS Hood-Wheel One and USS Rainier Wheel Two. Their suggested names were immediately accepted.

Bram passed on the names to Jeffrey and asked him to verify that these names would be acceptable.

Bram didn't know it, but the inspection was the calm before the storm. On the weekend following the completion of the inspection, almost two thousand demonstrators showed up at the gate leading to the hanger where the crafts were housed.

Bram was on what he had declared was his recovery weekend at his new Dalles home when he received Jose's call about the demonstrators. Bram felt near the point of exhaustion and was planning a hike in the Mt. Hope National Forest with Amy and Pat.

He watched the video Jose shared and read the signs the demonstrators carried stating in large letters that the world would end if the project continued. He noted that the demonstrators had a large banner showing Earth exploding. He listened as they shouted that the project would be the end of the world. He wondered how the demonstrators had found out about the project and how they had learned where construction was taking place.

He called Jeffrey about the leak. Jeffrey said he would investigate where the leak occurred but made the point that leaks were hard to track down.

Bram shared his thoughts of where the leak might have come from. He shared them in the order of probability; President Natorly's office, someone in the Boeing construction group, someone in NASA. He was certain it had not come from anyone on the designated Fold team.

After Jose's call he drove out to the new Fold site and toured the facility. He took in the massive six-inch thick powerlines that swept down from a series of towers. They curved gracefully down to two dozen transformers each the size of nine sea containers standing on end next to each other. The power lines ran from there to the hanger that dwarfed all other structures in the area.

Almost everything was ready for the bubbles to be moved in. The remaining item was the installation of the ten-gas powered two hundred fifty kilowatt generators. Their mounting pads and power hook ups were ready and waiting but it would be another two weeks before the generators would start arriving and another month to get them all installed.

However, if all the power from the dam were utilized, Bram figured he would be able to transport the vessels from the Seattle hanger site to their Dalles hanger launch site.

Bram called Jeffrey to suggest they accelerate the day for moving the crafts to the launch site. It could be done as soon as all the current power being generated by the dam was made available.

Jeffrey agreed with the timing change and said he would have Erica make the power available.

Bram immediately called Amy and Pat and had them take their copilots and get their Wheels ready to move. He called Elizabeth to let her know about the move of the Wheels and asked her to take command of both wheels. He told her it would be their first Fold and she would be in command.

He let her know that he was staying in Dalles to control the move. He wanted to make sure everything was in control on the Dalles end.

Erica bent arms and called in favors. She faced what seemed to be a wall, but she made the power available. More and more she was becoming a fan of Bram's bold moves. She loved the action that seemed to follow his development of space travel. She was happy that he had stuck it out even when she had been extremely frustrated.

A few hours later after getting the OK to go call, from Erica, Bram listened as Pat hailed Amy over the ship-to-ship communication system. She looked around to the six people behind her. Her copilot gave a thumbs up. Pat declared the USS Mt. Hood, Wheel-One ready.

Amy declared that the USS Mt. Rainier and Wheel-Two was ready for Fold.

Elizabeth stated that as commander of the fleet she was ready.

Bram at the Dalles launch site checked that everything was ready at his end. He had walked the entire power system with the power supervisor and decided that everything that could be done had been done.

Bram looked at the two crafts at the Seattle launch site. They appeared on the left side of the Dalles's auditorium forty-foot by sixty-foot screen. The right side showing the inside of the Dalles receiving site was blank.

Bram was seated in the back of the auditorium with his auxiliary control system running on his computer. He decided he needed to install a more substantial control booth at the back of the auditorium.

Pat would be the first to activate the Fold from her Mt Hood control system. This was a duplicate of Bram's back up.

Bram told Pat to activate whenever she was ready.

Pat had practiced the simple act of pushing the activate button at least a hundred times. She knew that a monkey could be trained to perform this simple act.

Yet her palms were sweating.

She pushed the button.

She thought it had not worked.

Then she looked out the window to see a group of cheering people.

The lights in the hanger dimmed and the giant screen blinked. Then a cheer went up as the Mt Hood appeared in the Dalles hanger.

A cheering group rushed out to the Mt Hood, Wheel-One. They were the ground support crew for the Mt. Hood.

Bram had a very different experience than everyone else. A shiver had run down Bram's back when the lights dimmed. He had experienced this when he lost power and lost his three-foot steel cube. He had never recovered it and had no clue where in the universe it might be. It was not at the coordinates that he had set for it to go.

He was keenly aware of the loss that would have been suffered if the power had failed. He called the power crew and asked them to check the condition of all the lines and the transformers used for the transfer.

Not much later he was informed that power lines and transformers were at the top end of their temperature ratings and one of the transformers had cycled to prevent itself from blowing up.

Bram called Elizabeth and Amy and told them there would be a delay in the Fold of the USS Mt Rainer, Wheel-Two.

He let them know that he would authorize the next Fold when the local power system reached its normal operating range.

Amy asked if the Hood was OK. And then she asked of the Rainer what the crew should do?

Elizabeth ordered everyone to go for a walk and then have lunch.

She was not about to sit while waiting. She knew it would only make her nervous.

Bram joined the power crew for a tour of all the equipment that had been stressed. He ordered fans and cooling systems be deployed to bring temperatures down and keep them from going offline on the next transfer.

In Seattle, Jose stood on the back of the flatbed truck and looked out across the entrance gate to a gathering that had continued to grow to at least ten thousand protestors. He had been sent out to reassure the crowd that they would be able to go into the hanger to verify that it was empty. His loudspeaker comments to the crowd had been met with jeers, boos, and Bronx cheers.

A short time later he was appraised about the delay. He was now worried about losing control.

He decided to broadcast the local music over the speaker system. He then had his support team contact all the vending food trucks they could and asked them to come out and feed the crowd. However, he specified that no alcohol was to be served. He made sure that the trucks knew that the food tab would be picked up and paid immediately and she should give the vendors the code to get paid.

He was hoping to delay any aggressive actions by the demonstrators.

He hoped that the transfer of the wheel would take place soon. He did not want a riot or the crowd trying to break in.

The arrival of the food trucks had an immediate calming impact on the demonstrators. The scene, though still tense turned into more of a large party atmosphere. People were eating hot dogs and hamburgers and talking with each other.

Back in Dalles, it became clear to Bram that the transformers that had overheated were the original older ones. The new transformers that had been installed were temperature controlled and had both air coolers and air-conditioners. They had stayed in their control range.

Bram immediately called John to see if the older transformers could be replaced with newer air-conditioned versions. He knew that he would need to manage with what he currently had but was pleased to hear that John would have it on order immediately.

Though it seemed like a year for Bram, four hours later the second Fold was a duplicate of the first. He noted the power draw was at sixteen hundred megawatts and that the overheating occurred again. It was clear to him that the issue was the age of the equipment associated with the Dalles Dam facility.

Bram greeted each member of the Fold teams. Pat had asked about her Fold and about the delay for the second Fold. Bram told her that it had been a close call for both Folds. When Amy asked about the delay, he told her of the overheating of the power grid.

Bram's report of the two successful Folds sent a wave of relief through all members of the Fold program. The Fold team received calls from Jeffrey, John and at the top was a call from President Natorly. All expressed their pleasure and pride in the success of two successful Fold events.

From the bed of the truck, he was standing on, Jose announced that top management had finally authorized the opening of the facility. He apologized for the delay and had the gates opened. He had the food trucks move to each side of the hanger doors.

The hangar doors opened to show the vast expanse of the interior. The building was empty.

Jose stood looking at the emptiness and felt a shiver as he realized the magnitude of what had happened. He would have to ask Bram what had caused the delay.

He thanked the protestors and invited them to have drinks and snacks courtesy of the company. The demonstration changed tone and the gathering ended up looking like a fair event.

Bram looked at the two wheels perfectly positioned in the Dalles hangar. He walked around each just to take in their structure. He felt a sense of relief but also a nagging that he had overlooked something important.

Erica planned a success celebration. She had arranged for a canvass to hang from ceiling to floor and hide the wheels. On the outside, a catered dining area was set up. Excited conversations sprouted up between those mingling on the floor. The Fold success had everyone excited.

Erica had specified the menu that featured the choice of steak, local salmon, and shrimp or chicken as the main course.

Jeffrey, Erica, and John had all flown out for the success celebration. Jose and Ester had driven down from Seattle.

Bram had continued his analysis of the transfer. He was mentally exhausted, but adrenalin was still driving his energy.

Elizabeth came by to escort him to the dinner where he was the star participant. She knew that Bram was still reliving what he had referred to as the dimming of lights and lives of the Fold soul.

She was proud to have participated in Bram's achievement of the breakthrough he had promised and had the fortitude to act to defang the opposition. All the team members had expressed their willingness to take any risk associated with the first Folds.

Bram walked into the celebration area with Elizabeth on his arm. It was clear to him that she was currently in control.

He knew he was still overwhelmed by the Fold event.

He thought of the success as an Angel balancing on the point of a needle or a barefoot walk across a razor's edge.

He knew they had all been more than lucky. If they realized or not they had experienced a miracle.

He felt and breathed lightly as he thought on how close to losing it all they had been. He would needed to make sure that this risk was eliminated.

He took in the cheer of all those who had gathered for the celebration and let the grey thoughts be washed away.

He accepted the kind words of President Natorly and the praise from Jeffrey.

When asked to speak, he stood in front of the gathering silent for a few seconds and pointed to them and quietly commented that they had all been a key part of making it happen and that as a team they would continue to have success.

He sat down and then wondered what the next challenge would be.

Chapter 9: Mt. Jefferson Remedy

It was clear to Bram that he was in an after-success slump, and he needed to escape the environment of the Dalles facility. He wanted to do something with the team other than work on Fold.

He mentioned visits to the Mountains that the two wheels were named after. The team had discussed going to Mt. Hood but had taken the advice of a local Dalles born technician who said that the camping and fishing was better in the lakes around the foot of Mt. Jefferson.

Pat had researched the choice and had been impressed with the variety of activities available. She recommended that the team take the shorter trip and spend more time relaxing than sitting in a van. Her suggestion was accepted, and she made the arrangements.

They left the housing complex after an early breakfast. The white peak of Mt. Jefferson could soon be seen rising impressively up into a clear dark blue sky. It slowly disappeared as the van drove closer and the peaks disappeared beneath and behind tall soldier-like pines that seemed to be guarding them.

Bram, Amy, Pat, Jose, and Elizabeth sat in their comfortable captain chairs in the back of the conversion van.

Two of the four new bodyguards, Zoe and Eric sat up front. The other two, Bob and Thomas were following in a separate car.

Erica had pushed Bram to interview and select four permanent guards that would reside with him in his new home. He had done as requested and hoped that he had selected well and that they would all get along. They were all young agents that were looking for an assignment that would have some adventure other than always guarding an old man in an office.

Elizabeth had agreed to the fishing, but she wanted to have a nice shower and bed when the stars came out. She commented that she wanted to enjoy fishing not survive it.

She jokingly said she would save survival for the Folds like the last one that Bram had put them through. Everyone laughed and agreed with her.

After reviewing all the B&B's in the area, they selected an Inn along the Rushing river. Its location, the room availability and the surroundings made it the first choice. The friendly greeting, from Mary the owner, to a call from Pat sealed the choice.

It was a leisurely drive from Dalles to the Rushing River. They checked in early and chose to have a late lunch. Then those who chose to, each were on their own. They could do some fishing and gather later for dinner.

Bram passed on going fishing and chose instead to sit on the porch and relax. His B&B host, Mike, brought out the tea Bram had ordered and joined and engaged him in idle conversation. He shared the story of starting the B&B with his wife Mary.

Periodically Bram politely commented but he was deep in thought about the Fold activities. The constant nagging about having missed something seemed to be incessant. He seemed trapped in an analysis do loop.

Jose and Amy walked alongside the river and chatted. Amy had conflicting feelings about the situation she found herself in. She was struggling with her feelings for Jose and for Bram.

She had invited Jose so she could get to know him better.

Jose had made a very positive impression and it was clear to her that he was seeking to be more than just her friend. Her attraction to Jose clearly let her know that she welcomed his interest.

Bram attracted her, and she saw him as a true friend, but was he more?

She knew she was confused.

She decided she would seek Elizabeth's advice about the situation. She dropped back to where Elizabeth was throwing rocks into the river.

Elizabeth chuckled when Amy asked her for advice about her mixed feelings. She skipped several more, flat rocks across the water before looking at Amy.

She responded that she had no good advice. Her advice was to slowly stir the pot and examine what the spoon brought to the surface.

She advised to relax and let nature take its course.

Amy thanked her for such sage advice. It really did not seem to be of any help, but she didn't say anything.

She walked just upstream from Elizabeth and threw her fishing line into the river. She immediately hooked a large trout. She admired her catch but then unhooked it and threw it back into the river.

The simple act of unhooking the fish and letting it go helped her make up her mind in how to handle her situation.

His cup of tea in hand, Bram sat on the porch and rocked slowly back and forth in his rocker. His mind was racing through all his space Fold calculations.

His recent success and accuracy gave him confidence in his calculations.

But he knew that a small error in any of his numbers would be significant in the gigantic Fold of time and space across the galactic distances.

He concluded that he should first try a Fold across the solar system before proceeding to go across galaxies. Even then he worried about any minor miscalculations.

And the nagging feeling about missing something just kept growing.

Pat cast her line and in and began reeling it in with slow jerky motions. The surprisingly strong strike almost pulled her into the river, but her left boot found footing on a small boulder below her.

Her catch made a strong upstream run and then reversed course and tried going downstream. Pat continued to slowly reel her catch in. She was in no hurry, and she was enjoying the play of the fish.

Her patience paid off and soon she had an almost three-foot long salmon in the shallow waters at the edge of the bank. She decided it was a keeper that should grace the dinner table that night. She carefully slipped her hand into the gills to pick the fish up. She struggled to get it up the bank.

Elizabeth volunteered to take the pole and reeled it in. Pat struggle as she walked back toward the B&B.

The red hair, light green blouse, trim dark green shorts, knee-high socks, and black booted long legs caught Bram's eye, but it was the chest to ground length of the largest fish Bram had ever seen that kept his attention. The fact that someone as petite as Pat was able to hold it off the ground impressed him. She was much stronger than she looked.

He came down the steps to help her carry the fish to the side, kitchen door. There Mike greeted them and helped put the fish on a wood block table. He congratulated Pat on catching one of the largest fish he had recently seen coming from the Rushing River. He asked how Pat wanted the fish prepared.

Pat asked to have the fish scaled and served whole. She went on to ask if carrots, sweet potatoes, broccoli, and onions could be place around the fish and the entire tray baked in the oven. She described how she wanted the fish to be presented at dinner.

Once Mike agreed, Pat excused herself and said she was going to shower and change clothes, so she would not smell like a fish.

Bram watched as Pat walked out of the kitchen.

Mike commented that she would make a good catch.

Bram quietly agreed with Mike and returned to the porch to continue his musing. As he sat down, he watched as Jose and Amy walked toward the house.

He was aware of Jose's feelings toward Amy. He also took in Amy's relaxed and easy conversation with him. Emotional clarity came quickly to Bram, and he felt more relaxed than he had been for some time.

Mike and his wife Mary joined the team for dinner. The baked salmon was placed in the middle of the table. Mike had baked a potato and prepared a mixed salad for each person. He poured a glass of Muscat wine for each person and made a toast to the catch of the day.

Mary held up her glass and greeted everyone to the M&M, Inn and wished them all a good stay. She thanked them for filling the Inn in the off season and that they were welcome to come back as often as they wanted to relax and enjoy the area around them.

Bram looked around the table and knew he had the friends he had always wished for. He was not yet sure of his new bodyguards and was having to get use to them being somewhere in his presence wherever he was.

Later, as he was sitting and watching the day slowly ebb away into a grey that the Rushing River was disappearing into, Amy came out to talk with him.

He immediately knew what she was seeking. He clarified to her that he would always be her friend but that she was free to seek the partner that would be her soulmate. He said that he was all for happiness.

Amy gave him a hug and thanked him for making it clear and easy.

The rest of the weekend was a blur in his mind. He had gone fishing, hiking, and just relaxed on the veranda.

Pat carrying her giant salmon on that first Friday evening and his talk with Amy were the two events that stood out about the weekend.

His last thoughts were about his ability to ensure the success of the Fold project.

Chapter 10: Fools Rush In

The fishing and hiking had worked wonders in reducing the stress Bram had experienced after the two Folds to move the Wheels to their launch locations. It had also allowed him to clear the deck on the romantic side of his life.

Now he was back in his house. It was in the back of the new gated community built for the people associated with the Fold effort.

It had the highest elevation of all the homes and a had a good view of the apple and pear orchards to the South and the West. It also had the view of the power grid and transformer stations and the buildings associated with them to the North and the East.

He and his four bodyguards would all live in his five-bedroom home. It had been specifically designed for him and his bodyguard's occupancy.

It looked down on the entire fenced in community.

The large kidney shaped swimming pool and the spacious common dark green recreation facility had strategically placed parking lot designed for the electric golf carts that provided the transportation to that was use in the community. A small fire truck, an emergency rescue vehicle and another car were parked in the top corner of the lot.

He could see the playground equipment and the sand volleyball courts, one on each side of the rec building with the playground equipment next to the pool area..

He only had a glimpse of the baseball diamond located in the back corner of the grounds.

The soccer field was hidden behind the new row of maple trees.

The grounds had been transformed from a few old trees and a straggle of grasses to a series of three and four-bedroom homes and lush green lawns with tree lined streets. There was enough room for at least two hundred homes. About one hundred homes were completed and occupied.

A four-story apartment building on the backside of the recreation area and pool was almost complete.

The new community had a recreation leader, Melisa Etrius, that was an analyst by day and a neighborhood organizer by night. She was determined to get everyone to know each other. She had scheduled a series of weekend events for several months in advance.

She had come to Bram and asked him to fund these events.

Bram thought this was a great idea. He agreed to fund the expenses for the food and entertainment.

He gave these events visibility by having the community events highlighted in the weekly Fold News published by his staff.

Bram walked or jogged on the way to work each morning. His bodyguards participated each morning and joked that Bram was wearing them out and would need to replace them as they wore out.

He joked back that they needed to start paying him for getting them into shape. He was pleased with the attitude of his four bodyguards. He was relieved that they got along so well.

He had always been something of a geek and had often been excluded by his classmates. He knew that was why he had pursued and excelled in his martial arts classes.

He still practiced his Aikido moves but did so in the privacy of his spacious bedroom.

Since he often worked late, he was often driven back by his bodyguards. This cycle became a well-practiced routine for Bram.

Getting the electrical power system beefed up was the current delay in scheduling the next Fold. Bram had decided a Fold across the solar system should be the next step.

The pause nagged Bram, but he was using it to clarify what the two Wheels would be looking for and in laying out the analysis that would be a key part of the effort. The first Fold target was a location roughly ten thousand miles from Neptune.

In astronomical distances this target was like standing across the street from the Empire State building.

The Fold was delayed for a month until the new power generators were available. The delay would allow for the testing of the power systems that were being improved.

Elizabeth guided the teams to define the observation targets and the types of analysis to be carried out on Neptune and the surrounding area. The teams associated with each Wheel all participated.

Bram opened his eyes and let them get use to the dark interior of his windowless room. The lack of a window was one of the downsides of his security. A late sleep in was part of his Saturday and Sunday routine.

The dark seemed to amplify the question of what he was missing. He knew that he needed something to change but he did not know what.

Weekdays it was up at five, Aikido practice and then on to work. Breakfast on the workdays was at the site. There he always randomly sat with whoever he had not yet had breakfast with so he could get to know as many people as possible.

Today was Sunday and there was a community gathering planned that he was looking forward to.

He decided that he would fry two eggs over easy and make two pieces of dark bread toast with goat cheese and ham or sausage.

Bram got up and after brushing his teeth went down to get his first cup of coffee before making breakfast. He stood sipping it as he looked out the two-story high windows. One view looked out over the apple and pear orchards and the baseball diamond. The other view was out over the complex. At the center was the swimming pool, recreation center, picnic area and the new apartment building. He was looking forward to the grill out planned for lunch.

Bram turned to prepare breakfast. Zoe. She pouring a cup of coffee. She asked him if he were interested in a couple of over easy eggs. He was about to answer when Eric walked in and declared he would love a couple.

Bram watched the interaction of Zoe and Eric. It was clear to him that the two had hit it off and were becoming a pair. This he thought was good.

He knew that Bob and Thomas each were carrying on long distance romances with their interests back East. He wondered how that would work out.

Bram wondered about his own romance potential and decided it was time to relax.

He took Zoe up on the eggs and accepted two sausage patties and the toast that he had planned to eat.

After breakfast he retired to his office sat down with a book in the Alex Evercrest series by Ron Mueller about a black female detective in Cincinnati. He was about a third of the way through it. He enjoyed the flow of the stories and was always trying to guess how each episode would end. It was clear that the author had no idea where the story was going.

Bram always contemplated his actions if something like the story line would happen to him. He realized that the author and he had many of the same traits.

The pool party and grill out was well underway when Bram left the house a short time after that start time. Bob and Thomas had stayed behind with him. Zoe and Eric had gone down earlier to see if they could help in setting up and manage the outing. They had also wanted to get a quick swim in so they could be at pool side when he got there.

Bram was taking note of those sitting out by the pool. The only shade was provided by strategically placed umbrellas, but most chairs were out in the sun and occupied by those trying to get a tan. He saw Pat in the shade of one of the umbrellas. The bikini she was wearing made it clear to him that she liked bright lime green. And he couldn't help thinking that she also had a great body.

The parking area was full, and a few families were unloading their water floats and trying to get their kids in control and on the way into the swim area.

It didn't register that there was a strange pickup in the lot.

Suddenly, very loud shots rang out.

Everything seemed to go into super slow motion for Bram.

He briefly saw three persons at the top of the parking lot near the pickup before he was pulled down by Bob. Thomas was already firing at the shooters.

A mad scramble was going on around the pool. Zoe was in prone position also firing toward the gunmen. Additional shots came from the corner of the recreation center.

Bram saw a clear path to the side of the car just uphill from the shooter's pick up. He rolled downhill and then ran to the side of the car. The firing became a back-and-forth volley.

Bram waited until the shooting from his bodyguards stopped. He then jumped up and ran toward the shooters as they began their response fire toward the pool. He was within striking distance when the shooter closest to him sensed him and turned and brought the rifle to bear.

Bram continued his forward motion but turned his back to the shooter and stepped into the shooter's chest. He closed his left fist and forcefully slammed it back into the shooter's nose. He could hear the bones breaking. The force of the hit drove the nose bones into the shooter's brains. The shooter was dead on his feet.

The shooter's rifle had fired one shot that hit the back window of the car Bram had hidden behind.

Bram was surprised with the result of his attack, but he held the shooter up by the waist band with his left hand and grasped the rifle falling from the shooters hand, with his right. He turned and fired at the other two shooters. He missed both! They both began to raise their rifles to return fire. Bram was surprised as both went down in a fuselage of bullets. The back of one shooter's head exploded into a red blossoming spray. The other shooter's chest seemed to grow holes the size of large grapes.

Bram looked around to see his four bodyguards rushing forward all firing until their guns were empty. He would long remember Zoe in her blue string bikini firing her gun until she had clicked three times on empty. The two gunmen had gone down, and silence replaced the sound of gun fire.

Bram knew Zoe was on full adrenaline as she immediately went into the protect mode and asked what the hell Bram was thinking by rushing unarmed toward the shooters.

Bram replied that he was thinking about the kids in the pool.

He noted that his adrenaline was about as high as when the lights had blinked during the first Fold.

He turned and ran toward the pool area.

Two people sitting by the pool had been shot. Their wounds were serious, but the team doctor was immediately tending to their wounds as they waited for an ambulance to arrive.

Bram turned and went over to the grill and rescued the grill's contents that had been abandoned. He selected a brat and commenced to put relish, mayonnaise, and mustard on it. He then took a beer out of the cooler and sat down in the shade of one of the umbrella tables.

Melisa, the neighborhood event organizer, came and sat down with him. She pointed out to the kids in the water and quietly said, "I don't know if they saw what you did. I have it all here on my cell phone. You rushed in where angels would fear to tread."

Bram smiled and replied, "Yes fools rush in."

He lifted his beer and took a sip. He knew he was trying to recover from the shooting event.

Zoe went up to the house and got dressed. She returned immediately and located Bram. She shook her head when she realized he was sitting and talking with Melisa as if nothing had happened.

Most of the people of neighborhood were standing by the pool fence looking out to where the soldiers and the police had cordoned off the top part of the parking lot.

Zoe watched as two ambulances arrived. The Fold doctor and some helpers had moved some umbrellas to shade the two who had been shot. Both were conscious and talking with the Doctor.

Zoe decided that her role was back to watching out for Bram.

Bram asked Zoe if she was ready for a brat and a beer. He knew she would turn down the beer but was pleased that she asked for a hamburger.

Bram went to get the burger.

Melisa showed Zoe the action she had filmed. She commented that she had never seen an FBI agent in a bikini leap over a pool fence while shooting at an attacker. She asked where the gun had been kept.

Zoe took in the scene as Bram made his unarmed attack of the three shooters. He had been quite skillful in taking out the first shooter. It was clear he had been better in hand-to-hand than in firing at the other two attackers. She figured it was hard to hold up a dead body and shoot at the same time.

Bob and Thomas were immediately moving in, but Bram was blocking their ability to safely take a shot. She beat Eric over the fence. He was firing as he leaped and followed her. Their bullets were the first to hit the other two remaining shooters. Then all four were emptying their guns into the shooters.

Bram looked at the four of them as if he wondered where they had come from. He dropped the shooter he had killed. He looked out at the pool and then ran toward the pool entrance gate. He called out to the kids in the water. He took in the scene and then walked toward the abandoned cooking grill.

Zoe thanked Melisa and asked to have the video sent to her. Zoe knew that there would be a detailed follow-up and the video would help to clarify the situation. She asked Melisa to check to see if any of the other folks at the pool had gotten any video as well.

Eric was the next to join the three. He declined Bram's offer and said he would get it himself. He looked at Zoe and told her that the two of them had the watch duty of some crazy guy at the pool.

Zoe chuckled. "Crazy brave," she commented.

Her respect for Bram was at an all-time high.

The four were soon joined by Elizabeth who had just stepped out of her house when the shooting had started. Jose and Amy were the next to join. They pulled over another table.

When Pat appeared Bram immediately remembered why he had gone at the shooters. Pat had been sitting in the shade next to the two who had been shot.

He knew she must be suffering from shock. He had forgotten about Pat when he came down to the pool area after the shooting.

Bram got up and walked over and gave her a hug. It was clear to him that she had been crying. She responded by crying again. Bram was not sure what he could do other than hold her.

She looked at everyone at the table and simply said, "I was the next to be shot." Thank you for saving me.

Bram followed by saying that no one would get to shoot at one of his Wheel pilots and live to talk about it.

Chapter 11: Ready

Bram was not asked for permission for the erection of a ten-foot chain link fence topped with razor wire that went up the following week around the entire housing compound. The pristine housing complex looked very much like a deluxe prison camp to him.

He knew better than to object.

The army guards with their full body armor, machine guns, and night vision equipment was a step beyond what Bram had anticipated.

Again, he knew better than to complain.

The same fencing closed any open areas around the Dallas Power Station and the army had been tasked to guard the station.

Jeffrey called to explain the heightened security. He explained about intercepted messages indicating there were multiple groups trying to disrupt the Fold effort.

It was still not clear how the information had leaked but the heightened security had been a Presidential decision.

Elizabeth took the lead in getting the gas-powered generator installations accelerated. She was as eager as Bram to launch the next Fold. Her daily inspection tour became the talk of the installation crew. She was a tough inspector but when she arrived so did her crew with coffee, bagels, and donuts.

She promised the installation crew a full steak dinner for them, their significant other and their immediate family if they could beat their current schedule.

It was soon clear that she had inspired them to beat the schedule by at least a month.

Bram decided to use the extra time to test the whole system by moving each Wheel out of the dome to the open field immediately outside and then move it back in. He wanted to identify any significant issues while still in Oregon and not somewhere out near Neptune.

He made sure to have the field raked and all large stones removed. He toured and personally inspected each gas turbine generator unit. He made sure to include inspecting the fuel supply for each unit. He then followed through to ensure the fuel supply had been properly sized to last for a year.

He then inspected the power grid from the gas turbines and the connection to the Dallas hydro generators. All the transformers and power lines were new. They should not be needed but having them ready was a must for Bram.

Pat was accompanying Bram to work each morning. She had taken up Tae Kwon Do and was taking lessons at a local Tae Kwon Do Dojo, but it was the work out she got with Bram each morning that was accelerating her progress.

Her feeling of helplessness was slowly diminishing. She still woke up from nightmares of getting shot but those too were less and less frequent.

She and Amy were sharing a two-bedroom apartment and their evening routine include Yoga, which helped give her a deep sense of peace.

Bram seemed to understand and coached her in a calm and nurturing way that worked for her. She came over from her apartment for coffee and then went with the team on their jog to work.

She not only had a heightened feeling for Bram. She knew she was in love with him. She had watched the videos and it was clear that he had been the first to act to take out the shooters.

He had been unarmed but fearless.

The morning trips to work were more trying since the shooting. Bram had two personal bodyguards and two Marine guards in full body armor that accompanied him and Pat to work each morning. The Marines were impressive as they jogged in full body armor and a full backpack.

When he drove home at night, the Marines went in front in a Humvee with externally mounted machine guns that was also an impressive sight.

To Bram the Dalles environment had changed for the worse. He now felt super constrained and recalled his feeling in the original compound in Arizona.

Pat was slowly recovering from the shooting incident and coming back to the strong person Bram knew. This gave him a satisfying feeling.

He was in the wait mode in their relationship. He would wait until both upcoming Folds took place.

Amy noted the changes in the people and the work environment. There was a little more tension in the air, but everyone seemed to be focused on making sure their co-workers were OK. This was good to see and feel.

She too was a little more on edge, but her personal life had taken the direction she desired. She and Jose were truly meant for each other. They got along well and had fun being around each other.

Amy was as relaxed and calm as she had ever been. She was trying to help Pat get over what she knew was classic PTSD. Any unusual noise seemed to trigger Pat. She knew Pat risked losing her status as pilot if she did not overcome her current situation.

Elizabeth was very aware of Pat's situation. She had breakfast with her every morning for the last month. She saw a steady improvement and felt that Pat would be fine.

She discussed the situation with Bram. He suggested they touch base again after the Fold test they would be doing in the very near future. They would evaluate Pat's performance and decide prior to the Solar System Fold.

Bram extended an invitation to Pat to go fishing in the Rushing River. They would stay at the same Inn. He wanted to take her back to a time he had seen her full of confidence.

She asked who else was going fishing?

He replied, it would be just the two of them, Zoe, and Eric and two Marine Guards. He laughed and added that was as private as it would get for them. He went on to share that he had rented five rooms because Zoe and Eric would share one room.

Pat smiled and agreed to a weekend fishing trip. She said that she would love her *"private"* time with him.

The Marines drove their Humvee. Zoe drove their black SUV. Bram and Pat sat comfortably in the back in the captain chairs and enjoyed their iced sparkling water. They all listened to some jazz and hardly spoke a word on the way.

Bram was mentally reviewing the coming week's Fold. He had made sure the timing was such that no satellites would be able to spy on them. He mentally reviewed his discussion with Jeffery and John. Both had voiced their concern about Pat.

Bram had staunchly defended her and assured them he would have her ready.

The Humvee driving into the parking lot made a statement that was hard to miss. The armed Marines that jumped out caught Mike and Mary by surprise.

Bram rushed forward and apologized for not having given them any warning. He went on to introduce Zoe and Eric as two additional bodyguards. He finally pulled Pat into the group and recounted that Pat was the one who had provided the main course last time.

Mike asked what Bram had done to warrant such heavy protection. He went on to say that the Inn had no other guests, so it should be safe.

Bram suggested they all move into their respective rooms. He made the point that it was still early in the afternoon, and he wanted to go fishing.

He was soon out on the porch on the easy chair he enjoyed on his previous trip. Both Mike and Mary came out to sit with him. They were curious about the heavy security that was following him about. They knew that he was working on a secret project but that was all they had learned on his last trip.

Bram let them know that he was being protected from potential attackers. He reiterated that he really had come up to go fishing.

Mike chuckled and made the point that he had brought along the big fish catching lady, so he had to believe him.

He asked whose catch she was.

Bram smiled and replied that he hoped he had the big one this time.

Pat came out wearing the exact outfit she had worn on her first trip to the Rushing River. She too wanted to catch fish. One was sitting in front of her, and she hoped one was waiting in the river.

Zoe and Eric came out immediately behind Pat.

Pat waved her pole and said, "let's go."

Bram got up and followed Pat. They were passed by the two Marines who were still in their fatigues and brandished their two machine guns.

Bram called out to go left at the bank.

Pat flicked her line out into the river. She was in the exact spot of her previous success. She noted that she was in the exact same position with her foot on the stone.

Then her heart stopped as a helicopter flew past. It was flying low and following the river.

The tug on her line brought her back to the fishing line now moving swiftly upriver as if to follow the helo. She focused on her catch, but her ears listened to the two Marines. One was checking in and finding out about the helicopter. He kept repeating a four letter swear word over and over.

Pat kept her focus on her fish. The Marine hung up the field radio and turned and said they had to get out of sight. The helo that had gone by had been high jacked from the army group at the Dalles site.

Pat had her fish up to the bank. One of the Marines was about to cut her line. At the top of her voice, she shouted for him to stop. This caught him by surprise, and he stepped back. She reached down and lifted her catch by the gills.

Bram reached out and caught the other gill. Together they both lifted the fish from water. Pat then cut the line and tossed the pole to the still surprised Marine.

Bram led the way to the side kitchen entrance. Mike looked at the fish and smiled. He went on to say, "You have the touch. You only go for the big ones. I will prepare this the same way as the last."

Pat thanked Mike and told Bram that she was going to take a quick shower.

The two Marines told Bram that they would probably need to leave the B&B. They looked over to Mike and asked if there was a place close by that would offer protection.

Mary asked why in the world would they want a place of protection?

"Mam, a high jacked Army helicopter flew past us as we fished. It has enough fire power to totally demolish this Inn. We need to move to a safer location. We've called for backup. Both the Army and the Marines are responding but meanwhile we need to move as soon as possible.

Bram looked and Mike and Mary and asked again about a good hideaway location away from the Inn.

Mike looked at Mary and said in an inquisitive tone, "the mine shaft tunnel?"

"Yes, we have that set up as our storm and survival location. Let's go there," Mary replied.

"Let's bag the fish and the other things we want for dinner. We can cook everything at the mine," Mary went on.

The Marine Sergeant urged everyone to get moving immediately.

Bram was turning to go and get Pat. Her appearance in the doorway surprised him. She looked stunning in a black blouse and dark green khaki pants. Her red hair seem to be a flame illuminating her face.

She stood in the doorway and then asked, "What kind of trouble are we in?"

Zoe was the one that answered that they needed to immediately leave the Inn and go to a shelter that belonged to Mike and Mary.

Pat commented that thanks to Bram she was ready to take on the bad guys in hand-to-hand combat but now she would need to learn to shoot to be really ready. Then she asked what was holding them up.

The hike to the mine shaft entrance took only a few minutes. The night had enveloped the valley in a pitch-black veil. The Moon was behind the mountain and doing little to help them see the way. Mike was in front with Mary leading the way.

Mike took off the chain hanging across a three-inch thick oak wood door. He told everyone that he had made it himself. He had figured that the shelter would need a heavy-duty door if it was to protect Mary from a raging storm. He then opened the bolt lock holding the door closed. He led the way in with his flashlight. Mary herded the group into the shelter.

When everyone was inside, Mike closed the door and locked it from inside. He put a steel bar across the door. He then flipped the switch, and the lights came on. He pointed at the lights and commented that he had run underground power lines in. He also had a backup generator if necessary.

He pointed at a heavy-duty locker and commented that he also had a small arsenal to defend himself if necessary.

There was a table with four chairs, a full gas cook stove with an oven, an old refrigerator, a kitchen work area, two double bunk beds. The entire shelter area had a plastic plank floor, and the walls were stone. Mike was proud of the shelter. He had tried to make it as practical and as comfortable as possible. He had also put in a large supply of dry food that would last for a couple of months.

The Marine sergeant called in his coordinates, then signed off and turned off his radio. He looked around and gave a low whistle.

He commented that this was as comfortable of a hideout that he could possibly dream of. He went on to point to the entrance tunnel leading to the door and said he and his partner would set up their equipment there.

He went and set up his machine gun on a tripod and positioned it as close to the wall as possible. His partner did the same along the opposite wall.

Mike was already preparing the fish and vegetables to put into the oven. He commented that he and Mary had dibs on the lower two beds. The top two were available.

Bram looked at Pat and raised an eyebrow. She smiled and said she would love to share.

Zoe and Eric had already thrown their packs up on one of the beds.

Dinner was a spread-out event. Mary, Mike, Bram, and Pat sat at the table for four. Zoe and Eric stood at the kitchen counter and the two marines found boxes to sit on and positioned themselves at the entrance with their backs to the wall.

Pat thanked Mike and Mary for the great dinner and a wonderful place to hide out.

Bram climbed up into the bunk above Mike. Pat climbed in after him. This was as intimate as they had ever been.

Bram absorbed the warmth of Pat lying beside him. He looked at her and was pleased that she was looking directly back. Pat put her hand on his chest and leaned in and kissed him. Their eyes never left each other. Bram smiled and whispered, "so much for waiting until after the Fold missions."

He did not recall falling asleep. He only recalled feeling warm inside.

It seemed that almost immediately, Bram was knocked out of the bunk by a roaring explosion that ripped through the shelter.

He instinctively put Pat behind him as he moved in the dark along the wall toward the front part of the shelter.

Mike was thrown out the back of his bunk. He immediately made his way to the gun locker. He had two 308's, two shot guns and two forty fives. He sat on the floor and loaded them all.

Mary crawled up beside him and took one of each of the weapons and then crawled forward. Mike did the same.

Bram accepted the 308 that Mary handed him. Zoe accepted the gun Mike offered. He and Mary both preferred the shot guns. Pat took one of the forty-fives.

The sergeant had put the refrigerator on its side across the entrance area. His partner had tossed two grenades out through the entrance. For the moment all was quiet.

Mike began pushing crates of dried goods up to the marines. They immediately began positioning them across the entry way.

The dull deep thuds of a heavy-duty machine gun firing into the shelter area was followed by the boxes being shattered and exploding into flying splinters that flew back into the shelter.

Bram tilted the table on its side and positioned it, so they would be protected from the flying debris and ricochets caused by the heavy-duty gun fire.

The two marines suddenly stood up and let out a continuous round of machine gun fire. They must have been successful in hitting the operator of the heavy-duty machine gun. It fell silent.

They threw two more grenades and then went into a prone position on each side of the entrance.

Through the grey of the early morning dawn six dark figures rushed the entrance.

Bram and Zoe stood and fired their 308's. Eric was firing from a prone position. Bram ran out between the two marines who were firing from each side of the entrance.

He was firing his weapon as fast as he could work the bolt.

The dark figures in front of him went down in the hail of fire that they must not have anticipated.

The two marines jumped over the barricade as they continued to send short bursts of gunfire out. Zoe and Eric followed. Instinctively they spread out to the sides of the entrance. The marine corporal ran and secured what turned out to be a heavy machine gun (HMG) and verified that the three operators were dead.

The Marine sergeant checked out the downed attackers. He hit several with the butt of his gun. Three were apparently dead. There were two more dead by the machine gun location.

The Marine corporal zip locked the three live attackers' hands behind their backs. He then disappeared as he went into the woods to make sure there were no other attackers.

Three helicopters suddenly appeared. One swooped in and six armed men dropped down on lines.

The Marine sergeant shouted over the rotor noise and shouted not to shoot that they were friends.

Bram turned and handed his empty 308 to Mike. Mike took the 308 and then gathered the other guns and returned to the gun locker.

Bram turned and greeted Pat as she came out of the shelter that was now surrounded with Marines at the ready.

Pat said she did not know that being a Wheel pilot was going to be this exciting.

Mike returned and was looking at what was left of the door he had been so proud of. He pointed to Bram and commented that it was going to cost extra for the entertainment.

The entire group including the two marines went back along the trail to the Inn. Marines were now posted along the entire trail.

Bram was immediately thinking about how he would need to change the system test for the coming week.

Bram noted the two helicopters in the parking lot and that the Humvee and black limo were gone. He figured the third copter was probably parked in the open field on the other side of the river.

Bram knew the return trip would be on one of the copters in the parking lot. They had been instructed to gather their belongings and prepare to leave.

Mary gave them all a hug. Mike said he would love to have another salmon dinner with them, but he would meet them somewhere and bring the fish. He figured it would take a while to recover from their visit. He went on to say he was going to bill Bram for a new door interior cave refurbishing and a new refrigerator and stove that were now Swiss cheese., . And with a smile he said he was going to use top dollar wages to calculate the labor cost. cost.

 Bram replied that the next fish dinner would be at his house. He would send the invitation out in about a year. He took Pat's hand and followed his Marine Sergeant guard out to the waiting helicopter.

He would report that Pat was recovered and ready to pilot any vessel she was assigned to.

It was clear to him that his fishing expedition though much more exciting than he had planned had been a complete success

Chapter 12: Team Recovery

Bram jumped into the helo, took a seat, and put on the headset given to him by the copilot. He watched as everyone else took a seat and put on their headsets. Pat sat next to him. Eric and Zoe sat across from them, and their two marine guards sat across from each other on Pat's left side.

Mike and Mary guarded by two marines waved to them from the edge of the parking lot.

Bram took in Mount Jefferson and the surrounding mountains. The dark green Douglas-firs stood as straight as the Marine guards and seemed to be guarding the way to the brilliant white cap of Mount Jefferson. He put his arm over Pat's shoulder and pulled her toward him and pointed out and commented on the beauty that surrounded them.

The helo flight back to Dalles only took about thirty minutes. As they descended, Bram could see that cameras had been mounted along the fence and guard towers had been erected.

He saw an armored vehicle that seemed to be driving around monitoring the fenced perimeter. The equipment all had US Marine signs on them. He learned later that the Army guards had already been replaced.

Bram looked to the community complex and saw that cameras and guards had also been added. There were no corner guard towers at the community perimeter but two of the towers from the power facility looked down into the housing complex.

He knew he would soon be talking to Jeffrey and John about the upcoming test he had planned. He would suggest using the facility in Washington as the test location. That venue would make the test invisible to anyone watching the Dalles site. He wondered about who had ordered the change in security and who was managing it.

Only a few weeks earlier he would have been against it all. Now he realized that it was going to be necessary to ensure the safety of the people involved in the Fold effort.

They got out of the helicopter and were met by a Marine and told they were there to transport Bram and company to the VA Health Care Facility that was located only a half mile away as the crow would fly but about five miles by road. Bram could look out and see the facility from the power area parking lot. But he knew it was a five-mile ride by road.

The EMT briefed them that they would all undergo a comprehensive examination. A team of Marine doctors had been brought in and the VA facility was being used to provide medical support to the Fold team.

Bram became aware of the ringing in his ears. He was surprised he had not noticed it earlier. He looked around at each of the others and realized they all had scratches or other small wounds. His two marines as he was now thinking of them had several deep scratches along their cheeks and neck. They had been in the immediate area where the rocket grenades had exploded.

He followed the EMT to the emergency vehicle and got in. They all sat oriented in the same positions they had been in the helo. The lights came on and they were off to the VA facility that was within sight, but they would need to go around the highway to get to it.

It was Monday following his return from his "Fishing" trip. He resumed his early morning workout and then jogged into work. He was accompanied by Eric and Zoe as well as Pat. They were all led by their two marine guards.

He now began using the first names of his two Marine guards. The sergeant was Orlando, and the corporal was Caster. They smiled when Bram began calling them by name.

His support, Lacy, informed him that he had a ten o-clock morning call with Jeffrey, John, and a Major General Lester Tilson. She said that the General had been assigned to oversee security and team health care for the Fold project.

Bram thanked Lacy. He poured himself a cup of tea and then sat down and listed the topics he thought should be covered during the meeting. He planned to let Jeffrey lead, but he wanted to be ready. He placed a call to Elizabeth and asked her to come to the meeting.

At ten sharp the phone rang. Elizabeth and he each had a cup of tea in front of them. Bram had shared with Elizabeth some of the events that had led to their current situation.

Jeffery opened the call by introducing the General and letting Bram know that John and Erica were also sitting in on the meeting.

Bram replied with, may all be well with all of you," and let Jeffrey know that Elizabeth was on the line with him.

Jeffery then asked Bram to fill them in on the details of the attack that had occurred.

Bram jokingly asked if Jeffery wanted to hear about his recent fishing trip and the size of the fish he had caught. He went on and made fun of the Marine style of fishing with rockets and hand grenades and the type of fish they caught. Bram then claimed the Marines were mad at the Army for giving terrorists helicopter gunships, so they got pushed their Army friends out.

General Tilson laughed. He commented on the fact that he had received information that Bram had vigorously fished with his two Marine buddies and caught more than all of them put together.

That surprised Bram. He had indeed been shooting at the attackers, but he did not know that he had hit anything.

The General went on to compliment the entire fishing team on their resilience and ability to protect themselves.

He sent compliments to be given to FBI guards Eric and Zoe. They would earn gold stars in their evaluation reports.

His two Marines would also be recognized for their actions and probably get the promotions they deserved.

Bram replied that he was pleased with the recognition his protectors were receiving. He said they deserved every bit of it and more. He let the General know that he would appreciate having his two Marine fishing partners stick around until the Fold effort ended.

The General commented that he had talked to the two just before the call and they said they would like to do just that. They commented on the fact that they had never protected someone who attracted so much attention but needed so little protection. They figured that since they had finally achieved a first name relationship they should stick around for a while.

Bram chuckled and replied that indeed he wanted their protection, especially if he ever went fishing again.

The General asked if there was any concern with the security arrangements.

Bram looked at Elizabeth and raised his eyebrows. He replied that it certainly was an upgrade, but he had his eyes on making the success of the Fold project a reality and would leave security to the General.

The General went on to inform Bram of the fact the that the airspace above the Dalles Power Station area was now restricted. The landing and takeoff pattern from the Regional Airport had been changed to exclude the runway that utilized the airspace above the power transmission area.

Bram commented that seemed to be a very serious limitation and perhaps would affect the airport and the local economy.

The General commented that negotiations to build another runway would begin in a short time.

Jeffery then suggested they discuss the upcoming Fold test.

Bram suggested the hangar where the wheels were built be used as the place to Fold the two Wheels. They would stay there in the powered mode for a week and then Fold back to Dalles and stay in the powered mode for a week. Once back, Bram also wanted to test whether the Wheels would stay in position if power failed. He planned to position the Wheels a sixteenth of an inch off their holding stands and then cut power.

Elizabeth said she supported the tests as described. She wanted to add a disembark activity while in the Boeing dome.

They all agreed on both Bram's and Elizabeth's suggestions.

Jeffrey then raised the question about Pat's mental condition and readiness.

Elizabeth spoke up and said she had breakfast with Pat on a daily basis. It was apparent to her that Pat had come back from her fishing trip as the strong person she had been before the first shooting. The action during the fishing trip had strengthened her. Elizabeth left out the part about the new bond between Bram and Pat. Knowing Pat's feelings for Bram was the reason that made Elizabeth speak up.

The General reinforced Elizabeth's assessment. He quoted the Marine phycologist as having found Pat one of the strongest most balanced people she had spent time with.

The general went on to say he had asked the same phycologist about the stability of a certain Fold genius. She claimed doctor-patient confidentiality, refused to answer based on the persons obstinance.

Bram took the line and commented that he too had wondered about Elizabeth's genius stability, but that in the past he had let it pass. She seemed to him to be doing OK.

Erica had been on the phone all morning. She had talked to Zoe, to Elizabeth, to Pat and Amy and to Eric. She had gleaned the fact that Pat and Bram had stepped up to a new level in their relationship. She had sensed the old but now a much more powerful and confident Pat. She wanted to support both Pat and Bram and make sure there was no question about anyone's fitness.

She stated the fact that the Fold team was stronger and more powerful after the trying events that had taken place. She looked forward to the success of the upcoming tests and to the success of the entire Fold effort.

Jeffrey looked over at Erica and smiled. He saw a complete transformation and growth in a person that only a few months before he had been ready to replace. She was ready for more.

Jeffrey closed the meeting and said they would resume their normal weekly meeting on the following Monday.

Bram pressed the off button on the speaker phone. He looked at Elizabeth and commented that it seemed the call had gone well.

He then asked about her request to get out of the Wheel when at the Boeing dome.

Elizabeth gave a small laugh and said that she planned to take her crew to the best restaurant in Portland.

What was he planning to do with his crew?

Bram walked around the desk and gave Elizabeth a hug.

He asked if he could come with her to dinner.

Chapter 13: Fold Community Aftermath

℮ike a bear in hibernation, the Fold neighborhood quit its outdoor habitat and hid in their safe domains. The shootings by the pool had a dramatic negative impact on the outdoor neighborhood activities. It carried over into the work area. People were not interacting well.

Bram asked Dr. Serena Windal the Fold phycologist to design some group programs that would help them get relief from the shooting incident.

He also suggested she take on anyone wanting help.

Bram made a point of walking through the neighborhood after lunch each day. Since he was not allowed to walk alone, the group was made up of Orlando, Castor, Eric, and Zoe or on other days it was Bob and Thomas. Orlando and Castor were always out front.

The marine guards that patrolled the fence and walked the streets got to know and wave to all of them.

The fishing trip battle had made Orlando and Castor heroes to their marine brethren.

Bram noticed that all the Marines would salute him as well. He had participated in the shooting but did not have a clue at the time that he had any effect. It was only when Major General Tilson shared Orlando's and Castor's battle report that he discovered how effective he had been. He credited an adrenaline high for his actions.

Whereas the battle at the Rushing River had solved one problem, the shock of the pool shootings had created a major problem and had brought total paralysis to the once vibrant and active community.

Bram stopped by Melisa's house to talk to her and see if she would organize another grill out. He offered to make it a steak and shrimp affair with games and prizes for the kids.

She shared that she had been afraid to push for another event. She felt so bad for the two who had been shot. She was also a little intimidated by all the armed marines.

Bram agreed with her that it was a daunting situation that they had to overcome. He went on to make the point that she could play a key role in helping everyone deal with the situation.

He suggested the kids get to know the Marines by name. He proposed giving five one thousand-dollar prizes for the kids that submitted the most signatures of the marines first.

He said that he would talk with Edward Sharp, the site Marine Commander and make sure every guard wore a large name tag.

Bram said he would award the guard that got all the kids names in first a dinner out with a friend or better half.

Melisa agreed to invite everyone to another pool side grill out. She would make it a grand affair if he would also fund a music band to play.

Bram readily agreed with her request.

The couple that had been shot had recovered and had chosen to come back to work early. Bram met with them to ask for their help in getting the community back to its once active and fun lifestyle. He asked them to help sponsor the next outing. They each agreed to do so.

They thanked him for his action in taking the shooters out. They also ask Bram about what had happened to have the Marines come in to be the guards of both the Fold facility and the neighborhood. He briefly explained what happened when he went fishing.

Wow! So, there are more bad people after us, was their reaction. They asked if there was any other way they might be of help.

Bram suggested they share their experience on the Fold internal web site information system. This would help everyone process the shooting incident. He asked them to connect with Melisa and see if they could help plan the coming event.

Bram was surprised that the personnel on the Fold effort had not heard about the attack at the Rushing river. It spoke volumes of the tight control the Marines had over the situation.

Pat suggested to Bram to have a folk singer perform with any band that Melisa chose. She felt it would enhance the mood.

She joined Bram on his next neighborhood walk. This time Melisa came out to walk with them. She shared that Marine Commander Sharp had already agreed to support the next outing and he already had the Marines wearing large name tags. He also had established the contest to award a prize to the first five Marines to turn in all the kid's names.

There was also a prize for the Marine that turned in the most names of the residents. Melisa went on to share the fact that there were two marine bands in the guard unit. One was a pop band and the other was a country western band. The commander said he would make sure they were both available. Bram laughed when he learned that the Commander said that the fees for the bands would be covered by the Fold program budget.

That budget was Bram's budget!

Pat went on to ask Melisa to see if there was a folksinger among the Marines.

Dr. Windal was surprised that her individual patient schedule immediately filled after she started to have daily lunch session presentations on incidents such as the shooting by the pool.

She asked Bram whether it was appropriate to have morning and afternoon Yoga and Tai Chi sessions so that the people in the Fold program could attend.

She did not wish to upset the normal workday, but she thought it would make it easier for those who had kids to attend during the working hours. She suggested that the pool area facility be used. She made the point that in that way those taking the classes would be at the location of the attack.

Bram thought that it was a great idea and told her to go full steam ahead.

He approached Major Sharp and asked if any of the Marines would like to teach swimming. Bram had discussed this with Pat, and they had decided that having swimming lessons would be good for the kids and it would be an activity that got parents back in the habit of going to the recreation center.

Bram engaged the Fold team educators that had established a school inside the Fold community. They had classes set up for students of every age. Most of the classes were on-line but every student had a real teacher guiding them and interacting daily with them.

Lacy was studying the population of the Fold team that lived in the closed community. She, herself had recently moved into one of the new apartments. The move made it much easier to come to work and to work late if needed. She personally felt safer moving into the facility.

Bram wanted to know the demographics of the personnel. He was interested in the number of stay-at-home moms and their skills and talents. He wanted them to be able to contribute to the Fold effort at the level they chose.

Bram was also interested in the number of kids that resided in the Fold community and the programs to engage them. He was willing to sponsor fishing, hiking, and any other outdoor activity and to have the most popular movies brought in.

Bram knew he had ignored the community but was now determined to have it prosper as part of the Fold program.

On one of Bram's after lunch walks through the neighborhood, Melisa walked up to him and introduced him to a young lady, Maryanne and a young man, Terry. They were both in their high school senior year and were looking for a community project that they could put on their applications to the universities to which they planned to apply.

Bram greeted them and asked them to walk with him. He began to ask them questions about their interests and about their grades in math, science, and history. He asked them about the universities to which they were planning to submit their applications. Maryanne reminded him of Mallica or maybe a young Elizabeth. She was more interested in how people perceived and reacted to events around them. Terry was more into the technical aspects of how things worked.

Bram suggested that Maryanne have interviews with, Elizabeth and Dr. Windal. Once the interviews were complete, a project would be designed for Maryanne to work with one of them.

He went on to suggest that Terry have interviews with Lori Middleton and Remi Hardwood. Once those interviews were complete, he also would get a project assignment.

He then suggested they expand their applications to the Ivy League schools and perhaps to schools like Oxford or Cambridge in England.

Bram commented that scholarships and grants would be available if they were accepted into one of their choices.

Maryanne and Terry walked away excited about the projects they would get in the Fold program. They knew it would be a key element of their application strategy. They also were now thinking more broadly about their schools of choice.

Bram asked Lacy to set up meetings with the parents of both Maryanne and Terry. He wanted them to know that the program would pay for the kid's college expenses if they maintained a B average or above. He also asked her to write an article for the Fold news highlighting this benefit.

The Sunday picnic schedule began at eleven and was scheduled to go on past dinner time. Bram and company arrived early and helped to get everything set up. However, Lacy had arranged for her parents to cater the event and there was little to do but sit by the pool and relax.

Bram noted that Marines were posted around the parking lot and the pool facility. The neighborhood families began arriving and soon the pool was full of the kids splashing and playing.

Melisa joined Bram and shared that the folk singer turned out to be one of the stay-at-home moms.

Bram shared that Pat had commented on the singer's great voice and asked that when she stopped singing that she join the group for a drink.

Orlando and Castor had recruited two Marines to guard Bram and were in the pool enjoying a beer and talking to all the kids.

His four FBI guards were sitting all around him in their swimsuits. Each of them had a gym bag at their feet. Bram figured that was where their weapons would be.

Bram put his lawn chair back, took in the music and reached over and took Pat's hand into his. He imagined the commercial with two people, holding hands, sitting on lounge chairs on the beach, looking out to the ocean as the sun began its descent.

He fell asleep to the melody and the melodic vocal of the folksinger.

<u>Chapter 14: Fold Bubble Scouts</u>

*R*e-establishing a vibrant, happy community had taken longer than Bram had expected. The pool party and the involvement and help of almost every person in the community made a huge impact. The kids and young adults were surprisingly effective in changing the feel of daily life. The Marines and their engaging participation also made a huge positive difference. Melissa became her old self and took the initiative to schedule events out into the coming months, so people could see and plan out the coming six months. Bram was pleased to step away from the community issue.

The fence around the community and the marines patrolling the fence kept the community in isolation. But every home had one or more large screen monitors and linkage to the internet. The internet was strictly controlled to ensure that the outside could not "break" in.

Bram's primary worry, the power requirements for the project now received his full attention. The power requirements for the Fold was an enormous worry. It literally kept him up at nights.

He had been successful in the transfer of both Fold Wheels to and back from the Portland site. He had kept the power on for the entire time and was continuing to do so. He toured the electrical power supply every week. He talked to the maintenance crew to understand the maintenance requirements for such a system.

The gas-powered generators were running normally and showed no signs of stress. The new transformers were staying in their normal operating temperature range. The system had a fifty percent backup capacity just in case any component failed, and it was designed to bring the backup power online before the system power dipped too low.

The Fold to the edge of the solar system would stay in place for six months.

The Fold across the galaxy was currently scheduled to last close to a year.

Bram needed perfect performance from the power system.

The time frame and the need to have everything remain flawless bothered Bram. It made the mission dependent on what he considered a vulnerable power system. His original concept was to have the Fold power system be part of the Wheel. Bram's desire to have people in the Fold Wheel was the reason for the extreme power requirement.

Now that the time was near, he was having second thoughts. He was potentially risking the lives of people who he cared a great deal about.

He had not given them a choice.

Pat had become his confessor. She laughed when he first shared his concern. She commented that if he told the people who were assigned to the Wheels that they had a ninety percent chance of dying, every one of them would still want to go.

She then asked if there was a way that the risk of having a problem could be reduced?

That discussion resurfaced Bram's original design of having the power aboard the Wheels.

He replied that the ability to have an onboard power source or have shorter stays would reduce the risk.

Bram scanned the huge workshop that he had built as part of the Dalles structure. He had staffed it with one of every skilled profession from welders, electrician, electrical techs to computer geeks.

The staff of twenty in the lab so far had done little work. They had become familiar with their area and the equipment available to them. The manager of the area immediately reacted when Bram walked into her office.

In case you don't know my name, I am Lori Middleton she said as she stood up. She went on to ask if he had some real work for her team to do, to make, to build or to program. She said her team was going bonkers waiting to contribute to the Fold effort.

Bram took an immediate liking to Lori. He said that yes, he had an idea that he wanted them to help with. He asked if there was the possibility that the folks in the shop could meet?

Lori asked her support to call everyone into the meeting room. She went on to ask that lunch be brought in.

Bram followed Lori to the meeting room. There he got some help in hooking his computer to the large screen that dominated the one end of the room.

Bram looked around at the people in the room. He recognized many of them from having breakfast with them. He asked everyone to introduce themselves by giving their name and their specialty area.

Bram listened to each and repeated their name and specialty. Once everyone had introduced themselves, he shared one piece of information that would be new to all of them.

He had been fishing but had never caught a fish!

That caused some laughter, and someone commented that they had heard it was dangerous to go fishing with him.

Bram agreed and focused on opening a power point slide deck. A diagram of a sphere with a camera mounted inside appeared.

Bram stated that he wanted to build a sphere with a camera inside. He wanted the camera to be smart. It should focus on objects as specified by a computer program. The camera needed to be able to rotate to position to get the best shots possible. All of this should fit in a two-foot diameter sphere.

Once the first sphere was tested, Bram said he wanted a dozen more.

Lori asked Bram if he could give her team about an hour before the team responded. She wanted the team to brainstorm and see what they could come up with.

Bram replied that they could take as much time as they needed. He would be in his office working on what the camera would be recording.

Lori called Bram about two hours later and requested he again meet with the group.

Bram returned to the meeting room. Three easels had been put to use. One had a list of questions. The other two had diagrams of spheres.

Bram noted that the team must have several very good artists. The spheres and the camera looked almost real.

The first question was if the sphere was free to rotate in space?

Bram replied that he was not sure. They could test this in the lab. He would Fold a small sphere to a specific location and the team could check it out.

The next question was how long the sphere would be at its location.

Bram said that on the first placements, each sphere would stay long enough to slowly rotate and take pictures of all the surroundings. Then it would return. The time would be determined on the speed of the camera rotation.

A fourth question was whether any communications out of the sphere was required.

Bram replied that all pictures should be stored on memory and that at this moment in time he felt the sphere would often be so far away that it would return ahead of any signal it might sent out.

The final question was if the camera should be only in the visual frequency range?

Bram's reply was that the other camera frequencies would follow. This would either be in additional spheres or as separate cameras put into existing spheres. He stated he was open to their recommendations on all of his replies.

Lori asked the team if the answers changed any of the conclusions the team had reached.

All members were either silent or responded with a no. The only thing that was highlighted was that the behavior of the sphere would determine the final design.

Bram had brought the Fold transmitter he had used for the Presidential meeting. He asked if the lab had a sphere he could transmit.

While the team looked around the lab, Bram determined the Fold location of the table he had been shown.

He was handed a small Florence flask and was asked to send it out upside down.

The flask neck fit perfectly in the hole that was in the briefcase send location.

Bram pressed the Fold button and the Flask appeared floating two inches above the surface of the target table.

The entire team converged on the table, and each took a turn moving their hand around the floating sphere.

Remi the design engineer grasped the flask neck. He was able to move it but when he let go the neck and the flask returned to its original position. He did this several times and the flask always returned to its original position.

Lori looked around at the team. She turned to Bram and said that she could have his first bubble done by the following week.

Bram then asked if the team would examine the various size Fold transmitters and recommend the size that fit the bubble that was being built. There were three larger power supplies than the one in the suitcase in existence and they were all on site.

Bram returned to his office. He now had a clear plan on how to proceed. He would deploy the cameras as scouts. He would get the visuals of the location that he had selected to take the Wheels. This would allow for better planning and dramatically shorten the time that the Wheels spent in the Fold.

He located Elizabeth and shared his current thinking on how to move forward.

Elizabeth listened to Bram. She watched his movements and realized that he seemed relieved and energized. He began by sharing his fear of losing power while they were in the Fold. He went on to explain his current approach with a set of scout bubbles.

Instead of having the Wheels stay out for months, the scouts would go out and collect the initial data. The Wheels would follow and focus on the areas selected from the footage brought back by the scouts.

Her reaction was positive. The approach Bram had chosen was a very practical one and one that she could easily support.

The next day was Friday. Elizabeth called a meeting of the entire team to share the new approach.

She and Bram walked into the meeting together. She called the meeting to order and shared the new approach in how the upcoming Fold events would be managed. This change would delay the Wheel Fold about two to three weeks.

During the meeting Pat suggested that a Scout Analysis team be established. She volunteered to get it setup. Amy volunteered to help. Bram voiced his support and asked to participate in defining the Scout Team membership criteria.

Elizabeth agreed with setting up the analysis team. It would help her when she shared the change in Fold timing with Jeffery and Erica at the next leadership meeting.

At the end of the meeting, Bram suggested a Columbia River Fishing outing and asked who wanted to go with him.

The entire team, almost in unison, shouted, "You must be joking."

Chapter 15: First Catch

Everyone that had volunteered to go fishing met at Bram's house at five Saturday morning.

Bram had coffee prepared.

Three white vans arrived shortly after everyone had gathered. The vans would transport them to and from Celio Park.

Breakfast and lunch were part of the fishing trip package. Each seat in the vans had a box holding an egg, cheese, and sausage breakfast sandwich. A hot cup of coffee was in each cup holder of the van.

Bram and Pat led the way to the vans. Zoe and Eric were in the lead and Bob and Thomas walked behind Bram. Amy and Jose followed on Eric's heels. The rest of the group was comprised of Lacy, Lori, Orlando, Castor, Edward, and Ester. The outing would be comprised of three vans, three boats and twelve people.

Bram made a point to thank Lacy for her super ability to arrange the fishing trip on such short notice. She had pulled off a small miracle in successfully setting the trip up.

Lacy thanked him and made it clear that her father, uncle, and brother owned the boats. They had been the only ones available and were willing to do it for free. The vans were new and had been provided by the local car dealer and Bram owed the dealer advertising airtime. She said she would have arranged a fish for everyone to catch but she had no connection in that area, so she wished everyone good luck.

It was a short drive to Celio park where they would cast off. Bram was one of the few that stayed awake. His eyes stayed on the black waters of the Columbia river, that in this location was called Celio Lake. These were the waters above the Dalles Dam. It was hard to make out the far bank in the grey black of the early morning, but occasional lights appeared like low lying stars. The stars overhead were still shining, and they reflected up from the dark waters. Celio Lake became a mirror of the stars above. The heavens were still dominating the morning.

The bright lights in the parking lot and those casting their rays at the landing dock blocked the view of the Celio Lake but put the three sleek, low profiled, black fishing boats with 250 hp outboard motors in the spotlight.

Bram stopped to take a picture of the three boats and commented on how stunning they looked. The team agreed.

Lacy introduced her Father, Ted, her brother, Luke, and her Uncle Cedric. Ted said it was a pleasure to take the group out. He went on to claim that the three boats would show the group the best fishing they had ever experienced. He told them that Lacy had worked with him to assign everyone to one of the boats. He looked at Bram and told him since all the firepower would be with him, he would be in his boat, and it would be the most crowded.

Lacy then called out the names of the people in each boat. A safety discussion went on at each boat.

The proud boat owners also gave a brief tour of the boats. The live well and the bait boxes were the first to get shown off but the storage box with the makings of a variety of snacks got the most response from the team.

The plan was to return to the landing area for a picnic lunch. Ted's and Cedric's wives were bringing out spareribs, salad, and drinks.

Bram looked out to the East at the rays of sunlight chewing at the edge of the dark grey of the morning. The far side of the Celio Lake was still enveloped in black with a few lights twinkling their existence.

The captain of each boat lowered their propellers into the water and started their engines. Bram had expected a roar but heard the low purr of an angry lion instead. He relaxed and concentrated on Pat's warm head on his shoulder.

The three boats, in a triangle formation, cut smoothly through the water. The air rushed through Bram's hair. He was sitting with his back to the left side of the boat with Pat sitting next to him. Zoe and Eric were sitting together facing forward. Bram noted that they were wide awake. Orlando and Castor lay prone on the bow, and Bob and Thomas were sitting with their eyes closed.

Bram closed his eyes and cycled through the air blowing across him, the purr of the lion pushing the boat and the gentle pull toward the back of the boat.

The next thing he knew was Ted telling everyone it was time to get their poles into the water.

Bram looked at the flat platform at the bow of the boat and the one behind the L shaped seating area. He was unsure where he should go. Ted solved the problem by pointing to a seat he put up in the center of the bow. Bram went up on the bow platform. He stated that he had never been fishing before. He watched as Ted's eyes went wide and a smile spread across his face.

"My gosh, I have a virgin on my boat," Ted shouted out at the top of his voice as he pointed at Bram.

Bram had not expected the outburst. His cheeks turned red when everyone shouted that Ted must be kidding.

Bram listened carefully as Ted explained how to cast and slowly reel in the line. Ted asked Pat to fish from the center, out the open right side of the boat. He asked both Orlando and Castor to fish out the left side and assigned the rest to share the back platform.

After a few initial problems, Bram got the hang of casting and reeling in the line. He took a moment to look around and saw that everyone was focused on their own fishing. He relaxed and started trying to target his casts.

The sudden jerk and pull on his line almost caused him to fall out of the boat. He recovered and listened to Ted tell him to take it easy, keep the line tight but be in no hurry to pull the fish in. Bram immediately understood that keeping the line tight meant the fish was slowly being pulled in toward the boat.

Bram was finally looking down at what he thought of as a huge fish.

Ted handed Bram a large net with a long handle. He instructed Bram in how to bring the net up along the fish so that it would envelop it. He then instructed Bram to put the pole in the holder and use both hands to lift the fish up and onto the platform.

Once the fish was out of the water Ted opened the front live well and skillfully put the fish in.

Bram took out his phone and took a picture of his first fish. Ted commented that it was a good size and would make good eating. He went on to say that everyone wanted to catch the big fish, but the bigger ones had a stronger fish flavor that he didn't like. The size Bram had caught was just right.

Bram felt good and decided that it was time for another cup of coffee and a snack.

He asked Orlando if he wanted to fish from the bow.

The fishing was as good as promised and everyone caught a fish.

Bram went back to fishing and by eleven when it was time to head back for lunch, he had three fish to his name. He had caught the largest and the most fish on their boat. Ted praised him on his fishing ability and his luck.

Bram smiled and replied that in his case it was all luck and to being brought out to where fish were dumb enough to bite on his line.

As his boat and the two others approached the dock, Bram spotted a Humvee parked at the far end of the parking lot.

He looked at Orlando and asked if this was his doing? Orlando smiled and gave the excuse that the marines had been jealous and had come out to the park to fish from the pier.

Ted led the way to four picnic tables that were covered with food. He introduced his wife Rita and his sister-in-law Marial. Rita welcomed them and pointed to the table.

Bram looked at two trays stacked with barbeque sauce covered ribs, a tray of corn on the cobb, a large bowl of potato salad, a bowl of loose-leaf lettuce covered in tomato, cucumber, and onion slices, a tray of white, brown, and black bread slices.

Bram commented that this was beyond anything he had ever expected but he had no problem in digging in to such a feast.

He approached Rita and Marial and pointed to the Humvee at the end of the parking lot and asked if his Marine guards could take part in the meal.

They said they would be pleased to feed them as well.

Ted went to Orlando and asked him invite, the rest of his friends for lunch.

Ted commented to Bram that Lacy had shared the events of the attack at the pool and then the attack when he had gone fishing at the Rushing River. She had also shared that this was the first time since then that they had all come outside of the fence that had been put around the entire area.

He was wondering how Bram felt.

Pat was sitting next to Bram and looked at him. She knew that she felt safe inside what she now thought of as the compound. She was interested in hearing his take.

Bram had not thought about what the situation looked like from the outside. Only a few people from the outside community worked inside the compound. He paused for a moment before replying.

He admitted that he had never thought about the situation from the Dalles community's perspective. He went on to say that he embraced a supportive community.

He also pointed out that the work inside the compound was top secret but a very positive development for everyone on Earth. It had nothing to do with battle or war.

Ted replied that Lacy had said almost the same thing and that she could not say more. She did say it was not weapons work or war robots or anything like that. She had also made the point that she liked living at her apartment next to the swimming pool and the other facilities.

Bram told Ted it was a breakthrough, and he was making sure the world would benefit.

Ted said thanks for giving him this much information. He looked around and called out that it was time to get in some more fishing.

Bram walked over to where Rita and Marial were sitting and thanked them for one of the best meals he had recently enjoyed. He then joined Ted and they led the way back to the boats.

The sun was now on its decline but at the hottest point of the day. The wind coming over the bow and the wind shields pulled Bram's hair across to where it looked like a sheet of paper. Pat raised her left hand to play with it. She complemented him on his explanation to Ted.

Bram watched the Oregon shoreline passing by. It seemed to go downstream. The illusion was strengthened by the puffy clouds overhead that seemed to be flowing downstream as well.

Ted dropped anchor about fifteen minutes above the spot where they had first fished. He declared it as the spot to catch the big ones. He went on to say he didn't have room for any little ones.

Bram once again took the bow by himself. It was clear that the beginner was being given the space he needed.

Bram caught two good sized trout almost immediately. Then his luck ran out. He stopped to take a break and decided to watch how everyone else was doing. Orlando again willingly took the bow spot. Suddenly Pat let out a yell and was almost pulled overboard. Ted gave her a recovery hand but then stepped away.

Bram stepped over into the center area and put his arms around Pat's waist. It was clear to him that she was struggling to maintain her footing. He reached around and grasped the pole with his right hand.

Pat kept the line tight and was constantly pulling her fish in. Ted looked out from the bow and told Pat that she had one of the larger gars he had recently seen. Pat gave a gasp when the fish was finally alongside the boat. It seemed to be almost as long as the boat.

Ted pulled out a pole with a curved hook on the end. He asked Eric to help him lift the gar out of the water. Zoe, Bob, and Thomas got off the back deck to give the two more room. The gar put on a valiant fight, but Ted and Eric finally pulled him onboard, and Ted hit him on the head with a hammer. The gar spanned the entire width of the boat.

Bram snapped pictures with his phone and sent it to all on the Wheel team distribution. He had never imagined that anyone could catch a fish this size with a fishing pole. He pointed at Pat and put his arm out and made the motion of flexing his muscle. He asked Pat to lay down next to the gar so that he could take a picture of the two together. The gar was the same length as Pat was tall. It was another great picture to share with the team.

The team all caught fish. It was more than any of them wanted. Ted agreed to take all the fish that the team did not want.

Bram wanted to keep his first fish. He planned to bake it the way Pat had specified at the Inn. Most team members kept one of their smaller fish.

The all the extra fish, a big amount, went to Ted and his team.

The trip back to the pier was relaxing. Bram sat with his arm around Pat and took in the scenery of the surrounding area.

Chapter 16: Continued Threats

Getting the giant gar off the back of the boat became a three-person job. It took Ted, Luke, and Cedric to get the large gar off the boat and onto the pier. They set up a tripod stand to hang the gar. Bram took several shots of Pat standing by the tripod. His large salmon was hung up next and Pat took pictures. The picture taking went on for at least half an hour as everyone captured their catch on camera.

Pat and Bram returned to the house and carried his salmon in together. Pat had given her giant gar to Ted. She had asked for a small piece that she could try later. Pat, Bram, Zoe, and Eric all worked in the kitchen to prepare a dinner that would feature his salmon. Zoe and Eric had also kept a fish each. The two together had caught the most fish.

John and Thomas decided the house had enough fish and gave their catch to Lacy and family. They also made a point of staying out of the kitchen and enjoyed a beer as they watched the rest preparing diner.

Elizabeth had gushed about her catch and had brought home three smaller trout. She was glad to be home for a refreshing shower. She was looking forward to the salmon dinner at Bram's house. She would take over a bottle of white Muscat Wine.

Jose, Amy, Orlando, and Castor all came to dinner. Jose and Amy arrived with two bottles of Riesling. Orlando and Castor arrived with a cold case of beer each. They all made their way to the refrigerator. Orlando went over to the ice-filled cooler and put in as many bottles as he could. He then joined John, Castor, and Thomas to watch the dinner being cooked.

Amy and Elizabeth volunteered to set up the table. Elizabeth had John and Thomas put in the two-expansion table leaves so that the table would be large enough for it to seat all of them.

The fish had been much too large for the oven tray. It was cut in half and cooked on two trays. The dinner consisted of a tomato, cucumber, onion and lettuce salad, corn on the cob, grilled sweet potatoes, and a mix of other root vegetables and the baked salmon. The Riesling was served with the dinner and the Muscat as a desert wine. Desert was a mix of three ice creams: coffee, caramel vanilla, and raspberry chocolate chip.

Bram had invited the Stetson family, but they had declined saying they had a lot of boat and fish cleaning before they could think about eating. They made it clear they would love to come over on some future date.

The talk around the table was about the great fishing trip they had enjoyed. Elizabeth commented that the team needed three tries to get things right. This had been their third and very successful uninterrupted fishing trip.

The dinner ended, and the talk continued into the night. Finally, everyone realized how late it was getting and everyone went home.

Bram came awake on Sunday and knew that he had dreamt about the Fold. He wished for some other topic to command his dreaming, but he knew that until the next big idea came along, he was stuck with the Fold.

He got up and prepared a pot of coffee. He filled his large mug and decided to walk the perimeter of the housing area. He was on his way out the back door when Zoe yelled for him to wait up. She and Eric each carried their coffee as they joined him.

Zoe wanted to know if Bram was really planning to walk by himself.

Bram made an excuse about it being Sunday and besides there were enough marines inside the compound to defeat a small army.

Bram walked slowly as he mulled the problem that had been in his dreams. The bubbles were always anchored at the co-ordinates that they were given. A Fold to a planet moving at the speed the planet traveled around the sun would have only seconds of a few minutes of video. He needed to change the feature of being anchored to a specific co-ordinate.

Bram caught the glint of the Sun on some far object. He stepped behind a tree and looked again. The sparkle was still there. He told Zoe and Eric to casually move behind a tree. He asked them to look out directly across the fruit trees to the other side at the barn area.

Bram waved one of the perimeter guards over and asked him to look at the glint coming from the fruit farm barn truck loading area.

The guard took a quick look through his binoculars. He called in the suspicious glint.

Bram watched as a helo swept swiftly in from the west. It must have been on patrol along the river. There were several shots fired and two Marines dropped out of the helo to the ground. He asked the marine to share his binoculars. He was able to see the two marines climb up one of the semi-truck trailers. A body lay on top.

The guard tapped Bram on the shoulder and informed him that he was requested to return to his house.

Zoe and Eric took positions in front and rear as they walked back the long way down to the pool area and back up to the house.

Bram had refused to return immediately to the house and had chosen the long way back, so he could work through his idea that had formed by the blinking from the dead shooter. He spent the rest of the day mulling over various ways to implement his idea.

The next morning, in the dark grey of the coming day, six figures, only one looking awake, jogged along the road to work. Orlando and Castor in their full battle gear led the jog toward the office. Bob and Thomas jogged behind Bram and Pat. Bram was humming as he kept the pace set by the two marines.

Bram was eager to get to the office and work on his idea for moving the bubbles to keep up with their targets. One way was to manage multiple sequential Folds. This was his short-term fix. He continued to work through his Fold equations trying to see if there was a way to make the position fluid with time.

Bram entered the building and split from the rest of the team to go to the shop area. He was surprised to have Zoe and Eric follow. In the shop he found a partially complete camera and its multidimensional drive.

The bubble lay in two halves on another table. The computer lay next to it. It was clear to Bram that assembly was close at hand. He would try his multiple Fold idea with this first unit and evaluate the impact on the power system.

Zoe asked what he was building.

Bram replied that, it was a surprise, and it was time to get breakfast. There he saw Lori sitting down and asked if he could join her.

She laughed when he immediately asked how building the bubble was going. She responded that she knew he had already been to the lab and knew the answer to his question. Then she asked about his fishing trip.

Bram smiled. He liked Lori. She was easy to interact with. He told her about the trip and how good the fishing had been.

Lori responded that Lacy and she had breakfast on Sunday and that Lacy's father had said it was one of the best fishing days he had ever experienced.

Bram then asked Lori for a favor. He wanted to send some gifts to the Stetson family and wanted to go around Lacy, so he would not put her in the middle. He said that the gifts would be for the kids and grandkids in the family. He wanted to know what bank the family used. After Lori agreed to find out, Bram excused himself and went to the Monday morning leadership meeting.

Elizabeth was just finishing the normal good morning, how are you part of the meeting when Bram walked in.

Edward Sharp, site Marine commander was first on the agenda. The bright blink Bram had spotted on the previous day had indeed been a sniper. Ed figured the early morning sun was giving the sniper problems in seeing through his scope. When the Helo came in from behind the sniper, he turned and fired. The bullet glanced off the front of the Helo. The immediate returned fire killed the sniper. The who and the why were still being investigated. There was no identification on the sniper. The owners of the fruit farm were cooperating and had no idea who the sniper was. They agreed to allow the truck area to be monitored.

Bram knew that a small place like Dalles would immediately have a rumor with some version of what had happened. He suggested that a PR team come in and give an explanation about the Fold program and ensure the community that good stuff was being done inside the compound.

The message to the community had to be good.

Jeffrey agreed and asked if NASA might have a good PR team. John replied that he was sure NASA could do something along the lines suggested.

Bram requested that Laci, his support be included. She had grown up in the community and had a big well-known family. She would make a good spokesperson.

Bram brought up the point that he seemed to be wearing a target on his back. He felt that somebody in the know was guiding the attacks. The effort to get to him must be well funded and high up in the political ladder.

He asked if someone on the Fold team had good enough connections to get the FBI to investigate.

To the surprise of everyone Erica spoke up and said that she had the connection that the team needed, and she would call in favors to find out who was behind the action to subvert the team's efforts.

Bram gave a small chuckle and said, "Please let the investigators know I am the good guy."

Elizabeth guided the discussion toward the Master plan.

Erica then went into the detail of the power reliability trial requested by Bram that was coming to an end. It was very close to the time to make the first Solar Fold. The initial results indicated that the gas power generators had very high reliability and the backup switch over was accomplished with no power dip.

Bram chose to share the small bubble scouting Folds he wanted to throw into the mix. He went on to explain his idea about the scouting with the small bubbles and then strategically positioning the Wheels.

Erica asked how long this would delay the Wheel Folds?

Bram responded that there would be no delay. He did say that he might want some additional resources to staff the Bubble Scout Fold Program. Bram envisioned a Bubble Fold team that managed bubbles around each of the planets and bubbles that scouted ahead of the Wheel Fold.

The meeting ended with Elizabeth agreeing to a meeting in the following week to develop the plans for the Bubble Scout Fold Program.

Elizabeth took Bram's arm and guided him to the Wheel team meeting room. She called a meeting of both Wheel teams and asked Bram to explain what the Bubble Scout Fold Program was about.

<u>Chapter 17: Bramlets</u>

Bram looked around the meeting room.

It was hard to believe that he had just come up with this new concept and quicker than a bramble weed being blown across the desert in a windstorm, it had become a whole program.

He had gone to bed thinking about how to best utilize his, frozen in specific space coordinates, space balls and had gotten up to see if he could test his concept. What he had seen in the lab meant it would be possible to test the concept in a couple of days.

He still had to share his second concept with the lab team to see if they could quickly put together a self-powered version of a bubble that would still be significantly smaller than a wheel but could be programed to do multiple folds on its own.

The second bubble would need to be big enough to encompass the power transformer unit and a power source small enough to fit in the bubble. This would be a breakthrough if it did not have to return to the original Fold location.

Bram envisioned a ten-foot diameter sized bubble.

His final endeavor was to get help in the mathematics of the Fold equation to see if the Fold object could be moved without having to constantly Fold to reposition itself.

Bram wanted the object to be able to propel itself in any direction of interest. He either wanted to use a rocket system or perhaps a time altering technique.

He walked up to the white board and wrote down the three items:

Bubble Ball Scouts and their use

Multiple Fold Bubble Ball Scouts

Self-powered Bubble Ball Scouts.

He then thought about the resources he needed to pull in to help him review the math.

He wondered what Mallica had been doing for the last several months. He felt guilty about not having assigned her to do something meaningful. She was part of the team he had more-or-less abandoned in the original team space in Arizona. He had also left Marcus, another great resource languishing there as well.

He wondered if they were interested in coming to the Dalles site

The various members of the team began to come in and almost to a person they each asked what was up or don't tell them about another postponement.

It was clear to Bram that everyone was ready for some Fold action.

Bram listened as Elizabeth clarified the reason for the meeting as discussing and the enhancement to the Fold effort.

He was surprised when she clarified that they would do multiple shorter strategic jumps because he had developed the Fold Bubble Scout.

Bram looked around the room. He started his update by stating that everyone in the room was the cause of his development of the Bubble Scouts. He went on to state that his biggest concern was the safety of the Wheel teams.

He told them of his near heart attack when the power fluctuated on the very first Fold, when they brought the two Wheels to the current Dallas location. That event had caused him to demand replacing all the old transformers in the existing Dalles power grid and to wait on the new gas-powered generators for the next Wheel Fold.

He went on to share that the current test of the power system had increased his confidence, but he was still putting twelve people on the line on the next Wheel Fold. He went on to clarify that the longer they remained in the Fold the higher the probability of a problem.

The scout bubbles provided a way to look around at the site being targeted for a visit. They allowed for a way to take a best guess and then adjust once the scout verified the chosen coordinates.

They also allowed for the relocation of a specific Fold. If by bad luck the coordinates were in the middle of an object, no major loss, no lives lost.

The scouts could also reduce the time spent on any Fold by collecting all the general data before the wheels arrived. The Wheels would go in with a specific set of targets picked from the scout data.

Bram stated that he was mad at himself for not having started first with the Bubble Scout approach.

The question about Fold schedule was one common theme the team seemed to have and asked repeatedly?

It was clear to Bram that the team was negatively affected by the delay.

Bram explained that the Wheel Fold had been planned for six months. It was still scheduled that way. He however made it clear that he was now thinking each Fold would be more like two weeks, but perhaps each time at a different Fold location. He would let them know. It depended on how the scouts worked.

The next question was when would they know?

Bram answered that question by telling the team that the first bubble scout would go to the first designated solar location on the coming Wednesday. On the following Monday, the Wheels would go to the location the scout had visited unless he and the teams wanted to make coordinate adjustments.

Elizabeth and the team began reviewing what remained to be done to be ready for a Monday Wheel Fold.

Bram excused himself saying he needed to go to the lab to see how the first bubble scout was coming along.

He walked briskly down the hall toward the lab. Zoe commented that he seemed extra energized and wondered what he had eaten for breakfast.

Bram took in the entire lab crew gathered around the larger of the two stainless steel tables. There in what seemed a totally assembled state was the first scout bubble.

Remi proudly pointed to the bubble and declared that it was ready. He and several of the lab team had worked over the weekend to make sure they could get the bubble done.

Bram walked up to the worktable and put his hands on the two-foot diameter sphere. He suggested that the lab team name this first bubble scout.

Lori said she would work with the lab team on the name. She wanted to make sure Bram knew about a short coming to this first scout bubble. She pointed to the camera and the internal space and asked what Bram saw.

Bram looked at the bubble and its interior. He said it seemed a bit crowded but very practical and functional.

Lori made the point that the bubble had only a four-hour power supply. The battery would take almost four hours to recharge.

Bram agreed that was a limiting factor. He let her know that he had heard about a Japanese scientist that was claiming he had doubled the life of the conventional lithium type of battery. He asked Lori to follow up on that opportunity.

Bram went on and recruited the entire lab team to become the first Bubble Scout handling team. He made the point that there would be many more bubbles made of different sizes. They would all face the problem of having enough power.

Bram asked that the bubble be placed on a stand between the two Wheels. He declared high noon the next day to be the first Fold for the bubble.

Bram ordered a new power line to be brought in straight from one of the spare generators. He allocated an office, which looked out to the bubble, to be the new headquarters for the Bubble handling team.

Bram went to his office with the computer that controlled the bubble and programed in the coordinates for the Bubble Scout's Fold. He also programed in the camera motion for each of the four hours it would be at the Fold location.

Lori asked that he provide her lab team with some guidance on what he was expecting them to do as a bubble handling team.

Bram gave a chuckled and told her he would send his two lead Wheel Pilots and they would tell her what her lab team needed to do.

He made the point that one of the key actions was to get the Bubble Scout recharged and sent out again. He let her know that he had programed the computer for six launches and the camera orientation for that many.

He asked if the first scout had a name yet?

Lori responded that the vote was occurring at the very moment, and she needed to get back, so she could put in her vote.

The power line from the generator to the bubble launch location took much longer than Bram had allotted. The electrical maintenance manager refused to take any short cuts. He estimated that if the installation crew worked all day and through the night the power line would be in place by Wednesday afternoon. It was the best that he could do.

Bram had little choice and thanked the electrical crew for their hard work. He let them know that he wanted them to do it safely and to make the power source as reliable as possible.

He followed the electrical maintenance manager who insisted that Bram verify the work that would be done.

Later, while Bram was sitting with Pat, Zoe, Eric, and Amy in the cafeteria Lori approached. She had a large grin as she said she wanted to share the name given to the first Bubble Scout.

After a big pause she shared that it had been named Bramlet One. The one had been added because the team already knew that Bram was planning to have them develop additional ones.

Everyone at the table laughed. Zoe said it was so appropriate and right.

Bram knew his face was turning red. He said he wanted the lab team to know that he appreciated their naming the bubble after him. He wanted them to know how great it was to have them be able to turn his idea into reality in such short notice.

Pat and Amy engaged Lori about getting the lab team trained. They also wanted to know if the lab team would be making more of the bubbles and could the Wheel team members help.

Bram left at the same time Pat and Amy followed Lori back to the lab. He was on his way to his office to make a call to Mallica and Marcus. He now had a sense of urgency to get them out to Dalles to help him dig into the mathematics involved with creating the Fold. He felt that he had missed something important and continued to miss it on every run through the math and physics. He was somehow blind to what he knew had to be a huge, shortcoming.

Chapter 18: Problems with the Math

Bram returned to his office and placed a call to Mallica. Her surprise made him feel even worse than he already felt. He had forgotten about her and Marcus back in the original Arizona location. He asked how she was doing. After some reconnect chatter he asked if she were willing to come to Oregon and help him review the math associated with the Fold.

Her resounding, "Oh my god yes," made it clear that she felt left out. She made the point that Marcus would love it as well.

Bram told Mallica that she and Marcus could come out as soon as they wanted. There were two new three-bedroom homes available for them that had just been completed. They were available for immediate use. If they needed to get them furnished it would all come out of the Fold budget. He could hear Mallica saying, Yes, Yes, Yes, over and over again.

Mallica said that she would be there by Monday. Bram said that would be fine.

After hanging up Bram went out to Lacy and let her know about Mallica and Marcus. He asked her to work with them and get them moved into the new homes.

Lacy said that she would do so.

She then thanked Bram.

When he asked what she was thanking him for.

She said for the Stetson Educational Trust that had been set up. She let him know that she and her Dad had accepted being the trustees. She also made the point that having it designated for use with schooling and the future generation was the only way her Dad could have accepted the money.

Bram smiled and said that it was great. He let her know it was a forward payment. He was sure with good guidance the trust would do well. He wanted her to make sure her Mom and Dad got the credit. They created the money that was now in the trust.

Bram returned to his office. He sipped his tea and thought about how small gestures had huge impacts.

A short time later Elizabeth came to his office. Her excuse was that she wanted a cup of tea. She made herself a cup and took a couple of sips before she moved carefully into the topic she had come to discuss.

She was worried about what she perceived as his current protective attitude toward the wheel teams. She felt he had to disassociate his personal feelings from the role he was playing as the technical lead. It was her role to worry about the well-being of the teams. She wanted to know what his issue might be and how she could help.

Bram looked steadily at Elizabeth without saying a word.

He wanted to give her a hug. He decided to do just that. He was sure he surprised her and smiled as he sat down and took another sip of his tea.

He decided to share his current concerns about his Fold concept, its shortcomings and what he considered his biggest mistake.

It was not yet lunch time but close enough that he called out to Lacy and asked her to order in lunch for him and Elizabeth.

Elizabeth asked if this meant that Bram was going to talk a lot?

Bram smiled and replied that she had asked, and he was going to share everything that had been eating away at him.

First, he let her know that he had asked Mallica and Marcus to move out to Dalles.

She commented that it was about time. She had meant to bring that up some time ago, but their exciting fishing trips had always distracted her.

Bram said fishing had certainly distracted all of them. He went on to highlight that another concern he had was the fact that he was sure he was missing something in the math and the implementation of the Fold. The fact that he was missing something meant that the entire team could be at risk.

Elizabeth agreed with him.

She pointed out that the entire team knew there was a great risk in the Fold technology. She made the point that the team had talked about it, and they were willing to take that risk.

They appreciated his concern but reiterated the fact that it was not his role to limit them based on his concern.

Bram replied that she should assure the team that he had put their asses on the line several times already. He had done so with little concern and certainly had not limited the team.

He wanted Elizabeth to communicate to the team that he would continue to be aggressive in his deployment of the Fold. He also wanted them to know that if he found any problem, he could not fix, he would stop the Fold program until he could fix the problem.

His lack of knowledge should not be the basis for risks that need not be taken.

Elizabeth agreed to share that with the teams.

Bram then went on to describe the first problem he was trying to overcome. His Bubble Scout idea was his attempt to solve a problem that caused him concern.

He pointed out that the two Folds that the Wheels had experienced were short Folds in Earth's atmosphere. Earth was a clean environment compared to where they might end up, in an across the solar system Fold, or a Fold across the Universe.

He went on to state that now he would not allow a Fold to either location without scouts going first and checking out the area around the Wheel Fold coordinate

Elizabeth asked for clarity about the first Bubble Fold. She asked if Bram would call for a delay in the Wheel Fold if the Bubble scout trial failed?

Bram replied that if the bubble scout failed, the Wheel Fold would be delayed.

She made the point that no one would be leaving early on the following day. The Wheel teams would all be eagerly waiting for Bramlet One to return from its first Fold.

Bram made the point that he would certainly be there at return time.

Lunch arrived. Bram had ordered a half of a Reuben and a squash soup. Elizabeth had ordered a shrimp and scallop spaghetti in white sauce. They both took a moment to arrange their lunch before continuing.

Bram brought up his next concern about his understanding of the mathematics and science of the Fold. He knew he was missing something.

This made him worry about long Fold deployments. The unknown missing Fold problems or mistakes might show up with time or perhaps with the distance of a Fold. He welcomed anyone that wanted to get involved in the inquiry and investigation of the science behind the Fold.

Elizabeth chuckled. She said that Mallica and Marcus had been playing with the Fold math and were stumped in how you managed to get anything to work. She went on to say that she did not know anyone even close to Mallica's capability. She would open the door to everyone. She was sure there would be interest but that no one would last more than a few minutes when they got into the math.

Bram thanked Elizabeth for helping him unload his concerns.

Lacy came into the office. She apologized about having listened in, but they had left the door open. She went on and said that she might know of someone that could engage in the math.

She said that her sister, Linda, was a social worker who worked with kids that had special problems. Her sister insisted that this one kid had an exceptional mind but that the system was not equipped to handle her. Would Bram see if she was as brilliant as her sister insisted?

Bram was surprised. He agreed and asked when he could meet with the girl Lacy was talking about.

Lacy put up her hand as she got her sister on the phone. She looked up at Bram and asked when he could see her.

Bram thought for a moment and wondered if it could be done during the wait for Bramlet One to return from its Fold.

He wondered if the girl could meet here at his office during the time Bramlet One was out scouting.

Lacy replied that would be a great time. She would arrange for the transportation and the passes for her sister as well.

Bram looked at Elizabeth and asked if she would like to be present during the young girls visit.

Lacy brought in a card with the name of the young girl. She also let Bram know that she was physically misshapen, and wheelchair bound.

Bram spoke up and said that he would be glad to go to the girl's place to do the interview.

Lacy laughed and said that she had already heard from her sister, Linda, that the trip to the facility would be the highlight for her and for Zuri.

Bram suggested that they planned to start with Zuri meeting everyone that would be standing by waiting for Bramlet One's return. He went on to suggest that they make it into a waiting party. He asked Lacy to set up the event and send out the invitations to everyone.

Elizabeth stood up. She had a smile on her face. She always found being around Bram was full of surprises. A few were terrifying, but most were good surprises.

She left wondering how this interview of Zuri would turn out. She knew many social workers who believed in some poor soul but most often the individual was so damaged and limited that there was little hope. She hoped that it would not affect Bram negatively if it did not pan out. She would keep a close eye on this situation.

Bram knew immediately that Elizabeth was concerned about his interview of Zuri. He would know almost immediately if Zuri's mind was filled with brilliance or if there was only gibberish. It was clear to him that brilliance would not solve Zuri's problems, but it could open the door to a very different world for her.

Bram was glad the day was over. It was time to get home. He wanted to share his thoughts with Pat and of course his four bodyguards. He thought about the events that transpired in just one day. He knew that it didn't get better than this.

Chapter 19: Mallica's Arrival

He chose to walk home and enjoy the sunset. Pat was holding onto his elbow as they walked and talked about the events of the day. She had enjoyed working with the lab folks. She commented that it had been the most productive day since their fishing trip.

She let Bram know that Lacy had brought in a "small" chunk of the Gar she had caught. It was large enough to make two meals for all of them. She went on to say that she was planning on cutting it into steaks and grilling it in the oven for dinner.

She pulled on Bram's arm and asked if he was listening.

Bram looked at her and smiled. He replied that he was indeed listening and looked forward to eating her Gar.

He pointed to the Sun slowly setting behind the low mountains to the west. He let her know she was missing a beautiful orange, purple and gray sunset.

Orlando looked over his shoulder and asked if the dinner included the two most powerful and effective Marine guards on the ground?

Pat jokingly replied that the two he was talking about were probably already eating their dinner. She then asked if he and Castor might be interested in having dinner with the rest of the poor people that had to put up with Bram?

Bram's mind wandered back to Zuri. He had also been reminded that Marcus had a family that he was bringing with him and that Mallica had place of her own. Bram was pleased that Lacy had made the appropriate arrangements.

It reminded him that she was due a pay raise.

Bram seemed to be making a rapid run through all the events of the day and the forks in the road each of the events seemed to create.

He was glad that he was surrounded with very talented people.

He looked forward to dinner but by the time it was over he was dead on his feet. He excused himself and went up and after a quick shower fell into bed and immediately fell asleep.

Bram woke up to with Pat's head on his shoulder and her arm across his chest. He let out a slow breath and took in the warmth of Pat's cheek. He looked over at the large green numbers on the alarm. It was five in the morning.

Bram knew it was time to get up, but he allowed himself to absorb the feeling that seemed to embrace his soul. He slowly extracted himself from the bed and headed for the bathroom.

Bram thought he would be the first to the kitchen and coffee, but Zoe greeted him as he came down the stairs.

Bram said a polite good morning and headed straight for the coffee. It turned out he was just ahead of Eric.

He knew it was their turn on guard duty. A moment later Orlando and Castor made their appearance at the kitchen door. Bram commented that it seemed to be a waste of good talent in that it took four of them to get him awake and on the way each morning.

Pat added that it took five of them to keep him operational.

Bram gave her a hug and handed her a cup of coffee. He then called out five minutes and he was heading for the door.

Orlando began singing a cadence about Bramlet One this is your day, Bramlet One hey, hey, hey. Bramlet One to space today, Bramlet One this is your day. Castor took up the wording and added his own twist about Bramlet One was making hay, Bramlet One was on the way.

Everyone else but Bram added something additional and then they all sang the verses together.

Bram enjoyed the camaraderie but did not add any additional lines to the already ridiculous wording. His mind was on the events that would transpire on this day.

The cafeteria was empty when Bram and his guards entered. The Cafeteria had the coffee ready, and the manager greeted them as they all poured themselves a cup. She let them know that this morning the menu had waffles, sausage and eggs any style ready to go. Anything different would take a little time but the kitchen was ready, and she knew that oatmeal would be out shortly.

Bram asked that she let him know when the oatmeal was ready. He led the way to one of the tables and sat down. He was happy just to relax and watch the crowd slowly come in.

The electrical maintenance manager approached Bram and asked if he could sit with him for a moment. He wanted to share the progress in getting the power line setup.

Bram welcomed him and then listened as the manger proudly told of the super work his team had done. The manager went on to let him know that everything would be ready by one.

Bram thanked him and told him to thank the rest of the crew as well.

The next person that caught Bram's eye was a real surprise. Mallica stood in the entrance doorway looking around.

Bram raised his hand and waved until Mallica waved back. Pat got up and brought another cup of coffee to the table. She gave Mallica a hug and asked when she had arrived.

Mallica got introduced to all the people around Bram. She joked about the fact that Bram seemed to have increased the number of people it took to keep him going.

Bram stood up and gave Mallica a hug. He told her that it was good to see her, but she was not due until next week.

Elizabeth walked in and greeted Mallica and thanked her for coming out early. She looked at Bram and nodded and said that she was the reason Mallica had come early. She went on to say that she thought it would be a good idea for Mallica to participate in interviewing Zuri.

Bram let the implication sink in. He conjectured that Elizabeth was worried about the emotional toll that he might experience from the interview.

He valued Elizabeth and her instincts and figured she was probably right. He wanted Zuri to have that genius that would change her life and help him identify the barriers to his Fold vision.

A second opinion of someone of Mallica's mental capacity would be a good check.

Elizabeth engaged Mallica and soon led her away for a tour of the facility, the wheels and the Bubble Scout named Bramlet One.

He heard Mallica laugh as she repeated the name, *"Bramlet One."*

Bram turned his focus back on having breakfast and prepared his oatmeal. This morning he chose to use black pepper and mix in a soft-boiled egg. He noted that the cafeteria was doing a much larger business than usual. He figured that the word about the launch of Bramlet One had brought the folks out early to get their work done so they could relax at the Bramlet One picnic gathering.

Pat let him know that she and the rest of the team were going to the lab to assemble additional Bramlets. The lab had acquired enough bubbles to make a dozen. They were short on camera's and the wheel crew had relinquished the spares to get the scouts done.

Bram said freeing up the cameras was a good idea. He let Pat know that he would make the rounds as soon as he had met with Mallica and Elizabeth.

Lori arrived just as Bram was getting through breakfast. She wanted to make sure that the launch would be at two and that the computer seemed to be working well and that the battery was at its peak charge. She let him know she was nervous about being the person in charge of the launch of Bramlet One.

Bram smiled and assured her that he would not hold it against her if the Bramlet One blew up when she pressed the launch button.

Bram returned to his office and stood looking out the window. The sun had long cleared the mountains. It was a crisp clear cloudless morning. He cranked open two of the high glass windows and enjoyed the cool air falling in to embrace him.

He stood silently looking out at the far snow-capped mountain peaks to the East. He turned to the set of windows that faced west and the lower mountains that blocked his view of what he imagined would be the Pacific. He loved the landscape around Dalles.

The knock at the door brought Bram back from his mental travels.

Elizabeth led Mallica in.

Bram greeted them and asked how the tour had gone.

Mallica responded that she was amazed at the progress the team had made. The wheels were amazing. She went on to say that she thought that Bramlet One had quite a resemblance to him. Its interior was jam packed and its capability amazing.

Bram laughed at her dig and thanked her for coming early.

Chapter 20: Bramlet One

Elizabeth guided the discussion to the interview of Zuri. She wanted to understand how the two of them would know if Zuri had the potential to be of help.

Mallica looked at Bram and proceeded to give her thoughts. She would be looking for some understanding in basic math or in some ability to process a mathematical question such as the adding or multiplying two numbers. She did not expect her to be able to process complex equations, but she needed to be teachable. Zuri would need training to get to the level that Bram would be expecting so she would need to be able to comprehend new concepts.

Bram suggested they continue their conversation while they walked to the housing area and visited Mallica's two-bedroom apartment that she had requested versus a house.

Lacy had let him know that it was ready and Mallica's suitcases were in the apartment.

Mallica was surprised at the entourage that accompanied them. Orlando immediately made the point that he had changed his allegiance from guarding Bram and would look out for her instead.

Mallica smiled and turned to Bram and asked if his Marine guards were worth having.

Bram commented that Castor seemed OK, but he was not sure about the other one.

Zoe piped up and made the point that the FBI had decided to reinforce the protective coverage to four because of that concern.

The friendly banter went on until they approached the four-story apartment building. Mallica had a fourth floor, corner apartment. Lacy claimed it was the best one in the building.

The entire group crowded into one elevator.

Castor and Orlando were the first ones through the door of the apartment and told everyone to wait. They went in with their guns at the ready and checked out the entire apartment and the outdoor deck.

Mallica let out a long breath as she took in the exquisite arrangement. A plush cream-colored couch that had reclining seats on each end faced a huge, curved TV screen. A pale blue-gray patterned rug accented the space between the two. A matching cream-colored recliner was located on the far side of what Mallica immediately labeled the living room.

She looked at the table on a dark oriental rug just behind the couch in a large open area. A delicate, purple, and white orchid at the center of the table accented the space she labeled as the dining area.

Immediately inside the apartment door and slightly to the right was a large white marble island with a deep large single sink. To the right was a stainless-steel refrigerator, more white marble countertop, a microwave, and smooth surfaced stove and more white marble countertop.

This was Bram's first visit to any of the apartments. He was pleased that it immediately impressed him.

He led the way to the roomy deck. Lacy had pointed out that a screen blocking anyone from looking in had been put on the deck and all the windows. The person inside could look out and those on the outside would not be able to see them.

Mallica walked through the apartment and returned to the point between the entry and the living room. She commented that Bram should have invited her earlier.

Bram made the excuse that the apartments had just been completed.

She thanked him for having her now and then asked that she be given time to get unpacked. She would come back to the Bramlet One celebration later in the afternoon.

Bram agreed and told her that a car would pick her up at in time for the return party.

The black SUV dropped all of them at the entrance to the main office complex. Once inside, Bram headed straight to the Bramlet One launch area.

There, Bram encountered the electrical supervisor in the process of doing the final inspection of the power panel and the power line to the scout launch pad. The electrical crew was standing by so Bram took the opportunity to thank them for the great work and to invite them to stay around for the refreshments Lacy had arranged.

The electrical supervisor pointed to his watch and said that the crew wanted an extra beer for being fifteen minutes early.

Bram smiled and thanked him for the super effort and that if each person let him know the beer, they enjoyed the most, he would make sure they each got a case.

Lori was waving to Bram from the control room. It was clear she wanted him there.

Bram made sure everyone cleared the launch area and walked toward the control room. He looked up and saw Pat and the two crews of the Wheels all standing by in the observation area. He was sure everyone in the building was present to see Bramlet One disappear.

Lori greeted him and guided him to the launch table and pointed to the launch button. It had been appropriately labeled "Launch."

Lori pressed a button on her phone and a drum roll blared out. Bram looked at his watch and exactly as it turned to one, she pressed the button. Bramlet One disappeared and a loud hurrah could be heard throughout the building.

Bram chuckled because to him it was all a little too dramatic, but it was satisfying.

His phone rang, and Jeffrey, John and Erica complimented him on a successful launch. They along with President Natorly had watched via a video link.

Bram was surprised by the call since he had not thought about inviting any of them.

A moment later President Natorly called to compliment him as well.

Bram left the control room and went out looking for Elizabeth. She had to be the one who arranged for the remote viewing. She was doing a great job at making the Fold team look professional! He wanted her to know how much he appreciated her help.

By two everyone in the building and all the Marines not on duty were gathered on the far side of Wheel number two.

Lacy had arranged for three food vending trucks to come in to cater the event. One truck featured Mexican food, one truck feature Asian food, and one truck was all about steaks, sausage, burgers, and hotdogs.

Bram's observation was that the Marines were going to make sure every truck did a good business.

Major Sharp approached him and thanked him for making sure all of his Marines enjoyed this impromptu celebration. He emphasized all and let Bram know that he was rotating all the Marines through. The only restriction for those on duty was that there was to be no drinking.

 Bram wondered how much his impromptu celebration was going to cost. It didn't matter to him, but it peaked his curiosity.

Lacy walked up to Bram and let him know that she had invited her sister and Zuri to arrive early. She asked if he would be upset if the entire Stetson family made an event of it.

Bram almost choked on a sip of ice-tea. His first question was if the family had been cleared for the visit.

She pointed to Zoe and said that she had cleared them before the family was allowed to take them on the fishing trip.

Zoe saw Lacy pointing and walked over. Bram asked her about the Stetson family. Zoe assured him that all but the one standing with them had been cleared at the same time and had signed a confidentiality agreement. She smiled and said that Lacy had received a top-secret clearance.

At that moment Linda Stetson pushed a wheelchair bound Zuri through the door. Bram walked over and knelt to greet Zuri.

Zuri looked at him and through a twisted smile said hello and identified him as the man who knew how to Fold space and time.

Bram knew instantly that he had found the genius he was looking for. He replied that he needed her help in figuring out what he was doing wrong. Her smile sealed her fate. As far as he was concerned, she was in.

He described the foods that were available and asked her what he could get for her?

Elizabeth appeared and took the Stetson family in hand. They all got some drinks and then she took them of a tour of the hanger area.

Bram walked along and periodically got down on his knees to talk with Zuri. His observation and the questions that Zuri asked kept reinforcing his initial assessment.

Orlando escorted Mallica into the hangar area. He had picked her up early. Mallica thanked him for bringing her to the hangar. She picked up a glass of ice-tea and walked to where Bram was returning with Zuri.

Bram made the introductions and suggested they all take a table and chat. He went on to tell Zuri that Mallica was the resident mathematics genius that would be working directly with her. She would be the one that would spend the most time with her. He told Zuri to cut Mallica some slack because if she didn't like Mallica he would have to find someone smarter and that would be very difficult.

Zuri gave a loud, "Ha." She signaled with her hand for Mallica to lean in. She whispered that Mallica was beautiful and probably as smart as she looked.

Mallica was surprised by the comment. She thanked Zuri and looked around to see if anyone had caught what was whispered. The crowd had drowned out the whisper. It seemed clear to Mallica that the small person in the wheelchair was mentally in full control.

Five was the return time for Bramlet One. The catering trucks left the area, and the party broke up. The observation area was full of folks still enjoying the party.

Bram and the lab crew were in the control room waiting for Bramlet One to reappear.

The stand for Bramlet One seemed to flicker and then blank out. Then it seemed to slowly take shape.

Bram listened to the intake and gasp as the team absorbed what they saw on the stand. He also noted the absolute silence that followed.

He knew immediate action needed to be taken and shouted out orders.

Chapter 21: Bramlet One-Sad Return

Bram rushed out of the control room. He shouted for the transport cart and assigned six people to put on anticontamination gear. The cart was to have a nitrogen filled enclosure.

He approached the grotesque object that was part Bramlet One and a part that looked like a stubby moray eel trying to eat it. The black granite like boulder was slightly larger than the Bramlet. Bramlet One was half in and half out of one side of the black granite moray eel.

He noted that the observation area was almost empty. The Wheel teams were gone.

The wait seemed to take hours, but Bram noted that it was only a few minutes past five. It seem like hours to him but only a few minutes had passed!

Six alien looking figures in the anticontamination gear were rapidly pushing a cart toward Bramlet One.

Lori came to stand beside Bram. She commented how amazing it was that Bramlet One managed to return. She made the point that it meant the computer was still functioning and that the power source safety margin had been up to the job.

Bram agreed with her and commented that he would need to analyze what the computer had registered and what had been recorded. The shimmering and power surge were probably due to the extra power need to handle the mass of the boulder. He would need to know the amount of power consumed for the return.

Mallica brought Zuri out to where Zack was standing. She repeated the observation Zuri had shared that sending out Bubble Scouts was a wise move by a wise man.

Bram agreed to the wise move but added by a person who should have known earlier to do it in that manner.

He knelt and whispered that it had been pure luck.

He looked up as Pat, Amy, Elizabeth, and Marcus approached.

Pat and Amy said they would be glad to delay that Wheel Fold until Bramlet Two could verify a safe Fold coordinate.

Bram laughed and went on to poke some fun at them.

He pointed out that the coordinates for Bramlet One were the exact location in the Wheel where the crew sat. He went on to make the point that the coordinate was the coordinates of the Primary pilot seat. Pat and Amy looked at each other.

Pat made the comment that the coordinates he had chosen were diabolical.

As he looked at Pat, Bram was so thankful that Bramlet One had taken the hit.

The coordinates were not the pilot seat but the exact center of the bubble at the center of the wheel. None the less, the size of the Wheel meant that other debris could have been in the same location.

He looked at Zuri and told her that how an object moved to the specified coordinate was a mystery to him. It was a mystery that needed to be solved. Another mystery was how the power from Earth was able to reach through the Fold and power the object in the Fold. And why if the power made it why was it that communication could not also make it?

They all listened as Zuri responded that she would think about these questions, but she would need help in understanding the math and science Bram had used to create the Fold in the first place.

Mallica let Bram know that she was taking Zuri home. She had talked to Zuri about staying with her at the apartment. They would ask Zuri's parents for the approval.

Bram commented that it would be great if that could happen. He knelt and thanked Zuri for having stayed for the return of Bramlet One. He watched as Orlando pushed Zuri toward the SUV.

He turned to Elizabeth and asked her to arrange for a self-powered wheelchair for Zuri. He also asked her to arrange a total medical evaluation at the best clinic that handled cases like Zuri's.

Elizabeth gave him a hug. She let him know that she too was very impressed with Zuri. She agreed to get her the best care possible.

Pat took Bram by the arm. She led him toward the lab. She quietly told him she was taking him to look at Bramlet Two, Three and Four. She told him that the Lab team and the Wheel teams had been working on making more Bramlets.

She went on to tell him that even now as the lab team was examining Bramlet One, Lori was urging the rest of them to finishing another Bramlet to be sent out as early as the next morning.

Bram thanked Pat for letting him know. He had a surge of new energy as he realized that the next bubble scout into the Fold was that close to being ready. He let out a deep breath and gave Pat a hug.

Bram entered a lab that appeared to him to be a beehive in action. He noted that everyone was engaged and concentrating on their work.

Bram walked over to where Bramlet One was housed in a sealed containment where it could be handled without being contaminated any more than it had originally been. He noted that a small chip had been taken from the boulder and would be processed for its composition. It was clear to him that the lab team had the examination clearly in control. They had cut open the top quarter of the bubble and were extracting the computer. He asked that he be called when it was ready for examination.

Pat again took him by the elbow. This time she guided him over to an area where the wheel teams were gathered around three worktables. He looked at the center of each worktable and noted that each was almost at the exact point of completion.

Bram was surprised at seeing Remi the lead lab engineer supervising the completion of the three bubbles. He would have anticipated his wanting to be involved in examining Bramlet One.

He asked Remi as much. Remi replied that getting another Bramlet out was a much higher priority than figuring out how Bramlet One had survived.

Bram agreed with him and asked about the timing of the availability of another Bramlet.

Remi looked at the people around the three tables. They had all stopped to hear what he would say. He looked around and smiled as he said, "If the Wheel teams had applied themselves with more intensity earlier, they would have been ready now, as it is, once they saw what happened to Bramlet One they are much more enthusiastic about getting their Bramlets online. He said that there would be three Bramlets ready by the morning."

Someone added, "and it would go even faster if we had a better coach."

Remi groaned and asked who had come up with a way to double the battery capacity for Bramlet Two that would double the time a Bramlet could stay in the Fold.

Bram laughed and thanked all of them for their super effort. He would try to find better co-ordinates for the subsequent Bramlets. He also mentioned that he had a different scouting behavior he would share in the morning.

He looked at Marcus and asked if he would be able to help in defining better coordinates?

Marcus gave an affirmative shake of his head.

Bram announced that ten a.m. would be the launch of Bramlet Two.

He asked Pat if she was staying. She responded that she was. Bram thanked everyone again and walked out of the lab.

He had decided it was time to go home and continue work after dinner.

Castor stood by the Limo with another Marine. He explained that Orlando had requested to guard Zuri. His request had been granted and Corporal Donna was to be his replacement.

Bram welcomed Donna and told Castor to let Orlando know that he would not be invited to the next fishing trip. Castor laughed and said Orlando would probably not even notice. Castor pointed out that Orlando had his eye set on Mallica, and that Zuri was the official line for the change.

Zoe laughed and said that love conquered all and that Orlando, though a tough guy was no different. She took Eric's hand and got into the back of the SUV.

Bram agreed with Zoe and said he understood and knew the feeling. He asked Donna to tell them about herself.

Bob and Thomas had kitchen duty and were in the middle of getting everything ready. They welcomed Castor and asked who the new Marine might be. They invited both to stay for dinner.

They said they had been present for the return of Bramlet One and wondered how long of a delay that would cause? Would Pat be joining for dinner?

Bram answered the last question first. He suggested they put away a small amount of dinner for Pat just in case. He went on to announce that there would be no delay in the in the Fold program unless the launch of Bramlet Two suffered a similar fate.

Donna found it hard to concentrate on dinner since the team members grilled her.

Zoe commented that it was good to see a woman up front guarding Bram.

Donna joked that she had volunteered when she heard that going fishing with Bram was bound to be very exciting or very successful.

Bram was enjoying the dinner, but he wanted to spend some time in thinking about how best to scout out a Fold point. He excused himself and invited Marcus to join him in his study. Bob got up and led the way and Thomas followed in back. Once in the study, Bob walked over to the tea pot and asked who wanted a cup.

Bram replied that a tea would be great.

Marcus chose a bottle of cold water.

Together they then studied the location near Neptune. Bram decided that he had been too aggressive in locating Bramlet One at only three thousand miles from the surface.

Marcus suggested that something around one hundred thousand miles in front of the planets path would be aggressive enough.

They determined the coordinates that would place Bramlet Two one hundred thousand miles in front of and the same distance inside its orbit. They developed six sets of coordinates that would be used for the six folds.

The coordinates would be the center of a Wheel as it had been for Bramlet One.

It was approaching one in the morning when they finished programing everything into his laptop. He and Marcus agreed they would review their work in the morning before loading the coordinates into Bramlet Two.

Thomas and Bob had been playing cards while they waited. When they saw Bram closing his laptop they got up and cleaned up the coffee/tea bar area.

Zoe and Eric were still up and agreed to escort Marcus to his new home.

Thomas and Bob led the way to Bram's bedroom. It was strategically located and had no windows.

Zoe and Eric's bedroom was across the hall to the right side. Bob's bedroom was to the far end of the hallway and Thomas's bedroom was to the front.

Double curved steps on each side of the front entry area led up to a hallway that made a sharp right turn that was followed by a left turn. Bram had analyzed the layout and agreed that it provided him with maximum safety.

Additionally, the house had three safe rooms. One in the basement, one on the first floor and one in Bram's room. They were stacked one above the other and connected vertically so that Bram could, if necessary, go down through the safe rooms and get down to the basement and be whisked out of the house.

After Bob had cleared the room, Bram entered after saying goodnight to his two guards. He stood under the shower for a long time, as he once again reviewed the following day's agenda. He looked at the clock as he climbed into bed and groaned. It was almost two.

Zoe's knock at the door was the next thing he heard. Once again, he groaned. It was almost eight. Now he was late.

Bram jumped up and quickly got ready. By eight thirty he was going down into the basement to get into the SUV. He kept conversation to a minimum and was eager to get to programing Bramlet Two.

Pat and her team were in charge of Bramlet Two. Her bloodshot eyes spoke of having stayed up all night, but she and her team were exuberant that their Bramlet had earned the number two spot. She gave Bram an uncharacteristic public hug and a kiss on the cheek.

Bram thanked them all for their dedication.

Marcus had been in the lab ahead of Bram. Bram took a moment to introduce him and thank him for his help in determining Bramlet Two's coordinates.

Someone quietly commented that after looking at Bramlet One it was good that an expert coordinate definer had joined the team.

Bram looked around to see who had made the remark but laughed when everyone put up their hands.

He shared that Bramlet Two would make at least six Folds throughout the day. Except for the first that would last only ten minutes, each Fold would be an hour long with an hour between each subsequent Fold. The coordinates would always put Bramlet Two, one hundred thousand miles ahead of the planet.

Remi added that such a schedule would allow recharging the battery each time and Bramlet Two could continue such a schedule indefinitely.

Bram agreed that if more Folds were needed, he would certainly take advantage of the improvement of Bramlet Two.

After programing and closing of the bubble, Bramlet Two was ready for launch. It was moved out to the launch position.

This time the Launch was from a nitrogen filled chamber and each return would be back into the same chamber.

Bram suggested that the whole team press the launch button. He enjoyed the teams loud shout of Fold before they pressed the button.

He knew that the wait time would be like the ten minutes at end of a tight football game.

He decided to get a fresh cup of coffee.

<u>Chapter 22: Bramlet Two</u>

Small tables one for each person had been brought into the launch office. This allowed everyone to have a seat while waiting and provided a way to do some work. The room remained filled with Wheel Team One members. Elizabeth sat silently to the right of Bram and Marcus sat to his left. Neither said a word.

The anticipation in the room bubbled over like oatmeal boiling too fast and about ready to spill out of the pot.

It was heavy and tense.

Nerves were sparking like broken power wires in a storm.

Bram was sure that like his, every mind was on how Bramlet Two would return from its maiden journey.

Bramlet One had surfaced a huge problem. The environment in those far off Fold coordinates that Bram picked was an unknown. Up to this point the coordinates had not even been discussed.

The previous Fold successes had hidden the type of problem Bramlet One had suffered.

Bramlet One had gone out into far space. It had left the protection of the Earth and its risk-free environment. A new sense of danger had been realized and everyone wanted a way to reduce the risk of repeating the event.

Bram looked around. Most of the team was dozing. They had all spent the entire night getting Bramlet Two assembled.

The clock seemed to have gone on professional football time. It was on the last ten minutes of the game speed of a tied game.

He could feel his heartbeat match the beat of the wall mounted clock.

He realized that he was into an adrenalin high.

He felt Elizabeth take his hand and someone else put their hand on his shoulder as the last minute began ticking down.

He looked up to see Pat looking out intensely at the Bramlet launch chamber. The chamber was a nitrogen enclosed containment vessel like the one Bramlet One still occupied.

Then as if by magic a shimmering produced Bramlet Two. The suited crew ran out and wheeled the cart away toward the lab area where it would be briefly examined, and camera memory dumped.

An eager stream of potential examiners gushed out of the launch office, and everyone made their way to the lab.

It made Bram think of the scene one always saw of the football players jogging to their locker rooms.

The camera video from Bramlet Two was put up on the screen and the view of the blue planet was spectacular in its clarity and detail of the surface.

Even as they were enjoying this initial success, John Morgan, the NASA Director informed the group the Scout Bubbles would be equipped with more sensors. NASA wanted a more complete understanding of what was being captured.

He looked around to a beaming Remi and asked how big a scout bubble would need to be to have the equivalent of the sensors that was housed on a Wheel?

Remi replied that with the right camera capabilities and radiation sensors the bubbles might be in the three-foot diameter range. This would allow for more battery capacity needed to operate the additional equipment, but it would still limit the time a bubble could stay out.

Bram asked Remi to take the lead and get one ready as soon as possible. The target date would be to have it available before the Fold across the Universe. He commented that the current bubbles would be used for a Solar System Fold.

An hour later everyone was in the control room for the second Fold of Bramlet Two. This time Pat pressed the Fold button. It was not as dramatic as the previous Fold and the room emptied as soon as the launch button was pushed.

The Wheel teams all retired to their Wheels to get some sleep while they waited for the next hour to pass by.

Bram led the way to his office. He was tired but relieved. He asked Lacy to show Marcus to his new office.

The two agreed to meet back in the launch room for the return of Bramlet Two.

Bram called Mallica to see how she had fared.

Mallica said that Zuri's parents wanted to meet and speak with Bram and the other leaders of the program. They wanted to make sure their daughter was not taken advantage of, and they were very interested in what could be done for her. Their initial reaction was very positive, and she felt good about them.

Mallica commented on how much Zuri had taken to him.

Bram agreed that it was good that the parents would want to make sure their daughter got the best treatment possible. He asked Mallica about her evaluation of the parents.

She replied that they were well educated. They had both graduated from Ohio State. The mother had a degree in mathematics and the father had a master's in mechanical engineering. They provided a very positive environment for Zuri. They were struggling financially because of Zuri's medical needs.

He asked Mallica to investigate the availability of a house in the Fold community for the entire family. It would be good to give Zuri a stable home environment. He also asked that Mallica ask the FBI for top level clearance for all of them. He stated he would have a job for the two talented parents.

He and Mallica agreed to a weekend lunch at his house. Having it there would reduce the security effort and it would allow the family to see the community that would be available to them.

Bramlet Two made its multiple one-hour cycles. It performed flawlessly. The visual data that was captured was sent to the IT analysis team at the end of each Fold. It was being immediately reviewed by a host analysts. Word came back that it was beyond anything they had imagined they would be able to learn about Neptune in their lifetimes.

Bram was pleased with the enthusiasm the IT folks were showing.

He on the other hand was only taking a quick look at what was seen on each cycle. He was more concerned about making sure that Bramlet Two was executing all the commands as he had programed into it.

He was becoming more confident that he would have safe coordinates for the two Wheel Folds.

He asked about any additional Bramlets that were ready to go and was surprised that there were six more ready.

He looked at Marcus and asked if he were thinking what he was thinking.

Marcus replied he would not presume to try to guess what Bram was thinking.

Bram replied that they could send an array of Bramlets out and ensure each Wheel space was free of debris.

Marcus agreed that it would be a very good idea and agreed to set up the coordinates so there was a three-point clearance check for each wheel and one for Bramlet Two that took in the view of the six Bramlets. This would provide a double check of the chosen behind the moon coordinates.

Except for a crew of six from the lab, Marcus and he were the only ones to see the final four Bramlet Two cycles. After the last Fold he asked that Bramlet Two and the other Bramlets all be prepared for Fold instructions and be ready for launch on the following day.

The next thing Bram did was to verify that the current power supply was ample. He then asked the power superintendent to set up six more Bramlet launch power supplies.

Bram spent the wait time reviewing his Fold equations. He was verbally talking through the equations. Marcus was politely listening and pointing out the points where assumptions had been made. Bram noted several points where he chose to use a constant versus a variable to make the equations link. He wondered out loud which constants needed to be variables.

Marcus replied that he had no clue what he was being asked.

Bram knew these would be the areas he would seek Zuri's reaction and comments.

He then asked Marcus to pick a location across the Universe that he wanted to send Bramlet Two. The two of them would do a quick scouting trip to see if the Fold would take them to where Marcus chose the Fold to be.

Marcus whistled silently and said, "you seem to be able to expand scope, change actions, and just decide and then do what you want?" Has anyone challenged you on your independent, lone wolf approach?

Bram replied that if he asked permission there would soon be a whole group of people who had no clue about the Fold, trying to guide the program. He chose to act and then inform. He pointed out that so far it had worked. He also said that as soon as the Fold program was registered as a success, he would most likely be pushed back from the forefront. He said that he was almost ready for that.

Marcus said he would have the location coordinates by morning.

Mallica had spent the day and by late afternoon she knew she had run into a time barrier with having Zuri's parents being checked out by the FBI. Late in the afternoon she went to Bram's office to share her frustrations.

She nodded at Marcus and asked if she could have a moment.

Marcus asked if he should leave.

Mallica said no and started to vent her frustrating day.

Bram listened for a few minutes then put up his hand to stop her.

He called Erica and brought her up to speed on the issue and asked her to see if she could increase the importance of the background check and get it accelerated. He made the point that the family had been thoroughly investigated to get their US entry visa and they were both Ohio State graduates.

Erica readily agreed to go push the system. She was sure it could rapidly be done.

She informed Bram that he had the enthusiastic support of NASA and President Natorly and could get about anything he wanted. She made the point that his success was going to be a huge political boost for President Natorly in the next election.

Bram thanked Erica and went on to say he had also asked Elizabeth to seek all the medical help that was available for Zuri.

Erica replied that she had talked to Elizabeth earlier in the day and had connected her with a Mayo Clinic specialist in Minneapolis. She was sure Zuri would get the best care available in the world and that money was no barrier.

It was clear to Bram that his Fold successes had opened the resource door.

Mallica had taken the opportunity to make some tea. She handed one to Bram and smiled. She went on to say that success certainly opened many doors.

She recalled the year that Bram had walked out into the desert to determine the location of the compound at which all three of them were being held. His persistence then had made all this possible.

Bram looked at Mallica. He agreed with her and went on to apologize for leaving her and Marcus there for so long.

Mallica nodded in agreement and went on to say how demoralizing the lack of action on his part had felt. She said that Elizabeth had made sure everything was OK and had kept both Marcus and she connected.

Marcus had a harder time because his family was back in the Boston area, and he felt that he was not contributing to the Fold project while at the same time cheating his family. He almost dropped out but again Elizabeth assured him that he would be pulled in as soon as you realized you needed help.

Bram nodded.

He agreed and stated that now was the time he was seeking help.

He needed it with the math associated with the Fold.

He needed help with the astronomical locations to send the bubble scouts.

He needed help with the technical development associated with all the hardware and the power consumption the Fold required.

He nodded again and agreed he needed help.

He realized that the Fold effort was growing beyond his personal ability to control the many aspects that needed attention.

Elizabeth poked her head in the door. She asked if she were interrupting anything personal.

Bram smiled and got up walked around the desk gave her a hug and then went to get her a cup of tea.

He asked Elizabeth to sit down and share her good news.

Elizabeth wanted to know how Bram knew she had good news.

Bram pointed out that the smile on her face had broadcast good news.

Elizabeth went on to tell of her discussion with a Dr. Morgan Sewal. Dr. Sewal was globally known and recognized for working with children around the world who suffered many of the same problems that Zuri faced.

He had agreed to come out to meet Zuri and do a preliminary evaluation. Elizabeth said she took the opportunity to invite him to come out over on the coming weekend.

Mallica had told her of you arranging for the family to be at your house for dinner.

Elizabeth went on to say that she had invited Dr. Sewal to attend dinner.

Bram looked to Mallica, Marcus and then back to Elizabeth. He asked who was cooking?

Elizabeth laughed. She said she had thought about that and had asked Lacy to arrange for the dinner to be catered. She said that she had counted twenty-two people that would attend. That included Jeffrey, Erica, and John who were planning to fly out and to arrive on Friday.

Elizabeth went on to say that Lacy had asked whether her family would be allowed to cater such an event. She had given Lacy the preliminary OK based on his approval.

Bram put his hand on his forehead and said quietly that it seemed to be a good time to prepare for his background role.

He looked at Mallica and asked if she were ready to assume guiding the Mathematical review of the Fold equations? He wondered if Zuri's mother would be a good participant in that effort.

He looked at Elizabeth and asked if she would be OK with stepping back from being the technical supervisor and becoming the guide for Zuri's care and education.

She would retain her command of Wheel Two.

He asked Marcus to become the lead in determining the location and coordinates for the across the Universe Folds and to oversee all Folds.

He would ask Lori to be the lead in managing the Solar System Folds. Marcus would be her coach.

He would ask Remi to be the lead in developing and production of additional bubble scouts.

He would ask Jose and Ester, the previous project managers of the Wheels to retain those positions.

He looked at Elizabeth and asked her to identify and suggest people for the many other roles he was sure he was forgetting. He wanted folks like Amy, Pat, and their backups to be put in meaningful and appropriate Fold program roles. He went on to say he was totally biased and needed to keep his hands off their assignments.

Mallica agreed to lead the analysis.

Elizabeth nodded and said that the change would be welcome and probably be much more to her liking. She commented that it was clear to her that Bram was stepping back as well and that was good. It was time to utilize Erica's project management skills.

She suggested he should think about another fishing trip. He could arrange to take Zuri.

Marcus said he would agree to his role, but his family would need to be invited to go fishing.

Bram evaluated what he had just said. He had instinctively positioned the key people. He was determined to keep the Fold program moving forward as rapidly as possible. If its management was going to change, he would make sure it would fall forward as he envisioned.

He then asked Elizabeth the work with John Morgan anyone associated with the Fold effort be relocated to the Dalles site. He wanted to be able to keep the Fold information secret.

Bram stood up, stretched, and declared that it was the seventh inning, and it was time for a beer, a hot dog, and a bag of peanuts. He then walked out of the office.

Chapter 23: Leap of Faith

The grey light of the sun outlining the various peaks of the Rocky Mountains painted a black zigzag like surface ahead of Bram as he and his entourage of guards jogged on the road to the office complex. On this morning Marcus and Pat were jogging besides him. He had agreed with Marcus when he had commented that five thirty was an ambitious time to go to work. He asked Marcus if the opportunity to identify the point across the Universe where the two Wheels would make their maiden interstellar voyage gave him any energy to jog the distance. He pointed out that Marcus would personally press the launch button to send Bramlet Two and the other Bramlets to that location.

Marcus groaned and replied that he would try to keep up. He said he had the coordinates and maybe Donna or Castor could just take them and put them in.

Bram felt good about having engaged Marcus and felt bad at having forgotten him out in the desert compound for the past year. He wished Elizabeth had spoken up but with the flurry of situations that had happened he could not think of a time that he would have paid attention or cared.

He felt good. The Fold team had acted to keep the program on track.

He felt good. The people around him were great and they cared about the Fold program as much as he.

He felt good. He was sure that Zuri would provide the new insight and perspective that he was missing.

He felt good.

He called out to Castor and asked if he had a Marine jogging ditty about feeling good.

Almost immediately Castor had all of them chanting about feeling good to the beat of their jogging. The other marine guards they encountered as they got to the office area joined in as they went by. They called out that they felt good too.

Marcus, Pat, and he were the only ones at breakfast.

Marcus said he had asked his kids about where on the other side of the Universe they wanted to go.

They asked if they needed to stay in the Milky Way or could they go to another galaxy.

Marcus said that their question caught him by surprise. He decided that for now they should stay in the Milky Way.

He was aware that the power consumption of executing the Fold still needed more evaluation and decided they should take one leap of faith at a time.

His current thinking was that the order of the Fold sequence should be a Solar System Fold, then a Milky Way Fold to the nearest potentially habitable planet, and in the near future a Fold to another galaxy.

Bram commented that he was pleased that Marcus had such a bright group of resources to consult. He would be sure to thank them for their guidance.

Pat put her hand on Marcus's wrist and said that this was the highest praise he would get from Bram.

Bram smiled and raised his cup of coffee.

After breakfast Pat led the way to the lab area. Bramlet Two was parked in its nitrogen filled containment besides Bramlet One. The other Bramlets were contained similarly and were standing in a straight row along the wall. The sight of all the Bramlets parked side by side reinforced the need to be thorough in checking out Fold locations.

Bram logged into the local hub that communicated with the Bramlets. He asked Marcus to enter the coordinates that the Bramlets would go to.

Marcus explained that he had considered four locations. They were the most recently found exoplanets. They were Proxima Centrarui b at approximately 4.2 light years distance, Ross 128 b at about 11 light years, Luyten b at about 12. light years and Wolf 1061b at 13.8 light years.

He had let the distance be the guide to his choice. He wanted to send Bramlets to all the locations in the very near future. He commented that this would give them a chance to monitor the power draw as the distances increased.

Bram replied that Marcus should enter the coordinates of all four and that the Bramlets had the opportunity to set a new world record for distance traveled in one day.

Marcus let out his breath and replied that he indeed had coordinates for all the Bramlets.

Bram commented that if all the Bramlets made it through all four-Fold coordinates it would blow the lid off the everyone's expectations.

He went on to say that they would wait until the Bramlets made all their Folds before sharing any information.

He pointed out that if the Bramlet Folds were successful, Marcus would have his hands full in handling an ever-expanding Fold program and asked if he were ready?

Marcus made the comment that maybe he should have settled for the quiet life out in the desert compound.

Pat reacted to the banter by asking if the two were just going to talk or were they ready get on with the Fold.

Bram and Marcus replied, "let's go do it."

The power meter registered a significant rise in the power consumption as the Bramlets made their first multi-light year Fold. The power increase seemed in proportion to the distance of the Fold but well within what one power generator could handle.

Marcus commented that if the power draw was somehow proportional to distance then one generator seemed to be the capacity needed for the more distant Folds.

Bram agreed with Marcus. He took the precaution of checking with the power generator superintendent to ensure additional power would automatically come online if needed.

Bram returned to his office during the hour the Bramlets were deployed.

Lacy entered and said she wanted to give Bram a quick update on the dinner arrangements for the next day.

She shared the menu that would feature Salmon and Gar as the fish. Lamb would be the red meat. There would be a mixed fresh vegetable salad. Sweet potatoes and cooked carrots would round out the menu.

Bram said the menu sounded great. He wanted to make sure that this would fit Zuri and her family's diet.

Lacy said she would double check with Zuri's mother. She went on inform Bram about rearranging the lounge area in his house and setting up a long table to seat everyone.

Bram raised his hands and replied that he was OK with anything and everything. He laughed and said dinner was beyond his control. He would stick with the simple stuff like monitoring the Fold.

Lacy responded to his comment. She said that indeed the Fold was much easier and more like eating a piece of cake, "sometimes a little crumbly but it had frosting and was sweat as a piece of cake."

Bram agreed with her. He asked whether she could also arrange for another fishing trip for two weekends after the dinner.

He then excused himself so that he could get back to the Fold launch office and get frosting put on his cake.

Marcus had not only programmed in the coordinates for each Fold, but he had also provided guidance to the camera motion. His goal was to guide the picture taking so that the resulting images could be oriented. At this point Marcus had no clue how to aim the camera. Once these initial shots were examined future guidance could then be managed in a controlled fashion.

Bram agreed with Marcus's approach. Together they examined the results from the Proxima Centrarui b Fold.

Bram realized they could spend hours examining the footage they had brought back. He brought the viewing to an end by declaring it was time to send the Bramlets out to Ross 128 b.

The power draw for the Ross Fold increased proportional to the increase in distance but it too stayed well within one generator's power.

Bram now had the information to calculate the power draw for the bubble scouts based on their size and distance. He would soon have the similar requirements for the power requirements for the Wheels.

He decided that the first Wheel Fold would be out close to the Moon. This would give him two power requirement points for the Wheel folds and the opportunity to make sure that the Fold out to Neptune would be within the power that was available.

He mentioned it to Marcus and the two worked together to put the moon Fold location on the dark side of the moon. It would not be detectable from Earth.

Elizabeth, Amy, and Pat listened to Bram as he explained the change in the Wheel Fold sequence he was planning for the coming week. The fact that he had added a Fold close to the Moon was seen as a great precaution and well accepted. This was especially true when they learned that they would only stay at the Moon Fold location for two days. They would then take a day off and then make the Fold out to Neptune.

Everyone on the team thanked him for his caution but voiced the fact that they were ready.

Bram asked that the changes to the Fold schedule not be shared. He knew he was moving fast and adjusting schedules as the scouts provided additional information.

He and Marcus reviewed that footage the Bramlets brought back from Wolf 1061b. They had calculated all the upcoming Fold locations for all the Bramlets and the Wheels during the day. They decided that it was time to decompress and get ready for the Saturday dinner event at Bram's house.

Bram and Marcus walked back to Bram's office.

Lacy informed Bram that Jeffrey and Erica had just arrived and were in his office.

Bram took a deep breath and walked into his office.

Jeffery stood up and walked over to shake Bram and Marcus' hand. Erica did the same, but she gave Bram a hug.

Bram asked how the trip out to the west coast and the drive down had been?

Erica replied that it had had been a long trip but other than that it had been fine. She said that Lacy had been very helpful and had arranged to have their apartments ready for them. She went on to say that they had decided to come by his office before going there.

Bram replied that he was glad to see them. After asking if they wanted anything, he went on to say that he and Marcus had just finished sending Bramlets to four distant places that were from four to thirteen light years away.

He went on and said that Saturday evening's dinner would feature unedited views of Neptune and these four across the galaxy visits.

Erica gave a small laugh and commented that it was almost impossible to keep up with him and the Fold progress.

Jeffrey commented that he was pleased and that the speed of the Fold progress was taking everyone by surprise. He asked if Bram needed anything to keep things going.

Bram decided that this was the moment to share the changes he had decided on.

He looked at Erica and said that she was really needed at the Dalles site. He explained that he was stepping out of the role of managing the technical activities.

He needed more time to study and improve the Fold equations and the process. He was recruiting Zuri Juma, a seven-year-old savant, to provide an outside fresh evaluation of his work.

He had asked Mallica to manage the review and be a mentor to Zuri.

He had asked Elizabeth to step back from being the technical project manager and manage the medical care for Zuri. Elizabeth would retain her position as Captain of Wheel Two.

Marcus would determine the Galaxy and beyond Fold locations and coach Lori Middleton on her role as Solar system Fold locations leader.

Bram went on to explain that he had asked Elizabeth to work with Erica to make these changes and then make sure the remaining team members all got recognized and rewarded for all the great work by getting strong career building assignments.

He was staying on as the Captain of Wheel One. He made the point it was the only role that took so little time that he could afford to stay there for the near future.

He went on to say that Erica could have any home in the Fold complex that suited her and that was available.

Once again Erica commented on the speed of change in the Fold project but said that she would be pleased to take a bigger role in the Dalles location. She commented that it would be a relief from the haggling that occurred on the East.

Bram stood up and suggested they all ride together to the Fold community area. They could continue their conversation tomorrow over a late eight in the morning breakfast.

Chapter 24: Project Alignment

The short ride back to the Fold housing area allowed for only a brief follow-up conversation. This is what Bram had planned. He wanted Jeffrey and Erica to have the evening to think about the changes he had described. He let them both know that there would be a food menu in the apartment at which they were staying, and that the cafeteria stayed open until ten and would deliver the food to them.

They both thanked him and then exited and went to their apartments.

After dropping them off he let Marcus know he was welcome to the breakfast, but his presence was not required.

Marcus thanked him and said he and family would come over for the dinner and the space movie.

After Marcus got out of the SUV, Zoe and Eric moved from the very back and sat next to Bram. The SUV proceeded to the basement of his house.

Eric commented that he thought Bram had done an excellent job of managing his boss.

Bram gave a chuckle and added that it was not Jeffrey but Erica that he was trying to manage. She was excellent at her job, but she often wanted to step in and manage what other people were responsible for.

Zoe replied that while Bram was around, Erica would most likely stay between the lines of the road.

Bram thanked her for the kind words. He went on to say that Erica had been the one that had made first contact with him and at that time had greatly influenced his decision to work on the Fold project.

Jeffrey had sealed the deal by simply informing him that he had no other choice.

Bob greeted them as they came up from the basement. He let them know that he was just finishing getting dinner ready. He said the meal consisted of grilled chicken, mac and cheese, some grilled asparagus and a side salad of mixed lettuce topped with small tomatoes. He said it would be on the table in fifteen minutes and asked who wanted some Muscatel.

Bram said it all sounded good, could he have about twenty minutes so that he could take a quick shower.

The conversation at dinner was about the number of guests that would attend dinner on Saturday. One main concern was for the team to review the guest list and make sure everyone had been cleared.

The Juma family seemed to be the only guests that might not have their clearances, but Zoe felt confident that the family was not a threat.

Bram let Zoe know that Erica had indicated she expedited the clearance process, and that Zoe should look to see if there were any outstanding messages about that situation.

Zoe asked if Bram was willing to share what he had been doing with the Bramlets during the day?

Bram understood Zoe's curiosity and described sending the Bramlets across the Universe. The fact that the Bramlets had gone from four to fourteen light years across the Universe and brought back some astounding pictures was historic. He pointed out that those sitting around the table would be among the first to know. The Saturday dinner entertainment would be the showing of a few minutes at each location.

Pat had been silent until that moment. She looked around the table at the in-the-headlight kind of stares each of the protection team members exhibited. She commented that she too was amazed at the speed that Bram was using the Fold capability. It was historic and seemed to leap forward at the speed of a winning drag race car that did not have a stop parachute.

Bram asked who on the team would like to help him select the photo segments from each location.

Every hand including Pat's went up in the air.

Bram suggested that maybe the more fun thing would be for them to select the scenes and surprise him at tomorrow's dinner with the choices they made.

Pat and Zoe both said that the idea was a great one.

Bram smiled and said he would spend his time having breakfast with the boss and then go on with his reexamination of his math. He said he wanted to be sure it was safe before he got on Wheel One and let Pat push the launch button.

Pat joked that it was about time that he thought about the safety of the crew.

Bram got up and carried his dishes to the sink. It was his turn to rinse the dishes and put them in the dishwasher. He had insisted they all take turns at kitchen duty. He had designed the daily kitchen chore list of one cook and three of them as cleanup crew. During the week this only applied to dinner. On weekends it applied to all three meals. He was pleased with how well the team made it work.

After dinner Bram went to his office. Pat brought in two large mugs of tea and sat down beside him on the two-person recliner-couch. He chose to recline. Pat put her back to his side and opened the latest book she was reading.

Bram had his eyes closed and was once again going through the Fold math. He put his right arm over Pat's shoulder and absorbed the comforting warmth her body transferred to him. It was hard for him to concentrate on Fold equations, and he soon dozed off.

Pat felt the change in Bram's breathing and realized he had fallen asleep. She figured the events of the day had sapped his drive. She felt total contentment. It was a feeling she had sought. When she met Bram, her yearning was immediately satisfied.

At midnight Pat nudged Bram and suggested they go up to bed.

Pat guided a sleepy Bram up to their room. He threw his slacks on the chair and got in on his side. Pat soon came back to the bed and got in on her side and scooched over and put her head on Bram's chest. She gave him a kiss on the cheek and then settled in with his arm around her.

The next morning Bram fought through a dream about his Wheel flying off out of control and heading into a black hole. He awoke with a jerk. He decided his dreams were much too real as he wiped sweat off his forehead.

He went into the bathroom to get ready for the day. It was already eight. He was glad he had agreed with Erica for a late nine or nine thirty breakfast.

Pat was at the stove getting ready to cook some pancakes when Bram finally came into the kitchen.

Bram gave her a hug and said he was surprised they were the only ones up.

Pat corrected him and said their four FBI guards already had breakfast and were in the basement welcoming Jeffrey, Erica, John, and a Dr. Morgan Sewal. She went on to say that breakfast would be pancakes, bacon, eggs over easy and either coffee or tea.

Bram thanked her for being ambitious enough to feed ten people. Then he headed to the basement door to welcome his morning breakfast guests.

Jeffrey led the way with John close behind. Erica and Dr. Sewal were talking and briefly said good morning as they came in.

Bram said good morning to the FBI four and then led the way to the breakfast eating area.

John and Dr. Sewal had traveled down from Portland in an SUV that Lacy had arranged to pick them up.

Bram welcomed everyone and made sure everyone had been introduced and asked Pat to share the breakfast offering.

He then asked how Jeffrey and Erica had faired with dinner the night before.

Erica said she chose to just have a salad and now she was ready for a big breakfast. She said she would take one of everything and a cup of coffee.

Zoe brought the coffee and tea pot and filled each cup based on each individual's desire.

John said that he and Dr. Sewal had been on the same flight and had breakfast on board, but he was ready for some over easy eggs, bacon, and some toast.

Dr. Sewal said he would take the same as John.

Jeffrey said he would take what Bram planned to order.

Bram looked at Jeffrey and smiled. The two had in previous breakfasts discussed Bram's favorite breakfast being two pancakes, with two over easy eggs with three strips of bacon on top and drowned in maple syrup.

Pat had made brief notes of all the orders. She said she knew the last two orders by heart. She would add Erica to that list.

She began with John and Dr. Sewal's breakfast.

Zoe served them as soon as it was prepared.

Bram suggested that each person dig in as soon as they got served. He commented that breakfast was best when it was hot.

Erica dug in as soon as it arrived. She was on her second cup of coffee. Her comments about the breakfast were all positive.

Jeffrey got his next and immediately put the pads of butter between the pancakes and two on top. He then smothered it all in Maple syrup.

Erica copied his preparation on the three quarters that was still on her plate.

Bram did the same as Jeffrey had done. He looked to Pat and asked if she was going to join them at the table.

Pat sat down with just a cup of coffee for herself. She commented that breakfast was either very good or everyone was too shy to talk.

Bram saw that Dr. Sewal's plate was empty, and he was now just sipping his coffee. Bram thanked him for coming on such short notice. He went on to describe Zuri and that she was brilliant, probably a Stephen Hawking-like person. He hoped that Dr. Sewal would be able to improve her life.

Dr. Sewal replied that Elizabeth had made a similar comparison and had persuaded him to come out immediately. He thanked Bram for inviting him to dinner. He was eager to meet Zuri and he would certainly do everything in his power to improve her life.

Bram again thanked him.

He then turned to John and asked if NASA was ready to up their contribution to the Fold effort. Bram went on to specifically state that he did not want supervisors. He wanted contributing team members.

John replied that he had been waiting to be asked. He had a host of great people all chomping at the bit to get closer to the action. They were all wanting to be on the court and taking shots. He said that there were no bench warmers or sideline coaches.

Bram nodded and thanked John. He asked that all the current folks associated with the Fold effort be relocated to Dallas so that the information could me contained.

He asked John to help Remi establish bubble building contracts with some reputable companies. He pointed out that they had a leading company that had the Wheel building contract, but NASA needed to take a position on bubble building. At this time, the bubbles were being assembled on location. Remi Hardwood was the engineer leading that effort. He would be a great resource and potential future leader of such an effort.

He turned next to Erica and asked what she had decided about moving to Dalles.

Erica smiled at Bram and replied that if he would have her over once a month for a breakfast like the one she just had, she would make the sacrifice and leave the DC arena immediately. She said that she personally was ready for some field action and that the atmosphere back east was getting way too political.

Bram promised to give her as many breakfasts as she might want.

Jeffrey looked around the table. He commented that the Fold project seemed to manage itself. He wondered what he might do to help.

Bram looked at Jeffrey and commented that his role was going to get much tougher once the world realized how powerful it made the country that controlled the Fold process. He pointed out that even if it shared the results, the US currently controlled what was seen and how the program was managed.

He asked Jeffrey whether his support team back east was strong enough to influence and guide the US administration that was in power? He went on to ask which military branch wanted to control the program?

Bram's final comment was that Jeffrey should let Erica be his Fold Project manager and lock everyone else out and keep them on the other side of the fence.

Jeffrey commented that he had asked and gotten a clear message of what he should do. He agreed with Bram that the political aspects were getting tougher. It seemed that the Fold's early success had surprised almost everyone.

There was opposition for whatever reason, but probably they were financial ones, and that opposition seemed bent on stopping the program. A Fold success antiquated every space technology currently being use. It would put the rocket building business into the same situation that buggy making had experienced when Ford began mass producing automobiles.

He pointed out that Bram had introduced the next dramatic economic change and was continuing to do so at breakneck speed.

Bram looked around the table and saw everyone nodding their heads in agreement. He commented that the financial and cultural situation on Earth would take a momentary hit. He pointed out that John would be seeking to establish many business contracts. The world would quickly recover and benefit financially.

He then shared his major concern that he might expose Earth much like a prairie dog coming unsuspecting out of its den and being fanged by a rattlesnake.

He needed to ensure that there was not a rattlesnake waiting out in the universe that would sink in its fangs into Earth.

Jeffrey looked at Bram and agreed that the finances would quickly balance out and that the changes that had been suggested made the Fold effort much stronger. However, the short-term impact was a barrier that might prove insurmountable.

Eric commented that a catering truck was parked out front and that it was probably time for breakfast to end.

Bram stood up and thanked everyone for their participation in the Fold effort. He said he was looking forward to the dinner and a continuing discussion on how the world around them would change but benefit everyone.

Chapter 25: Team Problem

After everyone had left, Bram retired to his office. Zoe and Eric were his shadow for the day and sat on the sofa reading. Bram had spontaneously spouted his concern about exposing Earth. It had not been something he planned to say. He was now working through the various risk scenarios that some belligerent or scared, intelligent alien culture might pose.

He looked to Zoe and Eric and decided that they were probably always thinking about the various situations that's put him at risk.

Bram excused himself and asked them to help him identify the various risk scenarios that they would be concerned about and how they would prepare for each.

Eric said that would be great. Zoe agreed but she said that Thomas was the risk scenario freak among them. She suggested they invite both Bob and Frank to join in on the discussion.

Bram agreed everyone's participation was welcome.

Pat entered and became alarmed as Zoe ran out and called for Frank and Bob.

Bram signaled her over and explained that he had ask for help in identifying the risk scenarios that the Fold program could put Earth into.

Pat let out her breath and said the first risk would be the heart attack for the unsuspecting. She sat down in the recliner and sipped on her tea. She figured this would be a work session in which she would be able to understand and perhaps participate.

Eric, Zoe, Frank, and Bob took seats around the office. Frank expressed the fact that he had been discussing this exact point with the team. He wondered why it had taken so long to get to this critically important topic.

Bram restated his request. This time he asked that each risk that was brought up should be accompanied with at least one counter measure. The risk should be written down and pinned to the note bar that ran around the room. All the risks should be identified and then on a second round all would be reexamined.

Zoe agreed to be the scribe and to put each sheet up.

Bram listened as the four began their risk identification. He only intervened when they began to argue about a specific risk.

The risks were interesting and informative. They were,

- That a bomb would be attached to the scout and would explode on its return. The bomb might be big enough to blow up the earth.
- That an external tracking device be put on the scout and provide the aliens with a way to follow it back.
- That the aliens put germs or viruses on the scout that would then attack humans when the scout returned.
- That an alien computer Trojan horse be put into the scout and that it would spread around the world.
- That the scout would be captured and would give the aliens a technology they did not currently possess.
- That the scout would give Earth coordinates to the aliens. This would give them the ability to launch a variety of attacks.

Bram thanked the team for their morbid view of the alien culture. He had not thought about any of the scenarios. He admitted that he had been on "the raise your open hand and say friend," scenario.

He made the point that he could immediately implement having a sensor that made sure nothing was attached to the scout. Additionally, the scout was now launched from and returned to the inside of a sealed chamber, so any external viruses or germs would be detected. This chamber could be enhanced into a bomb explosion containment chamber. He would ask the computer experts about enhancing his software defense and a way to test the software for any changes on each Fold return.

He admitted; he was not sure about blocking any back tracking of the coordinates. He would put this on his list to work with Zuri as they reviewed the Fold equations.

He took in the expression on everyone's faces and commented that they had done a great job. He asked if they would they like to continue and lead a more thorough defense effort?

Zoe spoke up immediately that she would love it. It would make life so much more fun. They would need to get it cleared by their bosses. She pointed out that Bram's request would make acceptance an immediate reality.

Bram agreed to get Erica to make it happen. He then suggested they take a break and see if there were any snacks that they might enjoy prior to dinner.

Lacy greeted Bram as he came into the kitchen. She quickly re-introduced all of her family. She said that her Father was out getting the grill ready. Rita said hello from where she stood in front of the oven. Marial said hello from where she and her husband, Cedric were setting up a series of tables that would be pushed together to form one large table that would take up the entire recreation area. Luke, Lacy's uncle was busy erecting a large viewing screen.

Bram welcomed everyone and thanked them for responding to Lacy's request. He then asked if there might be a snack that the team could take away for an impromptu picnic down by the playground.

Lacy led the way out to where her father was at the grill. She asked what he was grilling? Ted responded that he had brats, hot dogs, and some chicken wings.

Bram shook Ted's hand and gave him a hug. He asked for a couple of chicken wings for each of them and a dog for himself.

Ted responded that it was great to see Bram and Pat again and that the Gar she had caught was still being eaten.

Everyone made a choice and the six of them headed for the playground. Almost immediately Bram caught sight of a drone hovering above one of the trees. He asked his four bodyguards if any of them had a silencer on their gun.

Zoe and Frank responded that they had.

Bram gave them the coordinates of the drone and told them that unless they had been informed that they should expect a drone they should shoot it down.

He watched as the two shot the drone out of the air. He thought that Zoe had been the one to hit it.

He called Major Sharp and informed him that a drone had been shot down. Then "Ed" as he liked Bram to call him said he would immediately send a team over to investigate.

Bram called one of the marine guards over and pointed to the drone and asked him to have all the guards look around for someone, inside or outside the fence that might be around with a drone control unit. He should guard the drone until the investigation team arrived.

Bram went to the nearest picnic table and sat down. He opened the basket of chicken wings and then took a bite of his hot dog. Pat sat down next to him, and Zoe and Eric sat across the table in front of him and Thomas and Bob sat one to each side of him and Pat.

It was clear to Bram that they were in their defensive protect positions.

No one at the playground noticed anything unusual. Melisa their neighborhood event organizer waved and walked over to say hello. She did not notice the Marine guard who was guarding the shot down drone.

Bram decided not to say anything and instead offered her some chicken wings.

Melisa declined and said she needed to get back to her kids.

Bram looked over at Zoe and said they needed to work on the risk scenarios associated with being a part of the Fold program and come up with additional counter measures. It was clear to him that so far, the Fold team was being naively defensive. He went on to say he wanted an offense.

He asked Zoe to work with Erica in setting up an FBI counter offensive unit.

Zoe agreed that something needed to be done but commented that she was not sure getting the FBI involved was the right step.

Bram watched as the Marine investigation team gathered up the small camera drone. They spent a few moments talking to the guards and then quietly left. Bram's request that the investigation team be discrete had been clearly followed and no one at the recreation center noticed anything unusual.

Eric made the comment that they were being watched. He suggested that all the dinner guests arrive by SUV and enter via the basement. He pointed out that the catering truck was parked in back and was out of view. He suggested that extra Marines be posted discretely and out of sight around the perimeter of the yard for the afternoon and evening.

Bram thought that Eric's suggestions were very appropriate. He asked Eric to make the arrangements with Major Sharp.

Pat suggested that they get back to the house and finish selecting the clips that they would show their guests.

Bram thought that it was a great idea to get back to the house. He stood up and headed up the hill toward his house.

He sought out Lacy and after explaining the situation he asked her to have the guests be brought in as Eric had suggested. He let her know about the extra guards and asked her to make the arrangement to feed them.

Lacy commented that he seemed to be a magnet for attention. She would inform the family of what was going on and then to make all the arrangements for the guests and those around that were guarding them. She said she was going to go ahead and arrange an escort for those leaving later for the airport.

She suggested that they needed a broader security net that was outside of the compound.

Bram was getting discouraged by the success of his adversaries and nodded his head in agreement. He decided that some of his Bramlets might be put to good use as perimeter snoopers.

The guests began arriving and were mingling around the kitchen, the eating area, the front entrance and sitting area. Marcus and his family were the last from the compound to arrive.

Then Zuri and her parents arrived.

Zuri was carried up the stairs by Orlando and Castor.

Mallica escorted Zuri's parents and introduced each. She made a point that Nuro, meaning born at night, had a master's degree from The Ohio State and Jina whose name meant victorious had a mathematical degree from the same university.

Bram shook hands with each of the parents and then got down on his knees and gave Zuri a hug and welcomed her. He called Dr. Sewal over and introduced him to Zuri.

Dr. Sewal got down on his knees and said hello.

Bram stood up and suggested that Lacy take control of getting everyone seated.

Marcus approached Bram and said that he really did not want to say anything, but his wife insisted that he tell Bram that she thought his greeting of Zuri was inappropriate. She wanted to let Bram know that she did not want him near her kids.

Bram was taken aback. He did not know how to reply. He looked at Marcus and then over to where Myla his wife was standing. He replied that he would seek additional opinions and get back to him.

He asked Dr. Sewal about the greeting and if he saw anything wrong with it.

Dr. Sewal replied that he would be doing the same once he got to know Zuri better.

He next asked Mallica and Orlando. They both said they had done the same thing he had done. Mallica wondered why Bram was asking. Bram explained about the message Marcus had given him from his wife. Mallica said she would talk with Myla and see what was up.

Bram thanked her and proceeded to take his seat. He knew that he had a real issue on his hand. He was almost sure there was a dark cloud in Marcus's wife's childhood. Bram made up his mind that it would either get resolved or Marcus would need a new assignment.

A name tag identified each person both with a name and a number. The number indicated the menu choice that had been selected. Salmon and Gar were the two most popular choices, but a few chose the Lamb. Zuri said that she had chosen Gar because she had been told that it was the one that Pat had caught.

Bram watched as the picture of Pat standing on the dock beside her Gar flashed up on the screen. He noted that she had on the same green blouse, shorts, and shoes that she had worn when she caught her record sized gar on the Rushing River. He also noted his own response with seeing the picture.

After a round of congratulations, the table went silent as everyone ate their meal. Small conversations would pop up and then once again there was silence.

Bram proposed a toast to the Stetson family and the fine cuisine they had prepared. Everyone raised their wine or beers and gave a Marine "Hurrah."

Pat then announced that they would start showing the journeys the Bramlet had made.

She showed the launch of Bramlet One and explained about the celebration that was held. She then flashed a picture of Bramlet One as it now rested in a container sealed in Nitrogen. There were audible gasps around the table.

Bram commented that the Wheel teams went from complaining about him being too cautious and worried about their safety to saying they were fine with the delay that sending out the Bramlets to ensure the area for the Fold would be clear.

Pat then showed the launch of Bramlet Two and explained how both Wheel teams and the Lab team had worked together to have Bramlet Two ready the next day for additional Folds. Marcus was lauded for moving Bramlet Two to a more distant and safer position out in front of the Neptune orbit. She explained that those present were seeing footage so far only seen by a few others in the room.

Then Pat shared that the next four slides would show views that went multiple light years across the Milky Way and that now there were seven Bramlets in existence.

She explained that the pictures would show the four planets that had been discovered in the last four years and ranged from four to thirteen light years away. She stopped and looked around the room and quietly pointed out that they were the first to see them. No one outside the room had yet had a chance. She pointed out that this was a historic moment for all of them.

There was a round of applause and an exclamation about having gone out into the Milky Way with no warning announcement.

Bram pointed to Marcus and gave him credit for having selected and determined the coordinates for the Bramlets' Folds. He complimented Pat and the FBI team for having selected the views that had been shared. He said all the information was safely stored and backed up multiple times on multiple storage hardware.

He closed by saying that it was time for dessert and wondered what it might be.

Lacy announced that the dessert was three types of her mother's secret recipe pies.

She described one as a strawberry rhubarb pie that was required eating before one went to heaven.

She said the second was an apple raisin pie that would make you want a second piece.

Lacy claimed the third, a caramel cream pie would instantly put ten pounds around your waist even if you just looked at it.

Bram had watched Zuri to see what her reactions had been to Lacy's dessert descriptions. It was clear she had enjoyed the banter and understood what was being said.

He waited until Zuri had ordered. She chose the last saying she could use a good ten pounds.

Bram said he did not need the ten pounds, but he was also choosing the caramel cream pie.

Mallica had changed seats so she could sit and talk with Marcus's wife, Myla. It was clear to Mallica that there was some personal history that might include abuse as a child that was affecting her reaction to Bram's hug of Zuri. This was not just a guess; she had experienced that type of abuse.

She knew that the dinner was not the setting to pursue the issue, but she wanted to make some personal contact.

The dinner broke up and everyone was chatting and marveling at the progress that the Fold effort had made.

Bram asked Mallica to meet with Dr. Sewal and Zuri in his office. Nuro and Jina joined the group going into Bram's office.

Bram watched as Marcus, his wife and two kids went into the basement to get a ride home. He would need to talk with Marcus on Monday morning.

He got everyone situated and thanked Nuro and Jina for participating. He said that he would step out and let Mallica, Elizabeth and Dr. Sewal talk with Zuri.

He went on to say that the interview by Dr. Sewal was to ensure that Zuri got the best care that was possible.

He introduced Elizabeth as the person who would manage getting Zuri every possible thing that would improve Zuri's life.

He pointed to Mallica and said that she would be Zuri's advanced math instructor.

He then said he was going to leave the office but would return at the end and would like to hear from the Juma family about being part of the Fold effort.

Chapter 26: Zuri Makes the Team

Ted was leading the break down effort of the tables and chairs. Rita was arranging the leftover food and supervising the kitchen clean up. The dishes were rinsed but would get a final wash back in the catering facility. The cleanup action would stop, and they would all talk about the pictures of planets light years away that they had been allowed to see. It was something beyond what they had thought was possible. They had commented that Bram seemed like just another guy, but he must have some brain to have figured out how to instantly send an object across the Milky Way.

Lacy came over to Bram and asked why he had left the meeting in the office.

Bram replied that he had something more important to handle. He had come out to talk to Ted about something even more important than what was going on in the office.

Ted heard what Bram said. He looked a little amazed and asked what in the world would he know that could be more important.

Bram smiled and replied that Ted knew where to take him to catch fish. He wanted to schedule another fishing trip.

Ted laughed and said that Bram could go fishing with him anytime that he wanted but he would have to bring along his better half who really knew how to catch fish or anything else she put her mind to.

Rita said she could provide lunch, but the weather would probably not be very cooperative. She suggested their catering truck and the use of an awning.

Bram said he wanted to take Zuri fishing. She would be in an outing wheelchair. It would be a light structure, but it would need to be fastened to the boat so that it was stable and would not roll or move around. He went on to say that he would pay for any modifications that might be required. He suggested that four eye bolts placed on the edge of the flat area would be a way to anchor the chair. He suggested that Ted figure out the best approach and let him know.

Ted chuckled and said that it was good that he had talked to him and not Luke or Cedric because they would have turned down any suggestion about putting eyebolts in the hull of their boats.

He, on the other hand, figured any person that could provide guidance to a disoriented person like Bram would be a person that he would modify his boat to go upside down and backward if needed.

He told Bram not to worry, leave the simple boat modifications to him and that his boat would be equipped to safely take Zuri fishing.

He suggested a date two weekends away.

Bram agreed to the date.

Pat came out of the office and said it was time for Bram to come back.

Bram entered as Elizabeth was pouring some lemonade and offering bottles of water to everyone in the room. It was clear to Bram that she had taken control and that all was well. When she saw Bram, she asked Dr. Sewal to share his diagnosis and his recommendations.

Dr. Sewal replied that he would like to have Zuri come to Minneapolis to the Mayo clinic for a full evaluation. He would then generate a plan for long term care. He would personally supervise the fitting of a motorized chair that Elizabeth had agreed to pay for.

Elizabeth looked at Bram to see if there was any reaction on his part.

Bram looked to Nuro and Jina and asked about their current thoughts and would they agree to having Zuri be a full working member of the Fold program.

Jina smiled and replied that she and Nuro had never dreamt of such an opportunity for Zuri. She said that the Fold team atmosphere seemed so positive, and Zuri was very excited about the work that was being done. She went on to say that having the best care for Zuri was a dream come true for them.

Bram said that indeed the Fold team culture and atmosphere was inclusive and positive. He asked if the two of them would also like to be part of the team.

Both Nuro and Jina had tears in their eyes as they looked around the room. Nuro said he did not know what to say. What possible job could he do? What would Jina do?

Bram replied that there were many jobs available and there was a house in the Fold community with the Juma name on the mailbox. Bram pointed out that the following day was Sunday, so they should be able to take tour of the house.

Nuro and Jina got down on their knees and shared a hug with Zuri.

He heard Zuri say see, I told you I knew a person who worked miracles.

Jina stood up and gave Bram a hug. She said that yes, she wanted to be on the Fold team and would sweep floors if Bram asked her to. Nuro gave Bram a hug and said that he would prefer a role that utilized his skills, but he too would sweep floors if asked. He was all smiles.

Bram replied that Jina would be part of Mallica's Fold equation review team. The objective of he team was to figure out how to make key improvements that he had no clue how to make.

He pointed to Nuro and said the Bubble design team was going to need his skills.

Bram pointed at the clock on the wall and suggested they call it a day.

He invited the everyone for a picnic lunch at noon the next day.

Dr. Sewal thanked him for the invitation but said that he had a flight to Minneapolis close to that same time. He looked at Zuri and told her that he would look forward to her visit in the next few weeks. He then got down and gave her a hug.

Bram again thanked him for having taken the time to come out and said that now he was their Mayo Clinic Fold member of the team. Bram said that the Sewal family was welcome any time and that they should think about a vacation in the area and plan to go fishing at that time.

Orlando was waiting outside the office. He wheeled Zuri to the steps where Castor joined in to carry her and the chair down the steps.

Elizabeth and Dr. Sewal said good night and followed them down.

Linda Stetson had waited to see how things would work out. She knew instantly that Zuri had made the team. She gave Lacy a hug and said that now she could go home.

Bram realized that Ted and Rita were also still present.

Ted said that the four of them were riding home together in a SUV that was blocked in by the SUV that was taking Zuri home.

Lacy grinned and said that was the family excuse for hanging around so they could all go home and celebrate the successful end of the Zuri saga that Linda had kept the family involved in for more than a year.

Bram looked at Lacy and said that maybe the Fold team needed a caring person like Linda.

Pat thanked the four and said their SUV was ready and pointed to the basement door.

Bram looked around at what was now as empty as the house ever got. He noted that Eric and Zoe were each standing on opposite sides of the room and that the Bob and Thomas must have retired to their rooms.

Pat suggested they go to the office and unwind. She poured each of them a glass of Muscat wine.

Bram agreed that her suggestion and the wine made a great combination. He commented that Marcus's message from his wife, Myla, was still eating at him and he wanted to discuss it with the three of them.

Pat said she was not sure to what the issue might be and asked Bram to explain the issue to the three of them.

Bram explained that Myla thought that his hug of Zuri was improper and that a man should not hug a young girl in that manner. She had expressed to Marcus she did not want him near her children.

Pat looked at Zoe and Eric and asked if they had seen anything that Bram had done that was improper.

Zoe commented that nothing improper had happened and the Marcus's wife must have a problem.

Bram said that Mallica was going to look into it some more. He said he believed Myla, might have been molested as a child by some man. He looked at Zoe and went on to say that he would like the FBI to look into Myla's background and see if there was any indication of her being molested as a child.

He shared that he had scheduled a fishing trip two weeks out. He had decided that Marcus and family would either be on the fishing trip, or they would be leaving to a new assignment.

He went on to say that to go on the fishing trip, Myla would have to agree to get help for her problem and realize that she was inappropriately projecting her experience.

The three of them agreed that it seemed a fair way to handle the situation even though it seemed he had put it on a tight timeframe.

Bram raised his glass and thanked them for listening to his problem. He praised them on doing a great job in selecting the pictures to share with the guests. Their selection had blown everyone away.

He admitted that he had experienced a ying-yang dinner. The company, the food and the follow up meeting had all been great. He put the issue with Myla on the dark side and that it had ruined the otherwise highlight of the year.

Pat said sleep might help the situation and they should go and see if they could get some.

Bram agreed and rinsed and put his glass on the bar towel by the sink.

The next morning Pat was up early and discussed the Marcus situation with Zoe. She shared that Bram was really taking the accusation hard. He was afraid that Myla would poison the community if she did not quickly get help. The two agreed that they would work with Erica to expedite the FBI background check and they should also arrange for immediate counseling for Myla.

Bram had reiterated to Pat that the only way Marcus would be allowed to stay was for Myla to get professional help in dealing with her issue.

Pat knew that Bram had planned to make breakfast for Zuri and her family. She had been kept awake much of the time by his tossing and turning. She was in the middle of getting things ready when Elizabeth came up from the basement. Jeffrey and Erica were right behind her. They said good morning and asked if they could help.

Pat accepted their offer and asked that the table get set and more coffee and tea get made.

Bob and Thomas were the guards for the day, and they helped everyone get organized.

Bram walked in just as everything but the final cook to order took place. He suggested that those who were ready should get their breakfast. He pointed out that it would allow the early risers to enjoy a leisurely conversation while he cooked breakfast for the later arrivals.

Pat said she would do the cooking if Bram took the orders.

He readily agreed and memorized each order as it was given.

Pat was always amazed at Bram's short-term memory. She also knew that he could retain whatever he decided was important.

It was clear to Pat that Bram had cleared his personal issue about Myla. He was back to the positive side that broadcast a warmth to everyone around. Sleep had been the right medicine.

Chapter 27: The Juma Home

Bram had put on his chef's hat and was busily filling the pancake, bacon or sausage and egg breakfast orders. Orlando and Mallica carried Zuri in on her wheelchair into the kitchen. Nuro and Jina entered behind the three.

Bram stopped what he was doing to greet everyone and to give Zuri a hug.

He stood up and asked everyone for their breakfast orders. He went on to boast that they had one of the best chefs in the world preparing their breakfast.

Jeffrey got up to greet the new arrivals and said there was plenty of room at the table. He took the chair at the head of the table and moved it to the side. He then helped position Zuri, so she could see everyone.

Zuri thanked him and commented that he seemed to be a very good boss.

Jeffrey replied that he was boss in name only and he was surrounded by bosses. He hoped that Zuri would be as good a boss as the rest.

The conversation between the two was the beginning of a rather long discussion about what it meant to be a good boss.

They all agreed that a good boss created a culture that valued, nurtured, and developed everyone. How the boss led by doing was another theme that was discussed.

Pat suggested they change the subject to what the Juma family wanted in a good home.

Jina commented that she had only seen the inside of Bram's home and it was beautiful. She would not expect such a wonderful house. She said that it appeared that all the homes were new, and she was eager to see the home with the Juma name on it.

Zoe came over to Bram and quietly commented that she had talked to Major Sharp and extra security had been put in place. She told Bram that he could walk over to the home that had been selected for the Juma family.

She volunteered that she and Eric would clean up after breakfast.

Bram thanked her. He smiled and commented that her offer to clean up was much more important than the info about security. He then carried his breakfast and took the seat by Zuri.

Outside grey clouds lay overhead in a thick blanket that made the day feel like the moment before sunset. A light intermittent drizzle blown by a slight breeze created the feeling that snow might be on the way.

Bram asked Zuri if she would rather be driven in the SUV. She replied that she wanted to see the neighborhood. A warm raincoat would be all she needed.

Orlando pulled out a poncho from his pack. He went over to Zuri and the wheelchair and slipped over her and the chair as if it had been designed for that function. He took out his knife and made two cuts so the handles on the wheelchair were exposed.

Bram smiled at Orlando and told him he had just earned a gold star and another fishing invitation.

Orlando commented that a good Marine was always ready but that fishing with Bram was always a bigger challenge than expected.

Mallica smiled and added that Orlando practiced being ready to a fault. She went on to say that he was always too ready.

Bram looked at Pat and quietly said that it seemed that Mallica and Orlando had bonded.

Elizabeth took Jeffrey's elbow and took the lead toward the Juma home. The single story, four-bedroom, ranch style home was located down the hill, below Bram's house. It was midway to the pool facility. It was one of two spec homes in the complex designed to house a wheelchair bound person.

When Bram asked if there was a home for Zuri, Lacy had immediately checked to see if one of them had been finished. She immediately designated it to be Zuri's.

Bram walked along side of Zuri and chatted with her as he pointed out the Fold neighborhood.

Jina was walking on Zuri's left side. She and Nuro shared one large blue umbrella and were commenting on the natural feel of the community and how impressed they were.

Bram noted that the ramp leading up to the front door was five-foot-wide and went across the front of the house and had only an eight-inch rise to the threshold. He admired the short deep green leafed hedge that edged the walk on the street side. It went around the eight-foot rounded landing at the front door.

The ramp was not visible from the street and the house seemed like any other house when viewed from the street. It was clearly a little longer and seemed larger than the two houses on either side.

He wondered about and planned to look at the ramp leading to the backyard and the one in the garage.

Orlando shouted out "here we go" as he rapidly pushed Zuri up the front walk, opened the front door and went smoothly into the foyer. He made a right turn and stopped in what he thought would be the living room. Beyond it was what he said was the dining room. He went through the dining room and to the left was the kitchen with an exhaust hood over a black glass stove top. The kitchen a refrigerator that was on its side and countertop high. There was as second one that was vertical and had bottom freezer , a vegetable drawer in the middle and the top had two vertical doors There was also an oven and microwave that could be operated by a person in a wheelchair.

The kitchen was open to the dining room but also open to a family room area. The circuit continued to another room to the left.

All rooms featured wide open areas that would allow a wheelchair bound person room to maneuver.

The way out to the back was through the kitchen eating area or through a wide door out from the family room. Both exits had a large landing area at door level with an eight-inch drop in a twelve-foot-long ramp down to a large tiled thirty by thirty-foot back yard tiled area that was surrounded by a flower bed. The tiled area had a wide walkway that went out to the driveway.

The home provided a wheelchair bound individual the ability to easily navigate all areas of the home and outside around the backyard and an easy exit to the driveway and garage.

Bram walked to the door at the back of the family room. It opened to the garage. The floor of the garage was at the same height as the floor in the family room. No ramp was needed.

He was impressed with the architect's attention to eliminating the barriers most wheelchair bound individuals faced.

Orlando took Zuri through a door from the family room into a large bedroom with a bathroom that included a roll in shower. He shouted out that they had found Zuri's room.

The roll in shower controls were outside the roll in area and at a level that could be reached by someone in a wheelchair. The sink and counter were also at a wheelchair height. The commode was in a separate room with hand bars and extra room around the commode.

Jina and Nuro came out of the front two bedrooms that share a common bathroom between them. They had gone through the master bedroom that was to the back of the house through a short hall from the kitchen eating area.

They marveled at the accommodations in Zuri's room.

Everyone agreed that the layout and the accommodations were appropriate for housing Zuri.

Once again Jina had tears in her eyes. She commented that the house was wonderful and more than she ever dreamt of living there but she said she was not sure they could afford the rent.

Bram had not thought about rent. As far as he knew no one living in the Fold complex paid rent. He made a note about the fact that it was a great work benefit that he had not thought about.

He replied that the house was part of the benefit of working on the Fold project. He was met with more tears in Jina's eyes.

He smiled and said that to qualify for such a benefit, Zuri had to be to work by ten the next morning.

He told Nuro and Jina to work with Stacy and arrange the move to their new home and that they should report to work in two weeks.

He then announced that in two weeks there would be a weekend fishing outing and a picnic in the park to celebrate the Juma's move into their new home and the Juma family's enrollment to into the Fold team.

Elizabeth suggested that they all return to Bram's home for some coffee and cake. Afterwards they would all go their separate ways for the rest of the afternoon.

Bram agreed. He was ready to spend some quiet time in his office to relax while he reviewed the Fold equations. He looked forward to having Pat sitting next to him reading.

Pat had watched Bram as he took in the home for Zuri. She realized that he had made a strong connection with Zuri and the potential he saw in her. She was warmed by his concern and his desire to open the world to the brilliant, but wheelchair bound young girl.

Bram noticed Pat observing him. He decided that once they were comfortably sitting on the office couch, he would ask her to tell him her thoughts about what she was so closely watching.

The grey of the morning was giving way to the sun that periodically flashed its rays through breaks in the cloud cover. The walk back up to Bram's house proceeded at a comfortable walking pace.

Bram looked at the smile on Zuri's face and decided that he would put this into one of his better days list.

<u>Chapter 28: Marcus Ultimatum</u>

Donna was running besides Castor and started singing a ditty about poor Bramlet One that had come back with something on its mind that just would not go away. Poor Bramlet One now locked away. She kept adding more miseries and then repeated the whole thing. The whole group went jogging through the dark misty morning repeating the ditty.   She ended with a shot at Bram about not caring for poor Bramlet One namesake of the heartless one.

Bram enjoyed the ditty. It distracted him from the cloud that he faced. Once again, he had been awake much of the night as his mind chewed through the issue with Marcus's wife. He needed to convince Marcus of the issue's importance and that immediate action had to be taken.

The aroma of coffee and the cooking going on in the cafeteria brought Bram to a better state of mind. He took two premade English muffins with cheese, sausage, and egg. He stopped to fill his mug with steaming dark black coffee and then went to his favorite table. The rest of the team joined him.

Pat, Eric, and Zoe took their normal seats.

Zoe was sitting across from Bram. She knew the agenda facing Bram. She shared her conversation with Erica. The two had met on Sunday and sent an urgent request to Erica for immediate action. They expected a quick report back by Thursday morning.

Erica had promised that it would be thorough and if the potential for abuse existed, they would know.

Elizabeth joined them and asked Bram if he wanted her in the meeting with Marcus.

Bram thanked her but said he would prefer to discuss this with Marcus alone. He was uncertain of Marcus' personal knowledge of why the hug had triggered Myla's reaction.

Pat wished him luck and let him know that both Wheel teams were getting ready for the Wheel Folds that would occur on Wednesday morning.

She also reminded him that he had essentially required Zuri be at work by ten.

Bram watched as Marcus came into the cafeteria. He went through the line and came out with two eggs and toast. He was going to sit by himself at another table, but Bram waved him over and pointed to the seats that Elizabeth and Pat had vacated.

Marcus was very quiet and commented that he had a notice from Lacy about a meeting with him right after breakfast.

He asked how Zuri's evaluation had gone?

He heard from Lacy that the family was moving into one of the units designed for someone in a wheelchair. He assumed that the evaluation had gone well.

Bram commented that things had gone well. He let Marcus know that Zuri was joining in on the review of the Fold equations. It would start at ten at his office.

Marcus figured the meeting in the office might be his last. It was clear that Bram had come to some sort of conclusion on Myla's threat about hugging children. He had personally been surprised at her vehemence. He had thought back at her behavior of him hugging the kids. It had become worse recently and he had no clue why.

He was worried about his meeting with Bram, but he was just as concerned about Myla's behavior. He needed to talk with somebody.

Bram led the way to his office and told Lacy that he did not want to be disturbed He would let her know when he would be available. He asked her to break in if Marcus and he went on too long. He wanted ten minutes before the ten am meeting started.

He asked Zoe and Eric to wait at Linda's desk. Zoe went through the security check of the office and then gave the "all clear."

Bram made one more request that Lacy find a large nearby room that could be made into a wheelchair friendly office.

Marcus and Bram entered his office together. Bram suggested they get a tea or coffee and sit on the couch.

Bram went straight to the point and commented that he had checked with everyone that had seen him hug Zuri and no one had any impression of impropriety.

He asked Marcus about his opinion of the situation.

Marcus looked in at his cup of coffee. For him, the dark black coffee was a reflection of his mind. He had argued with Myla much of Sunday as he tried to find out what had triggered her reaction.

He was lost about what to do.

He looked at Bram whose penetrating gaze always was disconcerting to him. He saw what he thought was real concern. He shared his confusion and that he was not sure what to do. He went on to describe his miserable Sunday.

He volunteered that he was mentally exhausted.

Bram pointed out that Myla's behavior was not acceptable. If she were to express her current opinion about the hug she would be poisoning the culture of the Fold community.

He made the point that he worked hard at making it a culture of inclusion, fairness and of treating everyone as one would expect to be treated. Bram pointed out that it was a culture that he had worked very hard to create and one that seemed to be functioning the way he had hoped it would. He said that he was going to protect that culture.

Bram then said that Dr. Windal expressed the opinion that Myla's behavior suggested that perhaps Myla had been molested as a young girl. Dr. Windal had gone on to suggest it might well be someone in her family.

Marcus said that he and Myla had never talked much about her family. He had met her parents before their wedding, but they had always gone to his family get togethers. Now he wondered about Myla's not wanting to go to her family's get together.

Bram went on to say that he had asked the FBI to do a background check on Myla's family and that the initial report would be back by Thursday.

He also pointed out that he thought Myla needed some professional counseling. He looked at Marcus and said he really wanted Marcus to be part of the Fold effort but unless Myla agreed by Friday to get counseling, he and his family would be reassigned to the best alternate job that could be arranged. He made the point that the assignment would be outside of the Fold community.

Marcus knew that Bram always worked fast.

He asked if he could get some help in talking to Myla. He said that he was afraid that she would shut him out.

Bram asked if Mallica, Elizabeth or if Dr Windal, who was a female Marine, might be of help.

He agreed with Marcus that it would be Myla who would need to come to grips with her past.

Marcus asked how much time he had to get Myla to agree.

Bram replied that he had a fishing trip planned two weekends away. The Smith family would either be fishing with the rest of the team, or they would be reassigned and moving East. The venue depended on Myla's agreement to therapy. Bram said that he expected the therapy to go on for a long time.

Marcus held back his astonishment at the speed for the agreement to action. He said as much but agreed that something needed to happen fast. He said he would take all the help he could get.

Bram reiterated the fact that he wanted Marcus to be part of the team. He stated that he was not expecting resolution in two weeks but the start of resolving Myla's problem. He suggested that Elizabeth, Mallica and Dr. Windal meet and decide on the best approach in working with Myla. He pointed out that they needed to connect on a personal level.

Bram shared that he was aware that Mallica had experienced sexual assault as a child and was able to identify with Myla's reaction.

Marcus said he would take all their help and let them guide him. He had already had his unsuccessful argument with Myla.

He shared that it was their first real argument that ended up in a shouting match.

Bram let Marcus know that he wanted this to work out well. He would free up all the resources at his disposal to make it happen.

He pointed at the clock and said they would soon get their ten-minute warning about the next meeting.

Marcus asked if he could miss the meeting and meet with Elizabeth and Dr. Windal.

Bram suggested they delay the Fold equation review until later in the day or until the next day. He and Zuri would look over her office space that he was sure Lacy had found by this time.

This would give Mallica a chance to be part of the meeting Marcus wanted to have.

Marcus had tears in his eyes as he got up. He was overwhelmed and as he looked at Bram, he knew that he had a friend that was trying hard to help but who insisted on fast and effective action.

Bram got up and gave Marcus a hug. He commented that Myla was a strong woman who when presented with the facts would measure up. She would connect with Mallica.

Marcus said hello to the Juma family as he walked out of Bram's office.

Bram gave Zuri a hug and then shook hands with Nuro and Jina. He invited them into his office.

He asked Lacy if she had an office space that would be Zuri's office?

He also asked for Remi to come to his office to meet Nuro.

He asked Zuri how the rest of the weekend had gone.

Jina answered that they had gone out for a treat at the local ice cream parlor to celebrate their good fortune.

Zuri asked if she was really going to have an office to herself?

Bram smiled at her and said that yes, she would have an office similar to his. If she was smart enough, she would probably soon have one bigger than his.

He looked at Jina and Nuro and said that they would have offices like their counter parts in their field. He smiled and made the point that Zuri was the one that got the biggest office.

Jina replied that her office could be a closet and she would be satisfied.

Bram smiled and said that they should all go and see the space that Lacy had located for Zuri. Afterwards, Nuro would go with Remi to see what he would be doing, and Jina would go with Lacy to her office.

Mallica and Orlando were standing outside the office when they came out. Mallica said good morning and then excused herself saying she was going to Marcus's office.

Orlando said hello to Zuri and gave her a hug and then pushed her down the hall as they followed Lacy.

Bram had a good feeling about how the week would go. He noticed that Zoe and Eric were missing and had been replaced by Bob and Thomas.

Orlando was whooping it up as he accelerated around the corner just down from Bram's office. Lacy called out that he had gone too far. She led the way into a forty-person meeting room. She said she had called in the architect, and he would be out to look at the space and then convert it to a wheelchair friendly office. He would use as much space as made sense and the rest would be turned into huddle rooms.

Bram said he liked her approach to getting the office ready. It should be at least as spacious as his and be wheelchair friendly. He said he expected it to be ready by the time Zuri returned from the fishing weekend outing. He reminded Lacy that Zuri would be back from the Mayo clinic and would be in her new motorized wheelchair by then.

He looked around and figured it was time for a tour of the lab and to review the Wheel readiness for the coming Fold.

<u>Chapter 29: Myla-Self Realization</u>

The walk out to the Fold Wheels was a welcome break from what had been a stressful morning for Bram. He took in the size of the Wheels and wondered if their full functionality would ever be used. His current plans made the Wheel living quarters almost useless. The Wheels might be useful for the longer across the universe folds or any longer-term exploration. For now, Bram wanted only the main bubble of the Wheel. The smaller bubble would mean less power use and would allow for more exploration at one time. It would also reduce the risk to those involved in the program.

He approached Wheel One and was greeted by Pat. She and the crew were doing a walk-through of the Wednesday Fold. Bram entered to look around and to see if there was room for one more.

He then went over to Wheel Two and was greeted by Harold Redat the backup pilot. He was taking the crew through a similar walk through. Elizabeth had assigned him the task while she worked with Marcus.

Bram was pleased with the readiness of both crews. He asked the two crews to procure HazMat type suits for the trip. When asked why, Bram explained that he wanted another layer of personal protection for the crew on the upcoming folds.

The lab was now a bubble assembly area. The lab team was divided into Bramlet One investigation and new bubble scout assembly. Remi was touring Erica and showing her the various bubbles under assembly. Nuro was busy with a team working on a three-foot diameter version. He took a minute to express his excitement of being part of the effort.

Bramlet Two through Seven were in their containment boxes. The team handling them commented that the Bramlets would be launched at noon to the location he had programed for the back of the Moon Fold area. They would Fold into the coordinates Bram had specified.

Once the Bramlets were back they would be prepared for the Neptune Fold.

Bram was pleased with the energy of everyone associated with the Fold effort. He decided to make a stop in the offices of the analysts. He had not visited with them for more than a week and wanted to hear from them about what they hoped they could get from the Wheel Folds.

Elizabeth had listened to Marcus and to Mallica, Zoe and the Fold phycologist Serena.

Serena had suggested a meeting between Mallica and Myla to see if Myla recognized she had a problem.

Mallica would see if Myla was open to talking to a professional trained to help her, but she did not want Myla to be defensive. Serena suggested she would hold off and plan to be a part of a second meeting with her if Myla was open to it.

Elizabeth asked Marcus to set up a lunch meeting between Mallica and Myla at some location away from the Fold area but that would provide some privacy. She said that lunch was on Bram.

Lacy called in the architect that she was working with on Zuri's office layout. Orlando was making sure that Zuri was in the right place as the architect first inspected Bram's office and layout and then proceeded to the large meeting room that was to be converted.

The architect commented that he would probably use the entire space for Zuri's office. He measured the room and said he would get back with some plans by Thursday for them to review.

Lacy thanked him and led the way back to Bram's office. She explained that Bram had changed his schedule and she was not sure what to do with the two of them. She offered to let them wait in Bram's office.

Orlando looked outside at the bright sunshine. He asked Zuri if she was interested in a tour of the outside of the hanger area.

Zuri replied that she preferred the outside to waiting in the office.

Orlando replied that he was the best tour guide in the compound.

After visiting with the analysts Bram decided that he would ask Remi to work with Pat to add some eye bolts to the floor of Wheel One. He had decided to include Zuri in the first human transit across the solar system and across the Milky Way.

He stopped by Wheel One to let Pat know of his decision.

She nodded and said that Zuri would be a great addition to the crew. She said she would get one of the support mechanics to put the eye bolts in the floor.

He went to the lab and met with Remi.

He asked where Erica had gone.

Remi said she had just left and was headed to Lacy and his office.

Erica approached Lacy and asked about Bram.

Lacy replied that she had lost control of Bram's calendar and his where about.

Erica took the time to inquire about office space for herself.

She had reached her decision about staying and agreed with Bram's project role clarification for the individuals he had named.

She recognized that the application of Bram's Fold breakthrough was rapidly expanding and as well as accelerating.

Lacy looked up to see Bram approaching. She commented to Erica that she would find an appropriate office for her and let her know. She asked if there was any specific location that Erica might prefer.

Erica thought about it for a moment and then replied that somewhere close to the Lab area or Remi's office. She went on to say that if there was no space in that area then show her the available offices and she would select one.

Erica greeted Bram and said she was impressed with all the practical work that was getting done. It was amazing that the lab had become such a good bubble assembly area.

Bram agreed with her and complimented Lori and Remi for their rapid response to his bubble scout idea. He commented that he felt that the bubble scouts were life savers. They were a great way to keep the human participants from ending up like Bramlet One.

Erica asked if all his Monday mornings were so active.

Bram replied that he hoped that they would not all be like this specific Monday.

He commented that he had not faced such a serious problem as the one involving Marcus's wife.

He thanked Erica for getting the FBI to quickly do a check of any family sexual abuse issues.

He shared that Elizabeth was facilitating a discussion with Marcus, Mallica, Zoe and Serena the Fold phycologist. He said that he was not sure where that was going but that he had given Marcus notice that the issue had to be resolved in two weeks.

Erica commented that it seemed to be an aggressive schedule but supported his decision.

Bram thanked her. He said such an issue could not be allowed to permeate the Fold community. His requirement was that Myla had to agree to counseling. He knew she would have a long way to go to fully address her issues.

Erica had expected Zuri to be in Bram's office and asked about her.

Bram replied that he had no clue where Zuri might be but that she was with Orlando and would be doing something fun. He described Orlando as a super Marine guard and a person that he would trust his life to. He went on to say that he had lost him as guard to Mallica and Zuri.

Lacy called in that Zuri and Orlando had returned from their tour around the outside of the facility.

Bram stood and walked to the front of his desk as Orlando wheeled Zuri in.

They were both laughing at something Orlando had said to Lacy. They turned to Bram and Orlando said in a serious low tone, "Ready for work boss" and they both laughed again.

Bram was pleased that they both seemed to like each other. He looked at Erica and asked if she would join them for lunch.

Zuri asked what there was for lunch. Orlando commented that Bram made the cafeteria serve only healthy food and that Zuri might be disappointed.

Bram replied that the problem was that Marines had such poor eating habits and probably did not wash their hands before lunch.

Orlando laughed and followed Bram and Erica as they walked toward the cafeteria. He commented to Zuri that the brains of the outfit was really going low when he started to attack the Marines about their eating habits, and he acted like he was whispering in her ear and said he did wash his hands before lunch.

Erica marveled at the atmosphere around Bram. It was fun to be around the people that worked on the Fold effort. She thought about the political intrigue and backstabbing she experienced back in Washington. It would be a treat to work in the Dalles area. She would not miss the pressure of her office back east.

Orlando took pains to point Zuri to the food that was the richest and the ones he thought Bram would object to most. Zuri had a problem seeing the food that was out on the counter.

Bram saw her trying to see the food and made mental note to make sure that her new motorized chair placed Zuri high enough to see the food.

Elizabeth and Dr. Windal entered that cafeteria together with Marcus. They saw Bram sitting with Erica and asked if they could join him.

Elizabeth asked if Bram had met Dr. Windal.

Bram replied that they had only met briefly when the facility had first opened and then again after the shooting by the pool area had occurred and then again when she became a lunch time lecturer.

But otherwise, he had no idea who she was.

He laughed and asked how she was doing and were her skills being utilized by the Fold personnel.

Dr. Windal in turn laughed and replied that she wished more people would come in and talk with her and when was he going to take the time to get treated for his lifelong affliction.

Marcus listened to the exchange and knew that he wanted to remain in the atmosphere that permeated the Fold community. He commented that the morning had gone well. Mallica and Myla were having a lunch meeting. He hoped that Mallica would be successful in her meeting.

Bram commented that it seemed they had made good progress and agreed that he hoped Mallica could make a positive intervention.

He looked at Zuri and tilted his head at Orlando and went on to say that after lunch he had a surprise for Zuri. He asked Orlando if he could push Zuri out to Wheel One.

Pat had skipped lunch and was relaxing next to the ramp leading up into Wheel One. She watched as the entourage that surrounded Bram approached. The mechanical support technician and she had just completed putting in the floor eye bolts that Bram had request. She had been surprised that he had decide to take Zuri along but liked the fact that he was doing it.

She stood up and greeted the group. She said that she would lead the way in and then Zuri and Orlando would be the next ones in. She said the rest could follow.

Orlando followed Pat and pushed the wheelchair up the ramp.

Pat led the way to where the rings were located and instructed Orlando how to orient the wheelchair. Pat then adjusted the hooks and bound the chair to the floor.

She then stood in front of Zuri and gave her a salute and welcomed her as a crew member of Wheel One as a performance analyst first class. Zuri was to analyze the crew performance on the upcoming Folds to the moon and the galaxies beyond.

Zuri shouted out, "no way! Is it really true? Am I a part of the crew?

Bram knelt beside her and answered that it was true, and her real role was to think-deep and think-hard about what was happening during the Fold. The performance she should be thinking about was the Wheel One-Fold performance. He said that he still needed her help in making sure her parents were OK with her going out with the Wheel Fold on Wednesday.

He gave Zuri a hug and welcomed her to the Fold Team and to the crew of the USS Hood Wheel One better known as Wheel One. He told her she was the Admiral, and he was the Captain of the ship.

Chapter 30: Time to Step Up

ℒunch for Mallica was a walk on thin ice. She needed to connect with Myla and get her to understand that she was fighting her own demon and overlaying it on other people. She needed Myla to accept help via counseling. Mallica knew that failure to connect and get agreement to treatment would result in Marcus getting reassigned. Her similar personal experience helped on how to approach Myla.

Mallica began by sharing her own personal experience of being molested as a young girl. In her case, it had been an older cousin and it had devastated her. Her mother had finally believed her and had acted to get her out of the situation.

She asked if Myla might have had a similar experience.

Myla sat silently looking at her.

The moment lasted longer than anticipated and Mallica went on.

She let Myla know that if she did not get counseling, Marcus would be reassigned to a job outside of the Fold program.

Myla got mad and stated that was not fair to Marcus.

It was a reaction that Mallica had anticipated.

Mallica agreed but said there was no other option.

Myla said that she wanted to talk to the boss of the program. Mallica responded that the boss had already been informed and agreed to the requirement of her getting counseling.

Myla broke down and began crying.

Mallica breathed a sigh of relief.

Myla admitted that she had just recently recalled being abused as a young girl. She had suppressed it for so long she had forgotten about. Seeing Bram hug Zuri had been a lightning bold that brought it all back. It had gone to the bottom of her soul and ripped open a memory that she had suppressed. It was a shock.

She was afraid to tell Marcus.

Her safe warm world had shattered in that one moment before dinner on Saturday.

Mallica gave Myla a hug and told her she was with a friend who understood. She had a similar experience but had gotten help and still regularly sought that help. She went on to let Myla know that Marcus had been part of the team that had sent Mallica on the mission to get her to agree to get counseling.

She shared that Bram had been the one driving all of them to resolve the situation in a way that would help everyone.

And that Bram wanted her to be happy and that he wanted Marcus to be on the Fold team. Then Mallica made it clear that would only happen if Myla agreed to get on the path to getting healed.

There was what seemed to Mallica to be an endless period of silence.

She kept her silence as Myla cried silently.

Finally, Myla took a deep breath and quietly agreed to get counseling and said she would meet with Dr. Windal and learn what was needed.

She wondered if she could speak with Dr. Windal on the following day.

Mallica said that she would arrange it.

Mallica was drained but the outcome of the lunch made her eager to get back and share her success.

On her return to the compound, Mallica's first stop was Marcus's office.

When she walked in the tears in Marcus's eyes let her know that he had already talked to Myla. She and Marcus had become very close friends during their year at the initial Fold facility in the middle of the desert. She just walked over and gave him a hug. There was nothing else to add.

She asked if he wanted to come along to share the good news with Bram. He replied that he would join them in a moment. He said he did not want to go down the hallway crying.

Mallica said she would wait in her office until he was ready. She told him that he should be the one to inform Bram that Myla had agreed to get help.

Lacy had informed Bram that Mallica had returned from lunch and that she had gone to Marcus's office.

While he waited to hear from Mallica, Bram had called Nuro and Jina to his office to request their permission for Zuri to be part of the Fold team that would visit the back of the Moon on the coming Wednesday and then would Fold to Neptune and the Galaxy in the following weeks.

Nuro and Jina were chatting with Zuri. It was obvious Zuri had her heart set on being part of the Wheel One crew. She said she trusted Bram because he would have the seat next to hers.

Nuro and Jina looked at Bram and they told him that he had not played fairly but they were so proud that Zuri would be one of the first humans to make such distant trips. They just wanted to make sure he would bringing Zuri back safely.

Bram agreed that he had in his excitement rushed ahead and he apologized for not having checked with them first. He went on to say that sometimes he forgot how young Zuri was. He commented that he thought that her mind was well beyond his own in capability and interacted with her as if they were partners working on the same problem.

Lacy announced that Marcus and Mallica were waiting to meet with him.

Bram thanked Nuro and Jina and told them to take Zuri home and that they should all report to their workplace at the normal time the next day.

Marcus led the way in and simply said that Mallica had accomplished her mission.

Bram walked over to Mallica and gave her a hug and thanked her. He turned and gave Marcus a hug as well.

He went on to say that there would be a prize for the biggest fish and the most fish caught on the upcoming fishing trip. He stated that he expected the Smith family to win one of those two prizes.

He looked at Marcus and told him to go home and give Myla a hug and comfort her. He could take the next day off if that would help.

Marcus had tears in his eyes. He thanked Bram for pushing to get help for Myla. He would talk with Myla and decide about being with her on her first day of counseling.

Bram put his arm around Marcus's shoulders and guided him to the door and said, "see you later," and gave him a gentle push out the door.

Mallica had quietly observed how Bram handled Marcus. She knew why she had stuck around in the desert even when she had felt abandoned. Bram exuded a positive aura even when he was pushing everyone to work faster, smarter, and harder.

Bram turned to Mallica and asked for some more detail and her feeling about Myla's acceptance.

Mallica replied that she felt Myla had come to realize her actions were driven by her own demons.

Bram shared that Myla had sent him a message of apology and said that she had agreed to the counseling and had expressed the desire to start immediately.

Mallica let him know that she had arranged with Dr. Windal for an appointment in the morning.

Bram closed his eyes and took a deep breath. He looked at Mallica and ask what she wanted as a reward for having saved the day.

Mallica smiled and said that she wanted a seat on the other side of Zuri during the upcoming Folds.

Bram laughed and replied that she was lucky that he had not yet recalculate the power draw expectation for the added weight on Wheel One. He told Mallica to check with Lacy and to report for her weigh-in at the same time that Zuri was getting weighed in.

Mallica gave him a hug and then asked if there was room on Wheel Two for Marcus.

Bram shook his head and replied that Marcus should weigh in with her but since she had extracted such a big reward, he was not sure she qualified for the fishing contests. He would have to think about that.

Mallica was all smiles as she walked out to check with Lacy.

Bram looked at the clock it was a little early but called Pat let her know that he was ready to call it a day.

Zoe and Eric came into his office and said that they realized that he would need FBI protection even when on the Wheel. They asked if he had he made allowance for the two of them to be there to protect him?

Bram rolled his eyes and said he would see but he felt that he was getting to the Fold power limits. He would let them know in the morning. He asked for their weights.

Pat walked in as he finished his comment and asked about weights for whom?

Bram replied that the FBI guards were pressuring him to accept protection even when on the Wheel.

Pat replied that he would probably need protection from the chief navigator.

Bram replied that is what he had told the FBI representatives making the request but that they had insisted.

He said he was going to walk home to clear his mind. On the way out he asked Lacy if the home service was going to be doing the cooking that evening. She replied that indeed the Stetson Catering service had arranged for a chef and kitchen crew to be on duty that evening. She said that by the time he got home dinner would be ready.

Castor and Donna were in the lead. Zoe and Eric followed behind. Bram walked silently holding Pat's hand.

Bram was tallying the various scenarios that were unfolding around him. He had pulled back just in time. It was time to let the Fold program grow. It was going to grow well beyond his ability to managed it. Once he had done the initial set of Folds, he would need to retreat into deeper development research.

He hoped that Zuri would be the mind that would provide or trigger new insights.

He needed to advance the capability of the objects being Folded.

He needed more sophisticated scouts.

He needed to work with Marcus in selecting the future targets.

He needed to get Jeffrey to expand the program and to get Erica to manage it.

He had brought the Fold breakthrough to the world. It was time for the world to step up and engage the future.

Chapter 31: Fold Virgins

Bram got home and realized that his first Fold to the back of the moon could not be scheduled for two days. The Wheels would be exposed within hours. They could only stay for the length of time the moon would shield them.

He talked to Elizabeth, Pat, Amy, and Marcus and together they agreed to multiple Folds. The new Fold schedule would be a better test of the power system than the original Fold sequence. He asked Elizabeth to explain the change to the rest of the Wheel crews. He smiled and suggested that the teams should have picked up on his mistake.

It was hard to describe his frustration. He found it hard to accept the fact that his Fold location was static and not dynamic. He was really looking forward to the additional research work that would occur when his equations were tested and revalidated.

He was sure that the different perspective that Zuri might trigger would change his understanding of how the Fold occurred.

Bram had no doubt that the design of the magnetron would be impacted, but at the moment he had no clue what that impact would be. He tried to imagine what physical change was needed to allow movement of the object in the Fold.

He wondered if an alternating current source in the Fold objects, would make it possible to create mini folds that would act to propel the object. In space, once motion was established it would be maintained. He decided that the way to create physical movement could be immediately tested in the lab.

Bram found it hard to contain himself. He called Remi to see if he were willing to do a little early evening bubble modification. After describing what he wanted to do, Remi suggested that he would do it early the next morning. He had to locate a dc to ac converter that could be put into one of the bubbles. He suggested they use one of the new bigger bubbles since it would have enough room to add the converter and the Fold transmitter.

Remi recommended the test be held after the two Wheels completed their Fold behind the Moon.

Pat had listened in to the bubble discussion and agreed with Remi's advice. She reminded Bram that he would have his hands full for the entire day. Their first Fold was scheduled to be at nine in the morning.

The evening seemed to pass slower than a duck trying to take off into the record headwinds of a one-hundred-year storm.

Bram felt conflicted. He was certain that his scheduled Folds behind the Moon would be successful.

What he was now eager to try was the concept of mini-Folds as a propulsion concept. Then he wanted to see if modifying the design of the magnetron could be the means of channeling the power flow to provide not only the Fold but also propulsion for the object being Folded.

Bram decided to spend the evening investigating the equations that led to the design of the honeycomb like magnetron. He wondered if his math might be expressed in a slight variation and if in that manner change the design.

Pat could tell that the morning Wheel Fold was not a concern to Bram. He was off into a world of his own. He was scrolling through the endlessly long Fold equation on his computer.

She wondered if he knew that he periodically talked to himself. He not only talked to himself, but he became two different persons that argued the different sides of a problem.

At this moment it was clear he was having a major internal struggle with himself. She had never seen Bram in this state.

A light was blinking in her mind reminding her that Bram really did have a different mind than the rest of the people around him.

She knew he she was seeing him during intense mental arguments as he envisioned another breakthrough in his Fold environment.

She got up off the couch and walked over to him and gave him a hug.

Bram was brought up out of the haze that had enveloped his mind as he felt Pat's hug.

The haze turned to a warm glow.

He turned and pulled Pat onto his lap and gave her a kiss. He thanked her for bringing him back to the surface before he drowned in the depths of his mind.

Pat believed him. He truly had been in a different world far from her reality.

She looked him in the eyes as she again gave him a kiss. Bram was looking back as if he could see her mind. She wondered if he had the power to do such a thing.

Zoe had watched the entire scene. She looked over at Eric and gave him a smile. She knew he had also taken in the exchange between Pat and Bram.

They had talked about Bram's relationship with Pat and about his intense sessions when he was somewhere in his mind. It would sometimes seem that he was frozen. His eyes often stayed open, but Zoe had played games to see if he was seeing anything.

Eric always tried to stop Zoe when she began testing where Bram might be and what he was seeing. It was clear to him that Bram focused inward when in his deepest thoughts.

Bram recorded everything that went on around him. He knew of Zoe's tests and games she played.

He let it go. He figured someday he would play a game with her and get even.

Bram decided that he would try to get some sleep. He picked Pat up and then gently put her on her feet and led her out of the office. He saw Zoe jump up to get to the door ahead of them.

Once in their bedroom, Bram went for the shower.

He planned to get it as hot as he could possibly stand it and let the heat cool his mind. He was onto something, but he did not know what. He had to let it go so that in the following days he could find it again.

Pat joined Bram in the shower, but the water was so hot she had to stand to one side.

Bram reduced the hot water and then pulled her to him. He found the perfect release for his brain's conundrum.

After a few moments, he led the two of them out of the shower and slowly toweled Pat dry. She did the same for him and then led him by the hand to their bed.

Five thirty came early the next morning. Bram came up out of the depth and absorbed the warmth of Pat's cheek on his chest.

He gently raised her chin and gave her a kiss as he slid out of the bed.

When he got down to the kitchen the entire FBI guard group was there and said good morning.

Bram had put Zoe and Eric on Wheel One and Bob and Thomas on Wheel Two. Mallica was on Wheel One and Marcus was on Wheel Two. He figured if he was willing to put Zuri at risk then he would not deny the rest.

The crew would all go down in the history books. How could he deny them that privilege when every one of them had made great sacrifices to help him?

The entourage jogging along the road was led by three marines followed by Marcus, Mallica, Pat and Bram. His four FBI bodyguards followed behind. This morning Orlando started a ditty about hiding behind the Moon,

Hiding in back, the dark side,
Hiding in the dark, not ashamed
Don't want to be seen, Feeling sad
So sad to feel so bad.
Bram, Bram, Hiding, Hiding
But we are all smiles to be
Hiding in back, the dark side,

He went on then to repeat it and then everyone repeated the words.

Bram found it hard to keep jogging. He wanted to stop and laugh. He threatened to leave Orlando behind.

Orlando included the threat in the ditty being repeated by everyone. Orlando added, "No sense of humor, only threatens his friend."

Bram and the whole group entered the compound laughing and had all the Marine guards looking their way.

Orlando greeted the van arriving with Zuri and her parents. He gave Zuri a hug, greeted Nuro and Jina and pushed Zuri toward the cafeteria.

Bram took his usual spot in the cafeteria. He gave Zuri a hug. She had the end of the table, Orlando sat across from Bram. He thanked Bram for including him on the Wheel folds. It was special, and he would always be grateful. Bram looked at him and said that he had missed that day at the cave and some poor unknown had taken his bullet.

Orlando smiled and simply said, "Yeah I guess I am lucky at that."

Pat was the one that simply said let's go Fold and stood up and walked out toward the Wheel holding area.

Bram followed behind with Orlando and Zuri.

The countdown for the USS Hood Wheel One and USS Rainier Wheel Two was controlled by Lori.

Elizabeth had given Bram a hug and thanked him for making her dream come true. He had also gotten a hug from Amy with almost the same words. He had heard the same from Pat.

Bram took a moment to thank everyone for their dedication and hard work. He pointed out that most of them were Fold veterans and only a few were novices like himself. He described that their first Folds were intended to test some new concepts close to home but then in the following weeks they would all cross the solar system and then go out into the Milky Way. He made the point that Marcus, their destination identifier, had already threatened to go beyond to other Galaxies.

Bram looked up to the viewing area and saw that Myla was standing in the observation area with her two kids. She looked down and mouthed a silent "Thank you."

Bram waved at everyone and turned and walked into the Wheel One control center and took his seat next to Zuri. He held her hand as Pat closed the Wheel hatch. He listened as Pat announced that Wheel One was ready for Fold.

The next thing he saw was the glow of the sun coming around to the backside of the Moon.

He responded to the small hand that squeezed his and heard Zuri give him a quiet thank you.

He had tears in his eyes. He did not know how, but his mind had taken him to a place that embraced a magic that would forever empower humanity with travels to the farthest places.

The End

Preview *of:* The Message

Chapter 1: Success Celebration

This was Bram's first Fold. He, Zuri, Orlando, Eric, and Zoe were the newbies in the bubble.

Bram sat next to Nuri looking out at the surface of the far side of the moon. He was explaining to everyone that what was most often referred to as the dark side of the moon was no darker than any other part of the moon. In the course of a month, Sun light fell equally on all sides of the Moon and that the lunar day lasted about two Earth weeks.

He then shared the fact that they were being shielded from the noise of Earth and were in what was called the "radio dark." It was a location that was shielded from the noise of the Earth and the weak signals from the universe could be measured more easily at this location.

In fact, the systems on Wheel One were scanning out into the universe and when they returned to Earth the data would be closely scoured to see what they could learn.

He went on to have everyone look at the difference between the more heavily cratered backside surface and the fact that it lacked the maria or seas that made up the familiar man in the moon look.

He shared the fact that it was thought that the differences were caused by a wayward dwarf planet colliding with the moon in the early history of the solar system.

Orlando thanked Professor Bram for the great story that he had just shared.

Nuro squeezed Bram's hand and thanked him for giving them all a quick education about the moon. She said that it was all new to her and that she would have to do a little more study and research before the next Fold out to the edge of the solar system.

The Fold they were on was a top-secret Fold to test the ability to Fold over a long distance through space. In reality the distance to the back of the Moon was a miniscule distance as compared to the subsequent distances that were in upcoming Fold plans. The Fold implementation order was to go first to the edge of the Solar System, then to the nearest next solar system and finally to a different galaxy.

Since a Fold took relatively no time, it was possible to do the three planned Folds in the coming year. It could be done as quickly as doing them on three subsequent days but there was data analysis time put between each Fold. It would be important to analyze the data and apply any improvements that the data might provide insights about.

The successful Fold to the back of the moon pleased Bram. It was to have been the first Fold of the two Wheels but in reality, it was the third. The first two folds occurred in getting each wheel out of the Seattle area when a throng of rioters threatened to expose the technology that was a top US government secret. So, the official Fold that would be recorded for the history books was really the third one.

It was his first, but it was the second for each of the Wheel Crews.

He had let them all know that the people taking part on this Fold would have their names and biographies recorded in the history books.

He had been as inclusive as possible, but it was not possible to take everyone on the project. He took all the top players. He eventually would offer the Fold experience to all those who desired.

The Fold was a moment of relief for him but the lead up to it had been extremely stressful.

He had not intended the days leading up to the Fold to have been so hectic and stressful. He had envisioned a rather controlled, full schedule but one that focused on making the Fold to the back of the Moon safe as well as successful.

One concern was the safety of the crew members. Since relocating the Fold project to Dallas, Oregon he and his team had been attacked several times.

He and his close team had been attacked when they went on a fishing trip to the Mt. Jefferson resort along the Rushing River. He, his team, the Marines guarding him, and the resort owners fought and defeated a group of mercenaries that had arrived in a helicopter gunship and had a tripod large caliber machine gun on the ground. The battle had been fierce but ended in a few minutes as Bram and his two Marine guards took out the attackers.

The next attack had been at the Fold neighborhood swim party. Three gunmen opened fire from the parking lot. Bram, unarmed, took immediate action, and killed one of the attackers and his FBI bodyguards took out the other two.

He had gone into action when he realized that Pat was the next target after the first two people had been shot.

A third attack, by a gunman shooting at him from a boat, had occurred out on Celio Lake during a fishing party. Orlando and Castor turned the attacking boat and its occupants into Swiss cheese.

The final attack had been thwarted when he reported seeing a flicker from the top of a semi parked in the orchard that bordered the Fold community housing. A Marine marksman killed the attacker from a patrol helicopter before he could take action.

Bram figured that some rich and powerful people were trying hard to stop the Fold development from making any progress and he was the bullseye of the project.

These attacks had made him very cautious about everything associated with the project.

The attacks were disturbing and of concern to him but not as disturbing as being accused of being a child molester by the wife of his genius Astronomer and Fold coordinate planner, Marcus Smith.

He had worked hard at making the Fold community into a caring, sharing, and fun group.

The accusation if it was shared would have a very negative impact and he took action to immediately address and resolve it.

It turned out that Myla, Marcus's wife, had been molested as a child and had a hysterical reaction when she saw him hugging Zuri, a young autistic savant constrained to a wheelchair. He told Marcus to get help for Myla or both of them would be transferred to another project or job. It was a huge relief when Mallica got Myla to accept counseling to deal with the child abuse she had suffered. He was hopeful that with the counseling, she would resolve her mental issues.

After that he turned his attention to the planning of a celebratory fishing trip.

Lacy his secretarial support had worked out the schedule with her father for another fishing trip.

Bram had her invite several dignitaries all the way up to and including the President. He did not expect most of them to accept but he asked Lacy to make sure that she arranged enough fishing boats to handle everyone that accepted the invitation.

She let him know that her father, and brothers were all committed, and a picnic lunch would be arranged as well. They had all sent their greetings and had said that they hoped for another successful fishing outing without the associated fireworks of the last one.

On the Fold's return from the back of the Moon, Zuri commented that though she had learned a lot about the moon, she was a little let down that the Fold experience was no different than taking a ride in a car.

Bram gave a little laugh and said that he agreed with her and that the only thing that had made it the least bit interesting for him was Orlando constantly joking with her.

He said that getting the math and the means to make a Fold occur had been the part that had engaged him. Taking the ride out to the back of the moon had been very anticlimactic.

He asked if a fishing trip might excite her more.

That brought out an immediate and loud yes and she commented that the last time, her first-time fishing, had been a blast. She said that Orlando had really caught all her fish because she was too weak to pull them in. He would have her hold the pole, but he would reel in the fish.

She said that Captain Ted had done a great job in making the boat wheelchair friendly and he had made sure that she was safely strapped in. Then he had zoomed at top speed and made sweeping turns to give her a thrill sitting in her wheelchair. A ride in his boat was more fun than a ride in Wheel One to the back of the moon.

Bram said he agreed with her.

He then asked her if she wondered why the trip to the moon had been so short.

Zuri replied that she had no idea.

He then shared the fact that the current Fold was frozen to one coordinate location and could not move. He wanted to add the capability of motion to the Fold process.

Zuri looked at him and said that if he solved that problem, he would create a Fold wormhole that would turn Wheel One into a Fold spaceship. It would be a spaceship that could move through time and space free of the conventional limitations of the speed of light.

She asked what he was waiting for.

He looked at her and asked her for her IQ then reminded her that hers was much higher than his and that she was the smart one in the room that needed to solve the problem.

She gave a little laugh and joked that he was the smart one she was just the clueless one that asked the right questions.

Pat, Amy, and Elizabeth walked into the office and commented that the journey of Wheel One and Two had been anticlimactic and that it seemed surreal as if it had just been a dream. They commented that getting the two Wheels out of the hanger in Seattle into the Dallas hanger had been more exciting.

Bram said that Fold had been more exciting for him too since he had almost left them somewhere in-between. He made the point that he had no idea if an in-between existed or if the wheels would have just disappeared and never been found again.

Elizabeth looked over to Zuri and told her to watch out for Bram because he might have a great mind, but he often moved faster that the technology around him. She shared that she had gone and looked at the charred power transformers that Bram had fried when the first Fold was done. She said she had gone out and bought a dozen lotto tickets hoping to cash in on her good luck at being alive, but the lotto had won, and she was still poor.

Zuri smiled and said she would pay close attention to what Bram was concocting since even his fishing trips were more exciting than she had expected.

Lacy called and asked if Bram was able to meet with Myla.

He was surprised but he said that he would be free in about five minutes.

Pat said that she would take Zuri and look to see if anything had been done with her future office area and that afterwards she would have Orlando take Zuri home.

Elizabeth said she was going to see about the new Bramlets that were being assembled. She commented that the next set of Bramlet scouts for the Neptune Fold were almost all ready for testing.

Bram asked Lacy to send Myla in.

When she came in he saw that her hands were shaking, and he knew immediately that she was very nervous.

He asked if they should shake hands or just go for a hug and put the past behind them and look forward to a long friendship.

Myla began crying but stepped forward and they hugged.

She began to apologize.

Bram stopped her and said that she should relax. He had no grudge and was not looking for an apology. He was looking forward to the long and good relationship the two of them would enjoy.

Myla thanked him and asked if there was anything she could do that would be appropriate.

Bram said that she should talk to Lacy on the way out and get the information about the upcoming fishing party and that he would expect the Smith family to catch the biggest fish.

Myla thanked him and said that she loved fishing, but she seldom caught one. She said that it was the sitting and enjoying the motion of the boat that pleased her.

Bram agreed with her and said that what he enjoyed most was to watch folks fishing, talking, and teasing each other about the one that got away.

He escorted Myla from his office and told her to stop by Marcus's office and let him know that his rather eccentric scientist was waiting to find out what the future travel plans would be.

He already knew the plan, but he wanted to have Myla stop and talk with Marcus before going home. He had told Marcus to finish up what he was doing and then go home to Myla. He figured Marcus would figure out that he did not have a meeting with him.

Pat came back and said that Orlando and Zuri had left. She commented that Orlando and Zuri seemed to have bonded and become fast friends.

Bram said that in fact he had replaced Orlando with a new Marine guard, Donna because Orlando had suggested that Zuri rated at least one person guarding her at all times and he was stepping up and volunteering to do so. Orlando had been the one to recruit Donna, who seemed to have her eyes on him.

Pat gave a small laugh and suggested that they both stay out of the love triangle.

He nodded and said he had all he could handle with his own love affair.

He suggested that since it was a nice day they walk home.

Walking home was not a simple affair, Castor, and Donna the two Marine guards, in full battle gear, were in front, and on this day, Eric and Zoe his two FBI bodyguards were walking in back and Bob and Thomas the other two FBI guards were driving the van that was most often the mode of transportation in the afternoon.

The morning always consisted in a slow jog to work.

The attacks aimed at killing him had resulted in the current mode of increased protection. This had been the routine for several months.

The level of security around Bram had always been high and though he sometimes felt constrained by it, the attacks that he had experienced made it clear that he was at the center of the bullseye to his adversaries and his adversaries seemed to have some deep political connections that surprised him. He wondered how he might find out who they were and see if there was a way to stop them.

The walk gave him time to think and to allow his mind to sort through what he needed to do to make the Fold program successful. He had stepped back from being the only one making it all happen and had split the responsibilities with various other members.

The Fold program's overall management on site was now being handled by Erica and back on the East coast by Jeffrey.

He had embraced the role of being the scientist that managed the data analysis and its interpretation, and he was the lead in making improvements to the Fold program.

Now all he needed was for his mind to open up and participate in solving the problem of developing a means to propel a Fold enclosure.

Chapter 2: Fishing

Almost every one of the team members signed on with Linda to go fishing. There was high enthusiasm among all the participants and a common groan when they found out the time that the fishing boats would leave the dock.

Lake Celio was really the Columbia River up stream of the Dallas hydro-electric dam. The river was somewhere around a mile across, and the current was slow and easy.

It was still dark when the boats left the Celio park docks. The moon light etched the far bank a dark black. Home lights twinkled as if the bank had its own stars competing with the millions of the ones overhead.

The rising sun was battling the night and slowly bringing in the day.

As it rose ahead, the seven boats went single file toward it.

Then the far horizon looked as if it had burst into flame and the sun rose red behind a thin layer of clouds.

The saying, "Red sun in the morning, sailors warning" went through his mind.

The rising white steam going up from the lake seemed to be trying to warm the cool and somewhat nippy air.

Ted gave a hand signal and the six boats behind him moved into a V formation. He began weaving back and forth and the other boats all followed and did the same. He was making it as exciting as he dared.

Zuri had thanked him for an exciting ride the last time he had taken her fishing. He planned to get her to thank him again. He was personally pleased that he had made a positive connection.

It was hard for him to treat her like he would anyone else. He needed to get rid of his lifetime feeling of alienation when he saw someone who was crippled. He needed to realize that the people in their wheelchairs had their own talents, ambitions, and dreams.

He loved fishing and so did Zuri. He figured that would give them a common bond. A good start. He shook his head; he was just an old foggy that needed to be around people like Bram and Zuri.

Bram was sitting next to Pat and holding her hand as they let themselves be absorbed by the moment. He alternated between watching the occupants of the other boats, enjoying the motion of Captain Ted's boat, and the feel the wind blowing his hair gave him.

The majestic scenery of the snowcapped mountains and the skirt of green forest that swept gracefully down to the edge of the water was spell binding. The experience seemed to tease his mind to let go of other thoughts.

The zigzagging brought him out of his daydreaming, and he paid attention to what was going on. He laughed when he realized that all the boats were copying what Captain Ted was doing.

He shout out to Ted and asked if help was needed in guiding the boat.

Ted smiled and said he had no choice because he was following Zuri's order to make fishing fun.

Zuri shouted out that she had not given any such order, but he should continue doing what he was doing.

Bram noted that the seven fishing boats formed a V as they made their way eastward along the lake. He wondered what the formation looked like from an arial view. He looked up to see a small drone following above them. He pointed it out to Ted who nodded and pointed to himself and to the drone to indicate it was one of his.

Bram later found out that Lacy was the one flying the drone. It had been her idea to film the entire fishing trip.

Lacy had informed him that Jeffery and Major General Lester Tilson would be joining in on the fishing trip. She also let him know that every one of the big shots up to and including the President had sent him and the fishing party good luck and that they regretted not being able to join in personally.

Jeffery had called when he had landed and let him know that he and the General had been parked out on the tarmac for almost an hour waiting for some gate keepers to get to work and work the bridge that connected the plane with the terminal. The Pilot finally let everyone off via the planes own steps.

The fishing had just started when Jeffery and Major General Lester Tilson arrived in the eighth boat. They pulled alongside and apologized for having been late

Bram let them know that no apologies were necessary but that they needed to get their lines in the water so they could try for one of three prizes, the largest fish, the most fish and the smallest keeper fish.

They both gave him a salute and their boat went out to the edge of the group and threw in their lines.

By noon everyone had caught a fish and Ted called a halt to the fishing and said it was time for the picnic to begin. He pointed to the darkening sky and said that it looked like a rain squall was coming in over the lake.

He called ahead and asked that the tent to cover the picnic area get set up in case they got rain.

The ride back was fast and straight. They all had their eyes on the black clouds slowly gathering down by the hydro-electric dam.

They had all just gotten out and helped finish putting up the very large tent when the rain started and soon it was pouring. The far side of the lake disappeared. It was hard to see to the end of the dock. The boats had their rain covers on, and all fishing poles had been put away.

Ted said that the amount of rain they had been getting was unusual.

The three grills were just outside of the tent and the three doing the grilling got wet every time they got a serving of what was on the grill.

Nuri was sitting by the edge of the tent looking out to the lake with her parents helping her eat. They were all listening to Orlando tell a story about the time he was on patrol and the rain had started. He made the point that the patrol was in the middle of the desert and had not come prepared for the rain that fell as heavy as the one that they were now sitting and watching. He went on to share that after the rain the desert was covered in flowers. It was as if a miracle had happened.

Bram enjoyed the story and noticed that Orlando had captured everyone's attention.

He took the opportunity to let everyone know that they would wait until after lunch and after the rain they would see who had qualified for the prizes that were being offered.

The tent and the food seemed to bring everyone closer. Pat commented that the rain only added charm to the event.

The thunder and lightning seemed to have the effect of making everyone speak softly. Rita, Ted's wife, asked if it was alright for her to play some music.

Lacy gave a small groan and then said that it would be country western, or old crooners singing songs of the sixties or before.

Major General Tilson said that it would be great to hear some music that he could understand.

The intensity of the rain lessened. The music was just what everyone needed, and the conversations seemed to well up like a dry sponge getting water put on it as everyone listened to Rita.

Bram then heard a loud explosion and as he looked back along the shoreline he watched what looked like a small atom bomb's plume rising brightly up into the grey of the clouds.

Everyone under the tent quit talking.

He knew immediately that the location was back at the Fold property.

The silence was louder than the thunder and lightning that seemed to have risen.

Everyone turned and looked at Castor as his phone rang. He put it on speaker mode and answered the call. It was the Marine site leader calling to inform him that an attack on the compound had taken place but had been thwarted.

The explosion had been one of the attack vehicles exploding in the back of the compound area and other than being spectacular, the explosion had killed all the attackers that had retreated to it, but it had done no damage. He said that each attacking van had four gunmen and all but one of the attackers were dead.

He reported that USS Hood, Wheel One had been tipped on its side, but it did not seem to be damaged.

When Jeffery asked if they should return to the compound, Bram was about to say no, when Pat spoke up and said that they should finish their fishing picnic. She went on to say that if the wheel was not damaged she would later do a Fold and then land to bring the Wheel back up right.

Major General Tilson asked the Site commander to have a twelve-person patrol sent to the picnic area and set up a defensive perimeter. He looked around at the group and said that it was just precautionary.

Bram looked out at the rain and the lake and said that if there was to be an attack they should be expecting the action to come from the lake.

Orlando suggested that they prepare for that possibility, and he asked if the Marine bodyguards had their weapons. He knew the answer but asked so that he could ask that of all the others would know that they had come prepared.

He then looked to the FBI bodyguards and asked them the same thing.

They all responded in the affirmative.

He then asked the boat captains if they would allow their boats to be used and got a unanimous response that they could but only if they were doing the driving and they got to shoot as well.

Bram watched in amazement as the boats loaded up and went out in the rain. He had been turned down when he had volunteered to go with Ted.

The General simply said that he could not justify risking either Bram or any of the other brains running the program.

Jeffery agreed and when he volunteered to go out he was also turned down.

Rita said that she wanted those that were staying under the tent to round up all the extra tables that were in the park and bring them to the edge of the tent on the lakeside and tip them so that they made a protective barrier.

She then went to the van and the trailer and returned with several shot guns and boxes of shells.

She handed one to Bram and said that she had heard that he was rather deadly in a gun battle and that her Ted had said that he was almost certain that once the rain let up there would be an attack.

Bram had a second set of tables tilted in the center of the tent and had Zuri and everyone else get behind the second barrier.

He asked that Lisa help Zuri to rest on the ground and instructed everyone to lay down flat if the fighting came their way.

The storm must have been listening because almost immediately after his announcement the rain stopped and as if it were providing better fighting conditions, the sun seemed to be pushing the clouds west along the lake.

Bram then saw what looked like a dark grey blanket being lifted from a fleet of boats coming in at full speed from the west.

Pat was looking through a set of binoculars and commented that there seemed to be more than a dozen and that two had what seemed to be heavy duty machine guns and two had mortars mounted on the bow.

Lacy excused herself and asked Linda to look after Zuri. She took the opportunity to launch her camera drone. She said she would take a closer look and she could help guide the gunfire from their boats.

Elizabeth said she would talk with Orlando and Pat said she would talk with Castor.

Bram had several tables moved to the two launch ramps and had two shooters positioned behind each.

Rita and Marial were also out at the two tables to help support them in case of a gun battle.

Amy, the helicopter pilot turned wheel two captain became the play-by-play announcer and shared what she was seeing on the computer screen.

Bram quickly realized that their boats were outnumbered and out gunned. The only advantage seemed to be that Stacey was an expert in flying the drone and in providing critical information.

The two boats carrying mortars were sunk in the first round of fighting. Then those out in their boats were able to take out one of the boats with a fifty-caliber machine gun.

The remaining boat with the fifty turned toward the docks.

All the attacking boats that remained had shooters with either AR 15's or high-powered rifles.

Bram realized that the one boat that had a fifty-caliber gun was fast approaching the ramp area.

Lacy saw the same thing and her drone made a sweeping turn and returned to the tent area.

When the first round of the fifty caliber was fired, the splinters from the first set of tables flew past Bram as if they were sent to make him into a porcupine.

Lacy flew the camera drone directly at the gunman and turned so close to his face that he turned to avoid getting hit. She then took the drone on a sharp turn and flew the drone toward the boat driver and crashed it into his face.

The boat swerved and hit the end of the dock. The fifty caliber gunman hit the grips of the gun chest first and was most likely critically injured but Bram's shotgun blast sent him flying back over the boats low windshield where the shooter behind him accidently shot him in the back.

Bram rushed toward the boat in a continuous pump and shoot fashion and then the click of the trigger made him realize his gun was empty and he was now a sitting duck. He was about to jump into the water when Pat handed him another shotgun as she took the empty.

Rita had done the same back up with a second shotgun for the grill master that had done the same thing as Bram, but on the adjacent dock.

Bram continued on toward the boat as he pumped and fired. There was no response, but he made sure everyone was dead.

Lacy ran down the pier, jumped into the boat, retrieved her drone, did a quick check, and used some duct tape and then launched it and sent it out to the boats where the battle was still going at an intensive battle.

Bram stood and watched as she flew her drone as if it was a combat plane.

Stacy's harassing drone seemed to turn the tide and the battle slowly came to an end as the only surviving attacking boat surrendered.

Stacy did a slow sweep of the boats and noted that all of their boats were full of holes, but the design of the boats kept them afloat. They might fill with water, but they would not sink.

Only Ted's boat had an engine that came to life and allowed him to slowly tow the other boats into the dock area. All the boats were tied bow to tail as Ted slowly pulled them back.

Bram had the ramp area cleared of the tables. He was about to get Nuri sent home when the Marines from the Fold compound arrived.

They took over. They had an EMT group with them and as the boats came in, they began checking on the wounded.

Almost everyone out on the boats had some sort of wound. They were treated and then those needing to get transported to the hospital were taken by the first unit. It was designed for battle conditions and could transport six and they were full as they departed.

Another EMT unit was on its way.

Bram was listening as Orlando was telling his version of the battle to Nuri. Castor kept throwing in color comments and Donna kept saying that they shouldn't try to pull the wool over a person's eyes who was ten times smarter than they were.

He saw that Nuri was really enjoying the banter.

Niro and Jina were standing next to him, and they commented that Nuri was really blossoming into a very social person and even with what had just happened they thought that she was where she should be.

Jina looked at him and said that she had not expected to see the dark side of such a bright mind, but she was relieved that he was a man of action.

Pat came over and pointed to Bram's leg and asked him if he knew he had a splinter the size of a chop stick that gone through his leg.

Bram looked down and realized that the shower of splinters created by the fifty caliper bullets had not all missed him. He was surprised by the size of the splinter and the fact that it was not bleeding.

Jina gasped when she saw the splinter.

They had all been so intent on listening to Orlando that Bram's injury was missed.

Pat had motioned to one of the EMT's and pointed to Bram.

He came over and asked Bram to come over to the Emergency Vehicle and get the splinter removed.

He wanted Bram to go to the hospital, but Bram refused. He asked them to remove the splinter and later he would go to the hospital.

The EMT went over to the General and after a brief discussion he returned and told Bram that removing the splinter was going to cause some pain.

By this time everyone was standing around watching.

Orlando was reassuring Zuri that Bram was going to be alright and that he was going to demonstrate the bravery of a Marine.

Bram reached into his shirt pocket and took out a large piece of hard jerky and put it between his teeth.

The EMT used some Novocain to numb the area around both ends of the splinter. After a few minutes he said that he was going to pull it out in one fast pull and that his assistant would put some gel and gauze to prevent the wound from bleeding.

Orlando began a chant.

> Fifty caliper no big deal.
> Bram is shooting,
> Bram is real.
> Fifty Caliper missed the mark
> Splintered the table,
> Angry table, Angry table,
> Tried for Bram but missed the mark.
> Little splinter, Little splinter
> Does not bother
> Bram is real.
> Bram, Bram is a true Fold hero.

Everyone at the outing took up the chant.

The EMT waited until "hero" and then swiftly pulled he splinter out.

The pain caught Bram by surprise. He bit down on the hard beef jerky and thought about a Fold to the Alien world.

Pat put her hand on his shoulder and asked if the contest was still on. She knew that Bram had used his powerful mind to ignore most of the pain and she wanted to distract him as the EMT's finished binding the wound.

Bram looked at her and smiled. He thanked her for being such a brave backup. It had saved his life.

Pat had not expected the reply, but she smiled and said that she always had his back.

He then replied that everyone had won and that they would all share first prize.

Enjoy

<u>The Message</u>
the continuing story of the Fold

About the Author

Ronald E. Mueller
remwriter95@gmail.com

Ron grew up fascinated by how things were built, put together and how they technically became more detailed and capable.

He went into the Navy with his eye on becoming a nuclear reactor operator. He served in Vietnam, became a Nuclear Reactor operator, and then volunteered to be on the hydrofoil USS Tucumcari and was both an electronics specialist and a helmsman during a tour around the European coast.

His developmental experiences continued during his thirty-eight years at Procter and Gamble and more than thirty around the world trips. He was a keen observer and his many experiences surface in the fabric of the stories he writes.

For the last ten years he has been writing both fiction and non-fiction books. His first-hand experiences are woven into the story.

<u>Listing of Fold Characters</u>

Amy	Wellington	NASA astronaut
Bob		FBI bodyguards
Bram	Nielson	Protagonist
Castor	Suarez	Marine guard
Cedric	Stetson	Fishing boat
Daryl	Nazda	Backup Pilot Bubble 1 Pat Pilot
Donna		New Marine guard
Edward	Sharp	Site Marine Commander
Elizabeth	Miller	humanist philosopher, .
Eric		FBI bodyguards
Erica	Wilson	Initial archrival
Ester	Mannerly	Nasa quality inspector for the two wheels.
Harold	Redat	Backup Pilot Bubble 2 Amy Pilot
Jeffrey	Mikelson	Boss that is patient,
Jina	Juma	Mom
John	Morgan	NASA director Jefferies Boss
Jose	Estrada	project manager wheel one and two
Lacy	Stetson	first office support. Ted's daughter
Lester	Tilson	Marine Major General Fold security
Linda	Stetson	Ted's oldest becomes Bram's support.
Lori	Middleton	Lab, workshop supervisor
Luke	Stetson	Fishing boat Ted's son
Mallica	Evenston	World class mathematician
Marcus	Smith	World class astrophysicist
Marial	Stetson	Brought Picnic lunch, Cedric's wife
Mary		Rushing River Inn Owner
Melisa	Etrius	Organizer of the Fold neighborhood activities
Mike		Rushing River Inn Owner
Myla	Smith	Wife
Nuro	Juma	Dad
Orlando	Gutieres	Marine guard
Patricia	Fleming	NASA astronaut Bram's mate
Remi	Hardwood	Direct bubble assembly Lab technical
Rita	Stetson	Brought Picnic lunch, Ted's wife

Samuel	Natorly	US President
Serena	Windal	Fold phycologist, Marine Therapist
Ted	Stetson	Fishing boat
Thomas		FBI bodyguards
Zoe		FBI bodyguards
Zuri	Juma	Wheelchair bound autistic mental savant,

Published by: Around the World Publishing LLC.